MIRIAM'S
·WELL·

MIRIAM'S WELL

LOIS RUBY

SCHOLASTIC HARDCOVER

Scholastic Inc.
New York

Library of Congress Cataloging-in-Publication Data

Ruby, Lois.
    Miriam's well / Lois Ruby.
       p.   cm.
    Summary: When Miriam develops bone cancer, a battle follows over
whether or not she must be treated.
                    ISBN 0-590-44937-0
    [1. Cancer — Patients — Fiction.]   I. Title.
PZ7.R8314Mi   1992
[Fic] — dc20   91-46301
                                                                        CIP
                                                                        AC

12 11 10 9 8 7 6 5 4 3 2 1   3 4 5 6 7 8/9

                      Printed in the U.S.A.   37

            First Scholastic printing, March 1993

For the people and ideals
of
Inter-Faith Ministries — Wichita

The ancient rabbis tell us of a well
that was created
at the twilight of the first Sabbath.
It was a rock which, when struck,
became a fountain of living water.
The rabbis say that Miriam, the sister of Moses,
was of such merit that only for her did this rock
follow the Israelites from encampment to encampment,
providing water in the treacherous desert.
After nearly forty years of wandering
with the children of Israel,
Miriam died.
The water ceased to flow.
And this miracle was called

MIRIAM'S WELL

CHAPTER ONE

Told by Adam

"Poetry is a bitch," Mrs. Loomis said that fateful day in October, and I wasn't sure I'd heard her right, since I'd been staring at the pie-faced clock that was groaning its way toward the end of English. But when Diana gasped, I knew I'd heard a word come out of Loomis's mouth that any of us would've been sent to the assistant principal for.

"Adam, how is poetry a bitch?" Mrs. Loomis asked. She had a habit of picking me for the big ones, because in her mind I was the classic under-achiever, like my brother Eric who managed to get in to law school anyway. I think all the teachers spent their lunch hour talking about me. My name was probably carved on the oak frame of the couch in the teachers' lounge, so that when I graduate, the Dwight D. Eisenhower High School teachers who never had me in their classes will hear about Adam Bergen, the one whose name is synonymous with wasted potential.

"Well, uh," I began, sliding my hand through my straight brown hair. My hair flopped right back into place, as I knew it would, because my hair is one

1

of the few things I can count on at least 94 percent of the time.

"Yes, Adam?" Mrs. Loomis's smile looked like it caused her great pain as it cracked the *papier mâché* of her face.

"It's kind of hard to explain."

"Ah, Adam, how true," Mrs. Loomis said. "And how imprecise. Take the word *literally*."

Literally? Bitch? I could think of a few at Eisenhower High. But I knew Loomis was looking for something bigger, something more Shakespearial. I looked around the room for a clue.

"Back to the clock, Adam? It can't possibly advance toward the bell without your watchful eye. We all owe you a debt of gratitude."

The class snickered, but a quick glance behind me told me that Diana wasn't involved in making me feel like the court fool. She was feverishly writing in her green notebook. Pretty soon her hand shot up; I felt the wind at my back.

"Yes, Diana?"

She cleared her throat and read from the loopy backhand writing I was always trying to decipher whenever she passed me a note in class. "Poetry is a bitch because her face looks sad, but her tail — that's T-A-I-L — tells a different story."

"Very good, Diana. Anyone else?" Behind her back (which was like the Great Wall of China), we called Loomis the Big Bang, largely because her polyester pants were so dangerously full that we expected an explosion at any time. Wasn't this how the world started? She'd start a whole new universe full of little creatures that instinctively knew the difference between a predicate nominative and an object. What a thing to look forward to.

Mrs. Loomis turned her back and tubbed her way over to the chalkboard. When she walked, the flesh followed a few seconds behind her. "People? Any ideas?" she asked, in that Sandy Duncan voice that couldn't have been her own.

"Where's the ventriloquist?" Diana had asked, that first August day in Loomis's class.

"Gentlemen? Have you anything to contribute?"

The guys in the class were all slumped down in the chairs as if, nearly laid out on the floor, we might not be spotted by Mrs. Loomis's X-ray eyes.

It was a big relief when Cynthia Turner raised her hand and read breathlessly, "Poetry is a bitch because, well, like a dog, she's real loyal, only she's loyal to language, not a master."

Mrs. Loomis gave Cynthia her cracked smile. Suddenly hands were going up all over the room. Not hands with motor grease under the nails, or with Def Leppard written on the palms like tattoos. No, these were all female hands.

"Yes, Katie?"

"Poetry is a bitch," Katie said, emphasis on the *itch* part, "because she gives birth to words that feed on her and grow into big, like, sonnets — no, bigger than sonnets, like, epics, like, big dogs, you know, German shepherds?"

"Yes. Well, you get the point, class. Those were some reasonably good examples. I'm still looking for something from you gents."

We slunk lower. Suddenly my friend Brent's voice shot into the silence. "I know a poem, Miz Loomis. It's the shortest poem in the English language, and it's about Adam."

3

Oh, no, here it comes.

"It's called 'Fleas.' It goes, 'Fleas — Adam had 'em.' " Well, Brent brought the house down. Even Loomis laughed, shaking the Jell-O in her polyester and maybe hurrying the dawn of the new universe.

"Thank you for that note of levity, Brent. And now, can we return to our lesson for today? Gentlemen, you can all sit up now, the heat's off. Pay attention. When I say 'poetry is a bitch' or 'my heart is a cavern,' what literary device am I using?"

It was metaphor; everybody knew that. Metaphor was whatever compared things but didn't have the words "like" or "as" in it. But I wasn't about to say it out loud. Rulo Número Uno of High School: If you know the answer, never, *never* volunteer it unless your graduation depends on it. This was like the thieves' code of ethics the guys always followed, and why not, since it's worked for generations, and men are still getting elected president and king and all that stuff.

The hand was clicking from one second to the other. Three more sweeps of the clock, and the bell would ring. Only another fifty-four minutes until lunch. The cafeteria had to be serving pizza, because it was Tuesday.

" — into pairs," I caught Loomis saying.

My mother had packed a huge, juicy pear in my sack. It was a Harry-and-David Fruit-of-the-Month-Club pear, and just thinking about it made my mouth water. A big wedge of cheese pizza, a piece of cake, chocolate milk, celery and carrot sticks (for tossing like wet spears across the lunchroom, into the geek camp), and my yellow pear. Not a bad lunch. I was a man of huge appetites. That's what

4

Diana said. But we're talking lunch here. I could eat and eat and never get fat. To tell the truth, I could have used about ten extra pounds, mostly in the legs and buns. "Buns are everything, Adam, *everything*," Diana said one night, and since then I'd been trying to figure out how to get my food to settle there, short of plastering pizza to my butt.

Pizza. Maybe I'd have two slices today. At a buck a piece? I tried to remember what was in my wallet. You see? I kept busy during English.

" — though I'm loathe to appear sexist," Mrs. Loomis said. My eyes snapped away from the clock. Certain words grab your attention. "I am pairing you by gender this time, because the ladies of this particular class seem to have a firmer grasp on poetry than the gentlemen. So, I've made my pairings for the poetry project."

No problem. She'd pair me with Diana, of course. Everyone knew we were going out together. Diana wouldn't push the poetry business too hard, and when we were parked in the back seat of her car, I can guarantee that poetry wouldn't be the main topic. But, even though one of Mrs. Loomis's favorite lines was "justice, justice shalt thou pursue," she didn't. I got stuck with Miriam Pelham.

How do I describe Miriam Pelham? The best word to describe her is "no." No make-up, no jeans, no T-shirts, no sneakers, no jewelry, no shape, no personality. Also, no friends. In the Who's Who of Eisenhower High, Miriam Pelham wasn't actually anybody. If you looked her up in the back of our yearbook, the *Abilene*, you'd probably see only her junior picture, her face and eyes and hair all one faded-out shade of winter gray. In class, you never knew Miriam was there. The only way you could tell she wasn't, was by staring at her empty seat long enough to remember who usually sat there.

Brent looked over at me and gave me the finger-down-the-throat sign. He got Ramona Ruiz as his poetry partner, and Ramona was at least a 42C, which made up for her moustache. Miriam Pelham. How lucky could a guy get?

It was Loomis's way of getting even with me, pairing me with the deadest girl in the class. What did Miriam need with a great extracurricular school like Eisenhower? She might as well have been in a convent. On the day the whole senior class cut school and went to Cheney Lake, Miriam Pelham and about five other social misfits showed up for school. The teachers couldn't wait to tell us the next day. And when we had assemblies, Miriam always asked to go to the library instead. I'm guessing she never went to football games, not that I noticed. At pep rallies, which you had to go to, she sat like a mute while the rest of us exploded with wild cheers like EISENHOWER POWER!!! and WE'RE PSYCHED FOR IKE!!!

Once I asked Diana, who is in charge of the entire Eisenhower world, if Miriam Pelham did anything normal, like sweat or drink carbonated beverages.

"Well . . ." Diana thought about it for a minute. "She suits up for basketball."

"Whoa, she actually gets out of those flowery skirts and starchy nun's blouses?"

"Don't be obscene, Adam."

"I'm not asking about her underwear."

"White, government issue. Little pink hearts. Just kidding. I never really noticed. I just thought it was

6

amazing that she even played sports, being so holy and all."

Around Eisenhower, we all knew she was a religious fanatic. There were three or four others in the school who met in Mr. Borell's classroom for some hearty Bible thumping before school started. We'd see them coming out just before first hour, their faces all red and sweaty, as if they'd just been to a Friday the thirteenth movie. Of course, they never had anything to do with the rest of us normal people, as though they didn't want to catch what we had. But they didn't have much to do with Miriam, either. She didn't even sit with the Jesus freaks at lunch. Sometimes I had to pass her in the lunchroom, as I looked for my friends. She'd take things out of a rumpled sack, and she'd be reading and twirling a strand of her mousy brown hair while she ate. As crowded as the cafeteria was, there was usually an empty space on each side of her. That's religion for you.

Religion, now there's something I take seriously. I seriously try to avoid it. Oh, sure, I had to go to Sunday School for eleven miserable years, and I had the standard regulation bar mitzvah a few years ago and the confirmation last year, but now I only go to the synagogue when my parents make it a condition of my surviving into manhood. Religion is their department, not mine. It's not that I don't feel Jewish; I do. It's just that in the things that define who I am, which is one of the more exciting things we used to do in Sunday School, besides making *succahs* out of tongue depressors, Jewish wouldn't be at the top of the list. The list would go like this:

(1) male
(2) citizen of the universe
(3) human being
(4) male
(5) American
(6) champion-quality debater
(7) underachiever
(8) too thin
(9) male
     and maybe, just maybe
(10) Jewish

So, since religion wasn't in my Top Five and was even at the lowest end of my Top Ten, you can imagine how thrilled I was to have a poetry partner who was first cousin to the Virgin Mary.

English was grinding to a close, finally. Even though I'd been staring at the bell, I jumped when it rang. All the kids were slamming their books shut, scraping their sneakers under their desks ready to bolt when Loomis gave the word.

"Before English tomorrow," Mrs. Loomis said, as though it were the Eleventh Commandment, "thou shalt get together with thy poetry partner." Then, when the Big Bang turned toward the board, we escaped.

In the next class, physics, Miriam sat in her usual seat, the front of the third row. I was over closer to the window and four seats behind her, so I had a good view of the back of her head, which she kept pointed straight toward Mr. Moran. Brent sat in back of me, tapping out some rap song on my back with the eraser of his pencil. Mr. Moran, A.K.A. Mr. Moron, was returning our tests. He had this cruel way of passing them back according to score. Diana's was always near the top, and by the time mine came, Diana had already corrected her few mistakes and handed the paper back to Mr. Moran. Miriam's paper, I noticed, was halfway down in the pile. She took the paper from his hand and stuffed it under her desk, without even looking at it. Then all of a sudden her head dropped to her desk with a clunk.

"Mr. Moran, look!" Arnita cried.

Moran ran over to Miriam, lifted her head by the chin, then eased it back down. "Terry, go get the nurse, pronto," he said, in his calm, even voice. Arnita, who was sitting behind Miriam, patted her back, but Miriam's arms hung lifelessly at her sides.

She's dead. I'll get a different poetry partner, I thought, then felt a jab of guilt. Brent had stopped tapping, and we all sat there silently embarrassed until the nurse came in. Mr. Moran and the nurse eased Miriam onto the floor, on her back. Arnita smoothed the skirt down over Miriam's knees. The rest of us crowded around. We'd all had CPR in gym. We all knew you were supposed to yell into the face of the victim, "ARE YOU ALL RIGHT? ARE YOU OKAY?" We watched the nurse check the airway for an obstruction, check for breathing, take her pulse.

Well, Miriam was alive. Pretty soon she started pulling her eyes open, as if they were stuck together with rubber cement, and when she saw us all huddled over her, she got this scared look on her face. "What did I do?" she asked.

"You fainted," the nurse said. "Can you sit up?" She could. "Can you stand up?" Unsteadily. "Can

9

you walk? Let's go down to my office, and we'll call your mother."

"No!" Miriam said. The nurse looked around at us all, while Mr. Moran motioned us back to our seats.

"All right, we'll talk about it," the nurse said, supporting Miriam firmly as they left the room.

"Back to our cogent discussion of velocity," Moron said, but it was useless.

Brent said, "Mr. Moran, what happens to Miriam Pelham is really important to Adam. See, he just got her last hour for a poetry partner." Brent kicked the bottom of my desk hard enough that I jumped with that old male instinct to protect my vital organs.

"Of course," Mr. Moran said blandly. "It is alarming when a student faints, but I'm certain she's fine. All right, people, let's take a few minutes to diffuse the tension." That meant he'd sit at his desk correcting papers, and we could talk.

"Well, on TV," Rachel whispered, "whenever a woman faints, it's because she's pregnant."

"No, no, sometimes it's because they got leukemia," Arnita said. "She sure looks pale." Some of the guys snickered, because Arnita was about as black as a tree stump. She snapped, "Whaddya think, I don't get pale when I'm sick?"

Diana, of course, had her own diagnosis. "Personally, I think she's anorexic. Anorexia nervosa is the disease of the '90s."

"Maybe it's PMS," Brent said.

Rachel shook her head. "Can't be, if she's pregnant."

"AIDS?"

"How would *she* get it?"

"We'd run out of diseases of the '90s, so someone started talking about a rock concert that was coming to the Kansas Coliseum, and the Jesus freaks that were threatening to picket it, and about the anemic record of our football team. Mr. Moron never did tune back in before the bell rang, and pretty soon Miriam Pelham's fainting spell was ancient history.

CHAPTER TWO

Told by Miriam

I don't remember fainting, only waking up on the floor and seeing the whole class hovering over me like a coven of witches. I remember snapping my knees together, and the nurse, Mrs. Elgin, saying she'd call my mother. "No!" I remember that.

I told Mrs. Elgin I was fine and pinched my cheeks for some color. Maybe that would convince her. Mama did that every morning, not for any nurse, of course, but so she'd look fresh and healthy as she headed for the church. It was Mama's job to send out all the mail and run off our bulletins. She didn't get paid much, not in money. What she got was something far more valuable to all of us — a sense of belonging, of being loved, a blessing from Brother James when we were feeling vulnerable to the dark spirit, a healing hand when that was what we needed most.

Right now I just needed some color. So I pinched my cheeks and smiled brightly.

"Miriam, I do not like the way you look. When was the last time you had a checkup?"

I could feel this band tightening around my chest. Brother James always said, "Lying lips are an abomination to the Lord," but I also knew that telling the truth now would cost us all way too much. Holy Jesus, forgive me just this once, I prayed silently. "Just a week or two ago," I said.

"And did everything test out all right?" Mrs. Elgin asked.

"Yes, ma'am."

"You had a blood test, the whole works?"

"Everything I needed, Mrs. Elgin." My face was hot, even though the rest of me was freezing cold. I felt bumps raising under the skin of my cheeks.

"Open wide," Mrs. Elgin commanded, and before I could protest, she shoved a cold, bitter thermometer in my mouth. I coughed and spit the thing out. It clattered to the floor, sending shivers up my back. But it didn't break, and she cleaned it and put it back in my mouth.

"Close your lips tight," she said, probing my wrist for a pulse.

I could barely breathe, and I was terrified that the hateful glass stick would slide down my throat and choke me to death. Finally, mercifully, she slid it out of my mouth and went over by the window to read what it said. "It's 101, Miriam. Have you had the sniffles?"

"No, ma'am."

"Any strange symptoms — going to the bathroom a lot or an itchy rash, vomiting, diarrhea?"

"No, ma'am."

"When was your last period?" she asked.

"Do I have to tell you? Does the school law say so?"

"No, Miriam, it does not."

"Well, in my family, Mrs. Elgin, we don't talk

to strangers about personal things like that."

Then she asked me, "Are you pregnant, Miriam?"

"No, I am not pregnant. I'm not even married." Mrs. Elgin smiled. Did she think I didn't know it happened to unmarried girls sometimes? But I wasn't that kind of girl. Brother James always says that our bodies are temples, and we must sanctify them and not defile them. One thing I've secretly wondered is, why is it okay to defile your body after you're married? Questions come into my head when I'm not concentrating hard enough. I swallow them all the time, praying that the questions won't show on my face, and praying for answers.

Mrs. Elgin sighed deeply. I didn't mean to cause her such grief. "I must call your mother, Miriam, because we can't keep you at school when you're running a fever."

"Please don't tell her about the fainting," I pleaded. "And don't tell her you took my temperature. And don't give her any numbers, 101 or whatever it was." Mama would have a fit if she knew I was even in Mrs. Elgin's office. I looked around at the padlocked cabinet with its shelf full of white bottles. I had to get out of there before Mama came for me. "Can I wait for her outside?"

"I'll tell you what. You can wait on the bench in the hall. How long will it take your mother to get here?"

"She has to walk from the church, which is about ten blocks away."

"She has no car?"

"The men have the car," I said. "My uncles, Ben-

14

jamin and Vernon." I couldn't tell her Mama didn't and wouldn't drive.

"Then let me do this. We'll call your mother, and I'll drive you by the church to pick her up."

"No! I mean, I don't think that's the best idea. Let me call my mother and tell her to walk home. If you want to take me home, I can be there waiting for her." Mrs. Elgin agreed, thank God. Why did He grant me that much, when I'd lied? Another question.

By the time Mama got home, I was sitting in front of the fire, wrapped in a granny-square afghan, and shivering. Mama took one look at me and lit the gas for a kettle of water. She put her lips to my forehead; that was how she could tell I had a fever. "What's happened today, baby?"

"I just haven't been feeling very well."

"Something happened at school?"

"No, Mama. Mr. Moran thought I looked peaked, so he sent me home." Mama put her arm around me under the afghan until the teakettle began to whistle. I drifted off to sleep while she made the cinnamon tea; it was the hot vapors that woke me up as she settled back beside me.

"Drink your tea, baby, and we'll talk." Mama's cup tinkled daintily, while mine seemed to clunk onto the saucer. I didn't feel like I had much control in my fingers. Pretty soon Mama took the cup and saucer out of my hands. "You lay down here on a pallet in front of the fire, baby," she crooned, spreading a quilt on the floor for me. "I'll give Brother James a call and see if we can't get him over here before the men come home." She pulled a soft cushion from the couch, and my head sank into it. Mama sat beside me, with her back up against the brick fireplace, reading the *Book in Gold Leaf*. Everyone else but us called it the Bible, Old Testament and New, but we found such beauty in the book that all our copies were in gold leaf, to mirror the treasure within the pages.

I heard the pages gently slap together as Mama looked for certain passages. I dozed and dreamed. I whirled through space, no, through a huge wooden room, spinning like a dervish, my hair flying behind me. Whirling, twirling, spinning, my skirt whipping around my legs — I was dancing! I awoke with a start, ashamed. Imagine, dancing. But then I was doubly ashamed to realize that it wasn't the wicked dream that woke me, but the telephone.

Mama knelt beside me. "Baby, it's some boy from your English class. Says he has to see you today." Mama's voice was dry and disapproving.

I stumbled to the phone. "Hello?"

"Are you okay?" asked Adam Bergen.

"Oh, sure. I slept a while, and I'm feeling much better," I said.

"Well, Mrs. Loomis says we have to get together with our poetry partners before tomorrow, and I thought maybe we should, because you're probably worried about your grade in there."

"Aren't you?"

"In English? Are you kidding?"

He didn't know me well enough to know that I was never kidding. "What do you want to do?"

"I could come over." He said it, but it didn't sound like he meant it.

I considered the possibility for just a moment. "Hold on. Mama," I whispered, "what time is Brother James coming over?"

"I haven't called him yet. You were sleeping so peacefully, I thought there'd be no need to bother him."

"Well, then, what time are the men due home?"

"Six-thirty, same as usual," she said, with that edge to her voice I'd begun to recognize when she talked about my uncles.

I heard Adam Bergen shouting something to someone on his end. It all came so easily to him — laughing, playing, teasing. "Are you still on the phone?" I asked.

"Still here." I pictured him sinking into our couch with the zinnia upholstery and weak, squeaking springs. Our living room with its small-scale maple furniture, its chintz and flounces, its dark, plaid drapes, would never contain anyone with the breezy style Adam Bergen had. The men hated the room, called it a woman's room, and refused to sit in there. The kitchen was where they sat to read the paper or the *Book in Gold Leaf*, when they weren't out in the garage working with their wood and tools.

But I couldn't take Adam Bergen into the kitchen. The simple polished maple table didn't join well at the seam where the table leaf would go when Brother James or one of the elders came to dinner. How would Adam Bergen feel reading Emily Dickinson at that table with the soulful eyes of Jesus watching him from the picture on the wall? And what would I offer him to drink? He'd laugh at me if I gave him cinnamon tea or tomato juice, or even caffeine-free Coke. To be honest, I'd never thought

17

about our house this way before, because no one ever came over except church people whose houses looked and smelled much like ours. But Adam was different, freer. I'd been noticing him for weeks, as he hung his lean body over Diana's locker or bounded up the steps two or three at a time or shoveled pizza into his mouth in the cafeteria.

"Adam, I really don't feel well enough for company," I said. My head was pounding. "I'm sorry if it's a problem for you with Mrs. Loomis."

"Doesn't matter to me," he said casually. That was the impression he always gave — a shoulder-shrugging "who cares?" Except when he was galloping after Diana like a lovesick pony. "Hey, but would you explain it to Mrs. Loomis, because she'd never believe me."

"I will. I have to hang up."

"Wait," Adam said. "Do you think you'll be at school tomorrow, before Mrs. Loomis skins me alive?"

With the secret pain growing in my back, how would I be able to walk all the way to school? And stepping up onto a bus was almost as bad. But, as Brother James always says, each day brings the miracle of a new dawn, and I promised Adam, "Oh, yes, definitely I'll be there tomorrow."

"See you," he said, so comfortably. It cost him nothing. I knew that his hands weren't sweating like mine when he put the receiver down, nor was his face hot. No doubt he'd already forgotten our conversation and had turned on the TV.

I wiped my hands down the sides of my skirt and lay back down in front of the dying fire. I wondered about Mrs. Loomis's motives. I'd listened closely while she announced her poetry pairs. I observed everything, because I was never distracted in class. It seemed to me she went out of her way to pair up the least likely teams — boy with girl, black with white, slow with smart, Cambodian with Mexican, Jew with Christian.

Adam was the first Jewish boy I had ever known. Though he never took things seriously, his voice was gentle. He wasn't at all like his friend Brent, who was such a loudmouthed show-off. Adam Bergen had nice eyes, kind eyes. I noticed his eyes sometimes at Rockwell Library, when he passed my table. Once I was scared to death that he'd take the seat beside me. That's the kind of person Adam was; he'd sit next to somebody he didn't like rather than sit alone. But he spotted his friends at another table and moved on by without even noticing me. I was relieved, then disappointed, then mad at myself for being disappointed, and I didn't get a thing done on my physics problem set. Then, to make matters worse, Diana came into the library. People at the other table scrunched up closer and pulled up a chair for her.

Diana was about the smartest and nicest girl in the school. She never passed me in the hall without saying hello, even if she passed me fifty times a day. If she did that to everybody, and I guess she did, she must have been hoarse by the end of every day. She and Adam looked just right together. Their skin tones were similar, sort of milky-olive, and she was half a head shorter than Adam. They were both slim and angular, in just the right proportion to each other. They could have posed for a magazine, one of the magazines I wasn't supposed to read, like *Seventeen*.

Diana and Adam should have been poetry partners, but somehow I got him. The idea made my stomach flip-flop.

"You shall love your neighbor as yourself," Brother James always said, but just as you would drown in pride if you loved yourself too immodestly, you also must love your neighbor with moderation.

This pairing, it wasn't what Brother James taught. But neither was Emily Dickinson, Robert Frost, and certainly not Walt Whitman, who were all on our poetry worksheet. And neither was Adam Bergen.

CHAPTER
THREE

Told by Adam

It's unnatural to get through a whole day without a trip to the mall, so Brent came by and got me, and we tore down Armour to Towne East. Some civic-minded parent once had the brilliant idea of putting traffic bumps on the street, to slow down drivers like Brent and keep small kids from getting smashed like mosquitos against the hood of a Toyota. But what they didn't take into consideration is that it's a lot more fun to do sixty over those bumps and see how fast the little kids can scatter. On a lucky day, you can terrorize half a dozen kids and get a good enough bounce to send your head up through the top of the car. But that takes some practice and an open sunroof.

Tuesday was just an ordinary day, rainy, no kids out, and a bump on the head barely worth mentioning. "What did you do about Ruiz?" I asked Brent.

"Caught her between physics and government. I told her to say something about poetry and to make it quick and dirty. She is some poet. She said, 'Okay, Jenkins, I'm talking alliteration here. Write this down.' Right there in the hall she came up with a half a dozen first-class rhymes." Brent stretched to get into his jeans pocket, pulled out a strip of paper ripped from a notebook, and read, "Pucker, plastered, pitch, pit, pock, and pass. Get it?"

"Sounds promising."

"So, what's the deal with you and the saint?"

"She's going to explain it to Loomis tomorrow. I'm off the hook for a while. Maybe I can study with you and Ruiz."

"No way!"

We hung around Camelot Music for a while, memorizing lyrics off albums. We never actually bought tapes or CDs there, because just about any other music store was cheaper. But it had nice ambience. That was a Diana word. She pronounced it in a French sort of way. When I said it, it was closer to ambulance. But so what; it's what Camelot Music had. We checked out a few other stores, read magazines in Waldenbooks, and played with the computers at Radio Shack. Then it was getting dark. Brent had to get home for *Wheel of Fortune* at 6:00, and it was close to dinner time at our house, so we left Towne East just as the parking lot lights were coming on.

After dinner, I called Diana, but her mother said she was at the library with Kunal, her poetry partner, who was offered $86,000 to marry a girl in India after he finishes college. Mrs. Cameron sounded pretty apologetic. She liked me. She didn't know my name was synonymous with wasted potential. "I'll tell Diana to call you when she gets home," Mrs. Cameron said, "if it's before nine."

I thought about calling Miriam Pelham back, but let's face it, I wasn't that dedicated to poetry. After a couple of physics problems, I stretched out on my bed.

"Adam, take off the bedspread," my mother said as she passed my room. She was everywhere at all times, vigilant against sloth and corruption. I kicked the blue quilted bedspread to the floor, put my headphones on, and fell asleep listening to Pink Floyd, "The Wall."

True to her word, Miriam Pelham was at school on Wednesday, though she looked like she should have taken another day off. In French she sat in the first seat of the first row closest to the door, so when the bell rang I didn't get to her soon enough to say anything about poetry. I don't know what she had second period, but it wasn't debate, which I took because it was an easy A and you got to leave school early on Fridays to go to tournaments in little Kansas towns like Kanopolis and Moundridge. I was late to third period English, and Miriam didn't even look up when I walked into the room. Mrs. Loomis, of course, had a few choice words for me.

"Adam, what a treat to have you drop by. Sit." (As if I were a Doberman pinscher.) "And tell me, how is your poetry worksheet going?" She glared at me. I wondered how the belt around her middle could possibly hold up under the supreme stress, but I had a speech ready on the subject of poetry. Debate was definitely paying off.

"You probably didn't hear that Miriam, who's my poetry partner, passed out in physics yesterday."

"I heard," Mrs. Loomis said. Yes, she and my mother were both tuned into a universal ring of truth.

"Well, I called her at home. Tell her, Miriam."

"He called me," Miriam said, in her mousy little voice.

"To what end?" asked Mrs. Loomis.

"So we could start right in with our poetry studying," I said, trying to fake as much sincerity as possible, "without loosing a single valuable day. But she was still sick. Tell her, Miriam."

"I was still sick."

"So you've both lost a single valuable day, together two valuable days. Hmmn. Perhaps you can both come here after school and make up for it. Would that be possible, Miriam?"

"Yes, ma'am."

"Adam?"

"After school?" That was my time, not the school's time. After school was for shooting baskets up at the park, for hanging around Towne East, for watching reruns of *Three's Company* (if my mother was still at work), and definitely not for doing poetry worksheets. It was strictly against my religion to tackle homework until after dinner.

"Adam," Mrs. Loomis said, peering at me above her glasses, "I've got a notice from Mr. Bennet that you need to be excused all day a week from Friday for a debate tournament in Dodge City. Well now, Adam, how can I sign the request until I feel certain that you have the poetry project well under way?"

"After school today's no problem," I said.

"Excellent decision." The Big Bang bent over to pick up one of a stack of books on the floor. "While you're working independently on poetry at home, people, we will be reading *The Stranger* in class," she threatened. "I want one person from each row to get a stack of books for your row." There was a massive rumbling as we jockeyed for position. It was an honor to pass out books. It meant you could toss them into someone's gut, smash fingers with them, flatten heads. No one wanted to miss out on the fun, but, thinking I had better maintain a low profile in the class for a day or two because of Dodge City, I let Patrick Davis beat me out this time.

Diana leaned forward and whispered in my ear. Her whisper was warm and moist, like the hiss from the hot air vaporizer my mother used to put in my room when I got a cold. "Kunal is a dunderhead," she said. "How did he ever make Honors English? I wish I'd gotten you as my poetry partner." Oh! Her lip brushed my ear as she pulled back. Promises, promises.

"Diana, you have something to say about *The Stranger?*" asked the Big Bang.

"Only that he's one of the most colorful characters in English literature," said Diana. Quick recovery.

Kunal said, "Hunh uh, it's French."

"But we're reading it in English translation," Diana said quickly. "Of course, I'd be happy to read it in French." There was a ripple of applause in the class. I couldn't turn around and look at Diana; I knew I'd crack up. Then I noticed that Miriam was watching us both, and she looked paler and stringier than ever, but there was a blurry smile on her face. So, even Miriam Pelham appreciated Diana for the incredible creature she was. During the opening paragraphs of *The Stranger*, I calculated exactly how many hours it would be until I got back from Dodge

City next Saturday and was in front of the TV in
Diana's dark library.

After school, while Mrs. Loomis erased the chalkboard, shaking like a prevolcanic mountain, Miriam
and I faced poetry. The worst was Emily Dickinson,
who was what Brent called a chick's poet. Miriam
read:

> Hope is the thing with feathers
> That perches in the soul,
> And sings the tune without the words,
> And never stops at all.

"How can Dickinson pass off 'soul' and 'all' as
rhymes? She's not such a great poet," I said.
"Maybe let's just try to figure out what the poem
says," suggested Miriam. " 'Hope is the thing with
feathers.' What has feathers?"
"Indians?"
"Or maybe a bird?"
"Vultures."
"Maybe a little bird, one that brushes your soul
with its soft feathers."
"Crapola."
Miriam blushed, which finally gave her face a
splash of color. But she hung in there. "It has to be
a bird, because it perches. Oh, look here in the next
stanza. It actually says it's a bird."
"So what do I write down? The question on the
worksheet is, 'What does the image of feathers suggest?' "
"Well, Adam, am I supposed to tell you the whole
answer?" asked Miriam, and suddenly I felt like the

dunderheads Diana's always talking about. Maybe Diana wouldn't have appreciated me as her poetry partner either.

"You write down your answer, and I'll write down mine," I grumbled. She wrote left-handed, with her hand on top of her lines, so it was pretty hard to copy it without her noticing. I wrote something about softness, mooshy feathers, I don't know what.

"Next question," Miriam said. " 'Does the narrator of this poem feel hopeful? Find the words in the poem that support your opinion.' "

"Well, it says hope, that's the first word," I pointed out.

"But does it keep on hoping?" Miriam asked.

"No."

"Why?"

"Yes?"

"Why?" Dead air. "Well, Adam, just look at the kind of words that are used. Look at 'sings,' 'sweetest,' 'warm.' Aren't these words that lift the soul?"

"Oh, yeah? Look at the last verse. 'Chillest' and 'strangest.' Those words dump on the soul."

"So then you put down your answer, and I'll put down mine." She said it this time.

"Mrs. Loomis, we're not getting anywhere," I protested.

"In fact, you are," the Big Bang said, her face buried in *The Stranger*.

Miriam sucked on her pencil eraser. "You know what I can't help thinking about when I think of poems of hope?"

I couldn't wait to hear. I also heard my stomach growling, because this was its sacred snack time.

"That line from Isaiah — "

"The Bible?" I could feel it coming. Hellfire and brimstone.

"Don't say it so contemptuously, Adam. Your name is from the Bible, you know. Listen to the line, 'For ye shall go out with joy, and be led forth with peace; the mountains and the hills shall break forth before you into singing, and all the trees of the field shall clap their hands.' Isaiah 55:12. What do you think?"

"I think you two have done enough for this afternoon," Mrs. Loomis said, and it was the first time I was ever glad to hear her voice. At Loomis's door, I waited to see which way Miriam would go, so I could take off in the opposite direction.

CHAPTER FOUR

Told by Miriam

Does Adam Bergen go out of his way to be immature and insensitive, or is it just a big cover-up? I thought about this all the way home. It took me nearly thirty minutes to get home, because I had to walk so slowly, and standing there waiting for the bus would have been worse. Each step caused a mean stab in my back, about where I thought my kidneys were, so I walked like I was carrying a pan of dishwater.

Vultures! Were those the only birds he could think of for such a delicate poem? Was it boys in general, or just Adam? Or was it Jewish boys who thought up such things?

He didn't look Jewish, whatever Jewish looked like. I used to think it had something to do with a nose and black curly hair and a very short neck. That wasn't Adam at all. Adam was lanky. Though he wasn't actually tall, he walked on the balls of his feet with a lot of spring and height and looked like a prizefighter prancing around the ring. His hair was brown, not black, about the color of Brother James's, and quite straight. It fell into his eyes; he always needed a haircut. And as for his nose, there was nothing extraordinary about it. It didn't dominate his face, because his eyes did.

Walking slowly down Thirteenth Street, I tried to get a clear picture of what Jewish looked like: Judd Hirsch, I thought, only Judd Hirsch wasn't Jewish, or was he? He never played Jewish characters on TV.

I was out of breath, so I stopped at the Amoco station a few blocks from our house and leaned against a Super Octane pump. An old man came out.

"Whaddya need? A dime's worth of gas for yer lawn mower? Free air for yer bicycle tires?"

"No, sir, just a minute to rest," I murmured, but I moved on. What if he recognized me and told the men next time they were in to fill up? I picked up my pace, trying not to wince as my heels hit the pavement. What was wrong? I'd had this pain for days and days. Growing pains, I'd thought, like the secret cramps I used to get in my thighs when I was in sixth grade and shooting up past most of the boys in the class. But after a couple of days, I admitted to myself that you didn't get growing pains in the kidneys. Something else was wrong.

Finally, I was home, and I collapsed on the zinnia couch with my shoes still on. "Dear God," I prayed, "You tell us that You listen to the small as well as the great. Brother James is the greatest man I know. He speaks to You on our behalf. I am just a small speck in Your universe, but I need You to listen to me now. I know that sickness is a curse that begins with Satan. I'm fighting it. The spirit is willing, but the flesh is weak. Please, whatever I've done, forgive me and cast out any unclean spirits that linger in me, because God, I'm not sure I can handle how much I hurt without disgracing myself." I lay back on the stuffed needlepoint pillow. "Please help. Please help please help please. . . ."

Mama found me there, I don't know how long afterwards, but the shadows across the living room were long, and the room had taken on a late afternoon chill.

"That does it, baby. I'm having Brother James come out. You are just not right." Mama went to the phone, dialed as fast as the numbers would come back around, tapped her fingers on the wall. "This is Sister Louise, I need to talk to Brother James," Mama said, as bossy as I'd ever heard her. But her voice soon changed. "Quite well, Brother James, yes. The men are well, also. But it's my Miriam I'm troubling you about. Could you find the time for a visit today? Bless you, Brother." She hung the phone gently on the wall. "He'll be over within the hour," Mama said. "We'll get ready." She slipped off my shoes, tucked the afghan around my legs, and put the *Book in Gold Leaf* on my lap. I thought about Isaiah, about the trees clapping their hands, but that would not be the passage Mama had in mind. Mama leaned across me and turned to a well-worn page in the Book of James. She read the first few words, to jog her memory, then recited the rest:

" 'Is any among you sick? Let him call for the elders of the church, and let them pray over him, anointing him with oil in the name of the Lord; and the prayer of faith will save the sick man, and the Lord will raise him up and if he has committed sins, he will be forgiven. Therefore, confess your sins to one another, and pray for one another, that you may be healed.' What have you to confess, baby?"

"Nothing, Mama."

"Darling, your body is telling you something. It's telling you that your soul and your mind are wracked with worry over something you ought not to have done, or ought not to have thought. Tell me, baby. We can face anything together."

"There's nothing, Mama." I tried so hard to think of the sin she was looking for, the thing that caused such a vacuum in my soul that pain and disease could seep in to fill it. Mama took my hand.

"We'll just wait for Brother James," she said.

I felt his presence even before he rang the bell. It was as though he surrounded our house with a protective cloak; no down-drafts from the flue, no breeze from the cracked window could get through.

A striking man was Brother James. Maybe six and a half feet tall, he made my Uncle Benjamin, who was an imposing man himself, seem puny. In the cooler months, except on Sundays, he always wore denim overalls and a blue plaid flannel shirt and western boots. The *Book in Gold Leaf* filled one pocket, penny candies that he passed out to all of us, the other.

Now he strode across the room. The floorboards were weak and creaking beneath his studded, black boots. He touched Mama lightly on the shoulder, and she pulled the maple rocker up for him, just across from me.

"Miriam," he said, and the sound alone filled me with the joyous certainty that I had the most beautiful name in all of creation. "Your mama tells me you're ailing."

32

"Yes, Brother James. I've been hot and peevish, that's all."

"And why's that, child?"

"I don't know, Brother James."

He turned to Mama. "Is it her time?" he asked, and Mama shook her head. I felt my ears go hot with embarrassment. He put his warm, work-rough hands to my cheeks. I was terrified that he would feel the lies in my face. "Something troubles her soul, Sister Louise." He closed his eyes, his face nearly touching mine. I felt the bristles of his dark beard on my nose.

"I am reading turmoil here, Miriam, anguish and doubt and terrible fear." It was he, it was he I was afraid of, my silent mind shouted. He'll know I've doubted. He'll know I've lied. I took a shallow breath and reminded myself: no it was not he that I was to fear. He was warmth, comfort, wisdom, kindness. He was my father as surely as if he had given me to Mama, the way men do, eighteen years ago. He had not, though. Eighteen years ago I'd had a real father.

He gently pulled his hands back from my face and folded them into the bib of his overalls. His eyes, nearly the color of robin's eggs, came to rest on me. We three sat in the fertile silence that I was too weak to fight, and soon it was all out, everything I had tried to hide from Mama.

"I've had this awful pain in my lower back," I cried, "and it hurts every time I move. I fainted in school yesterday. Fainted. I woke up on the floor, and everyone was watching me. They sent me to the nurse's office. She put a thermometer in my mouth and took my temperature. She said I had

33

101. I made her promise not to tell Mama, and now I've told everything," I said, wailing like a three-year-old. And yet, as miserable as I was, somewhere in my mind I wondered, What would Adam Bergen think of a scene like this?

"I swear, Brother James, I've turned to the *Book in Gold Leaf* for guidance, and I've read and read, but one passage keeps drifting to the front of my mind. Jeremiah, remember? 'Why is my pain perpetual, and my wound incurable, which refuseth to be healed; wilt thou be altogether unto me as a liar, and as waters that fail?' "

"Oh, dear God," Mama said.

"Sister Louise." Brother James moved his head ever so slightly, enough to tell Mama to go and leave us alone. She was reluctant, but we always did what Brother James said.

"I'm ashamed to think that way, Brother James. Please help me."

Brother James said, barely loud enough for me to hear through the pounding in my head, "We read in Matthew 21:22, 'And whatever you ask in prayer, you will receive, if you have faith.' Have you asked in prayer to be rid of this pain and fever?"

"Yes, Brother James."

"And nothing has changed?"

I hadn't meant to say it, but it slipped out: "It's grown worse."

"You have asked in prayer, and Matthew tells us whatever you ask in prayer, you will receive, is that true?"

"If you have faith, Brother James."

"Do you have faith, Miriam?"

"Not every minute of every day," I confessed.

"And each minute that you waiver, my child, is like a crack through which the dark spirit may be sucked into your soul. Each minute." He closed his eyes, and I knew he was praying. Finally, he said, "Let us speak to the Lord together."

"Yes," I whispered.

"Lord Jesus, Miriam and I ask Your ear. Say it with me, child."

"Dear Lord," I began, then faltered.

"You know the words." Brother James nodded his head, encouraging me.

"Lord, what am I to do? As You healed the lame, the halt, the blind, the dumb, and Miriam, my namesake, who suffered with leprosy, please remember me, too." I looked to Brother James; was my prayer worthy? I used to be able to pray so easily.

Brother James's eyes were closed. I saw his eyeballs working beneath his eyelids. For a second I thought he was asleep. Then his soft, dreamlike voice said, "Go on."

"Yes. Oh, Lord, You who made the heavens and the earth with Your outstretched arm, nothing is too hard for You. I don't think my meager little pain is too much for You to handle."

"Surely it is not," Brother James said. "Have faith."

"I'm trying."

"Ask Him, go on."

"How can I be stronger, Lord?" I waited, as though an answer might form in the ashes of the fireplace. I remembered the handwriting on the wall in the Book of Daniel. No message appeared on the wall for me; there was only the picture of a wheatfield, a barn, a silo, a lone horse.

35

Perhaps Brother James sensed my attention wandering, or felt the air of expectancy I'd breathed into the room. He opened his eyes and took my hands in his. "We have prayed for your faith to be buttressed, Miriam, and for your faith to be as sturdy as the cedars of Lebanon." He stood and placed both hands on my head, his fingers as light as hummingbirds. Lifting his own head toward the heavens, he said, "In the name of the Father and of our Lord Jesus Christ, who gave His life for our sins, and of the Holy Spirit. A-men."

"A-men," I whispered.

Brother James gave me a peppermint and told me he would see himself out. "God be with you."

With him gone, the down-draft was back, and Mama came with another blanket to wrap around me. I slept through dinner.

By morning I felt much better. The pain in my back was a faint twinge, probably just because I'd been favoring it for days. I sank to my knees beside my bed and thanked God and Jesus and Brother James for still another miracle, and I vowed to be faithful every minute of every day, if only I would be spared the shame of the pain.

At school, Adam was waiting for me in French. "I've got to have something to show her by third period," he said, thrusting his copy of the poetry worksheet at me.

"I thought you didn't care about grades." Did he read the unusual playfulness in my voice? I felt buoyant for the first time in weeks.

"I don't, but I've got to go to that debate tournament in Dodge City, and she'll screw that up for

36

me if I don't look like I'm working on poetry. What about the stupid Robert Frost poem?"

" 'Some say the world will end in fire, some say in ice,' " I quoted.

"Yeah, right, that one. What's this fire and ice stuff?"

"Let's say fire is passion, violence, apocalypse."

"What's that?"

"It's bad," I said, hiding a smile. This Adam, he seemed to be causing smiles, or was it that I was liberated from my doubt and pain?

"Okay, in twenty-five words or less, fire is passion, and ice is — what? — cold hatred?"

"Worse," I said.

"Worse? What could be worse? Quick, the bell's about to ring."

I said, "Worse than cold hatred is not caring at all."

"Yeah, I got it now. I'm not bad at this poetry stuff, am I?" He grinned, flashing the thin wire of his retainers, and I remembered only a couple of months before when his mouth was full of metal. But I hadn't noticed when he got his braces off. How could I miss a thing like that?

"Clahss, clahss, si-lahnce, s'il vous plaît," Mrs. Kearney said. We hushed like a symphony crowd when the maestro lifts his baton. *"Bonjour, mes élèves!"*

"Bonjour," we all replied.

"Bon Jovi," Adam said. Oh, it was a good day. He had smiled at me. No, that wasn't why it was a good day. It was a good day because Brother James had restored my faith, and because Robert Frost was almost as good as Emily Dickinson. And because Adam had smiled at me.

37

CHAPTER FIVE

Told by Adam

In about five years, Diana would be an architect. Most of us in the senior class were planning to start planning any day, but Diana had always taken the right courses to guarantee her a spot in one of the top architecture schools in the country. That's the kind of girl Diana was — she knew what she wanted. Me, for example. From the time we started going out, she couldn't see any point in wasting her time or hot, wet whispers on any other guy in the school. One word sums up Diana: efficiency. Efficiency, and ambition, and brains. Three words. And she was a natural beauty. She had brown eyes as big and soft as Bambi's. Usually they were laughing eyes, but she could make them wide and innocent when she needed to, or small and pointed when she was fiercely determined to blow a debate opponent into shrapnel.

She wore her hair in shaggy brown curls that fluffed out around her face — none of that sticky processed stuff that feels like wet cotton candy.

Everyone liked Diana, in spite of her incredible superiority and kissing-up behavior. She was never afraid to say whatever was on her mind or to stand up for the underdog. Come to think of it, she would have made a good socialist, except for the fact that she comes from generations of rich fathers who had rich fathers.

My family could have been rich, since my father's a lawyer, but he's always taking no-win cases, or cases that pay in what he calls *personal rewards*. That's his philosophy on my allowance, also, that the personal rewards of living in my family should compensate for the measly bucks. So I'm always interested in a good cheap date, not that I let girls pay my way, often.

One of the cheapest things you could do in this town was to go to real estate open houses. The first Sunday of the Poetry-Is-a-Bitch phase of my life, there was a model house open at a new development. It was furnished down to every detail, including a pair of ceramic dalmations like you'd win on *Wheel of Fortune*.

Of course, Diana and I had to pass as potential buyers, not kids, or we'd have been thrown out before she even opened her mouth. So we both dressed like Yuppies, in debate clothes, and I carried my debate briefcase, as though I'd just rushed over to the house after taking a deposition at a Senate hearing. I didn't wear my retainers, either. I took them off as soon as I left the house, even though my mother was always warning me that I'd end up with fangs if I didn't wear them.

"Oh, Adam, look!" Diana pointed to one of the homey touches the decorators had scattered around the kitchen — a ceramic pecan pie that looked like something a dog would leave on your lawn. There was also a machine pumping out a domestic aroma, like hot mulled cinnamon cider. A realtor approached; the plot thickened.

"Might I ask your names?"

"Mr. and Mrs. Wagner," I responded. "Might I ask yours?"

She shoved a card into my hand. She was Eunice Buntz. "Are you currently homeowners?" she asked.

"Just getting into the market," I replied, oozing self-assurance. The cider machine was pumping and hissing like a respirator.

Diana and I went up to check out the bedrooms. The kids' rooms were like Nike shoe boxes, but the master bedroom had a little sitting area, with a ceiling fan and a fireplace separate from the action center of the bedroom. In the main arena, the decorator had gone whole hog, with a wall of mirrors and a round bed that had a padded pink and green spread, and lush plants that set off my allergies, and a bathroom fit for a Roman orgy.

"There's no door on it," I said, between sneezes.

"That's an architectural affectation," Diana scoffed. "I'd never design a house with no door on the bathroom. Who wants to be doing her business with an audience? I mean really?"

But it was the bed that got me. "Which end's the head?"

"It doesn't matter. You just start anywhere."

"I've got to try this out." I slipped out of my penny loafers and crawled to the center of the bed, then flopped. "This is weird."

"Get up! Eunice is coming."

I scrambled to my feet just in time.

"You like the bedroom?" Eunice Buntz asked.

"It has some stylistic innovations," Diana said.

40

"My husband is intrigued with the concept of round-ness in the room."

"What does Mr. Wagner do?" Eunice Buntz asked.

"I'm an assistant district attorney," I said, slipping into my shoes. "Consumer fraud undercover, very confidential. My wife is an investment counselor."

Eunice was impressed. "This is a very well planned home for a young up-and-coming family."

Someone set off a tinkly bell over the front door to alert Eunice. She retreated to the first floor and the dog-crap pecan pie.

"Come see the view," Diana said. My shoes sank into the green carpet as I went to the window and stood behind Diana. I wrapped my arms around her; we could easily have been a married couple looking over our brown heaps of earth that weren't lawn yet, and the bones of half-built houses, and the twiggy promises of trees, if you lived long enough to see it all happen. But I'm getting ahead of myself. In those days I thought everyone lived forever, except Jimi Hendrix.

"It's not an inspiring view, Adam. Let's not buy this house. Hey, isn't that your friend Miriam Pelham over on the bike path?"

I dragged my lips off Diana's neck; it was true, it was Miriam, walking with a giant of a man in denim overalls.

"Who's the guy? What a wonderful bush of a beard. Why don't you grow a beard like that, Adam?"

"I've got a better chance of growing a second head."

"Could Miriam Pelham have such a dashing fa-ther? He looks sort of like Paul Bunyan on the chili cans. I would absolutely die if my father held my hand in public like that."

"That couldn't be her father."

"Why not?"

"Too young," I said. "Maybe it's a boyfriend."

"Too old." Diana shook her head, and her hair brushed back and forth across my lips.

"Do that again."

"Too old." This time she wiggled everything from the waist up.

"*How* old?"

"Not old enough," said Eunice Buntz, sneaking up on us. "You didn't fool me for a minute. I am trying to sell a house. Bye-bye, folks." She stepped back, clearly intending for us to pass her on our way off the planet forever.

"Thank you, Ms. Buntz," Diana said, with her sweetest puppy eyes glistening. "Adam, you can take me back to drug rehab now."

Dodging the sprinkler outside, Diana said, "Let's catch up with Miriam and Paul Bunyan. I want to get a closer look at that guy." Diana had the engine running before I was even buckled in. We headed up Thirteenth Street where we'd last seen them.

There are three places in Wichita where pimples in the road might loosely be called hills. Wichita, Kansas, is *not* San Francisco. Diana flew over the top of the zit of a hill on Thirteenth, and there was our prey, moving along at a good clip. Actually, it looked like Paul Bunyan was propelling Miriam along, like when you push a stalled car long enough that it takes off on its own. Diana honked, but the man did not turn around. Miriam stopped dead and leaned against a fence. We pulled into the service entrance of a clump of new house skeletons, and I jumped out over the door of the convertible.

"Hi, Miriam," Diana called. "We saw you walking by. Is this your dad?"

Miriam was tilted toward the fence, and it seemed all her weight rose to her shoulders and sank into the wooden panels. She looked gray and was sweating like a pig, even though it was only about 55 degrees. Trying to catch her breath, she said, "This is Brother — "

"Oh, he's your brother," Diana said. "Well, that explains it."

"What does it explain?" the man asked, finally acknowledging us. His voice had a golden resonance, like a radio DJ's. He fixed his sea-blue eyes on Diana and would not lift them.

"Only that we couldn't figure it out," Diana stammered. "Well, it doesn't matter." She moved closer to me, reached for my fingers.

I asked, "Are you okay, Miriam?"

"Yes," she said, but it was a lie.

"Who are your friends, Miriam?"

"This is Diana Cameron and — her boyfriend," she replied, not looking at us.

"What is Diana Cameron's boyfriend's name?" the man asked, and I had the feeling that his questions were like commands.

"Adam Bergen," I said, and I stepped forward to shake hands. His was so hot that I almost pulled my hand back. Remember the movie, *The Karate Kid*? My favorite part was when Mr. Miyagi, the old man, clapped his hands together and focused all his power into one hand, and then he put it on the

43

kid to relieve pain. But this guy with the reddish beard was no black belt in karate, and his hand shouldn't have been so hot. I glanced at my palm, as if he might have raised a welt on it, but it was still smooth.

"You have told me about Adam," the man said, and a little color rose in Miriam's cheeks, as she replied, "Yes, Brother James."

Brother James? Diana and I exchanged looks. Was he like a church deacon or something? We didn't have brothers and deacons in the synagogue, but I watched a lot of TV. There's always one of those lunatic religious types turning up on *Barney Miller* and *Night Court* reruns.

The Brother James guy said, "I will leave you with your friends, Miriam. Be strong." She didn't look like she could be strong enough to stumble over to the car. Brother James walked back toward Rock Road with even, giant steps, his hands in his pockets, and the chunky heels of his cowboy boots resounding off the pavement.

"You're both so dressed up," Miriam said weakly.

"Adam and I were just house-hunting."

"You really look nice." She said it to Diana, but she was looking at me. It must have been that famous phallic symbol, the Man's Tie, that got her, because she turned totally red. Then I wondered if my fly was open, but there's no way to check without drawing everybody else's eyes to the target.

"That big guy is such a hunk," Diana said.

"A hunk?" Miriam leaned her head against the fence post.

"A babe. A fox. A study. You know, I mean he's a tall, meaty man."

"Jesus, Diana, the guy's her preacher. She's not supposed to notice."

Diana snapped, "Ministers aren't supposed to be without gender, Adam. Only Catholic priests are into celibacy."

Miriam's face, which had been flashing red like a neon sign a minute ago, was now as white as a puddle of Elmer's glue. "Has he rounded the corner?"

I told her I didn't see him, and Miriam slid to the ground. Her head fell back against the fence. I saw the wood vibrate with the impact. Diana crouched beside Miriam. What if there was something wrong with her that only women tell each other? I circled a bush and tried to look invisible.

"You need a doctor," Diana said. "You look positively terrible. Adam, don't you think she needs a doctor?"

She looked more like she needed an undertaker. I'd seen people look healthier at Halloween parties.

"Come on," Diana prodded. "Adam and I are taking you to a minor emergency center."

"No," Miriam protested weakly.

"That's stupid, and I have no patience with avoidable stupidity. You're as limp as a wet towel. Adam, help her up."

Diana and I each took an arm and tried sliding Miriam back up to her feet, but she was like dead weight. Finally she stood up and let out a whelp like a dog whose paw's been stepped on.

"What's going on?" Diana asked, as we settled Miriam into the back seat of the convertible.

"I don't know."

Diana flipped her hair off the back of her neck, her sign that she was through fooling around and was coming in for the kill. We drove to the emergency center, back over the hill and right through a red light at Rock Road. Brother James had turned off somewhere; anyway, I was relieved that we didn't have to pass him. Miriam made some lame attempts to get us to drop her at home, but Diana was determined.

At Mediplex, we eased Miriam into one of the plastic chairs in the waiting room. Diana, of course, did the talking.

"This is Miriam Pelham, P-E-L-H-A-M. She needs to see a doctor immediately."

The nurse, a Ms. Doolan, asked, "Is she a minor?"

"Well, sort of."

"Do you have written consent from her parent or legal guardian in the form of a notarized letter authorizing medical examination and treatment?"

"Well, not exactly."

"We're just her friends," I said. "She needs help, look at her."

Ms. Doolan nodded crisply. She must have been able to see that Miriam was the color of an old sweat sock. "And is either of you over twenty-one?"

"This is ridiculous," Diana cried. "You call this humane medical treatment? I'm writing a letter to the editor."

"I'm over twenty-one," I said, hoping the suit and tie might sway Ms. Doolan. "I'm an assistant district attorney. Would you like to see an ID?"

"No," the nurse said with a faint smile. She slid the consent form across the slick counter and buzzed for a doctor.

CHAPTER SIX

Told by Miriam

The doctor had a foreign accent. I could barely understand him, but I heard him say I should be in the hospital. Mama would never consent. I didn't want her to consent. I locked my eyes shut, praying for strength, while the little dark man poked and prodded me in private places and asked me questions no one should have to answer.

Please God, I said to myself over and over, get me through this, and a voice from inside my head, very much like my own, but not my own, said, But look where you are, child.

A nurse came in, and the foreign doctor told her to find Mama. What would Mama do if they phoned her? Especially if the men were home, and where else would the men be on a Sunday afternoon except home, puttering with their power saw and knotty lumber? The nurse fixed a tight thing, a blood pressure cuff, she said it was, on my upper arm, pumped air into it, and watched the little clock face on it. She obviously did not like what it said. She gave the doctor some numbers that made no sense to me, something over something. He mumbled. The nurse laid me down and put a hard crackling pillow under

47

my knees, which helped the pulling at my back. Her cool hand brushed my arm. The panic rose in my throat; I swallowed and swallowed, afraid I'd throw up. She asked me about school, about what clubs I belonged to, about my friends. I don't remember what I answered, and I don't think it mattered to her. Minutes passed. She would not leave me, but she'd run out of questions. She kept rubbing my arm; I felt the hair stand up on it. Finally, I heard a loud commotion out in the waiting room — my uncles.

"I want the girl out of here," Uncle Benjamin roared. "It's against the law, you keeping her here. You never signed, did you Louise?"

I didn't hear Mama's response, but I knew she'd never signed.

Then the doctor was out there talking to them. He slowed down and pronounced everything distinctly for their benefit. "She is very sick. She must be transferred to a hospital. She must have tests. I suspect she is dehydrated. Her blood pressure is dangerously high."

Uncle Vernon said, "I'm going in to get her," and I heard the swinging door slam against the wall. Uncle Vernon yanked back the curtain on my cubicle. The nurse clutched my arm tighter. "Little girl, we're going home," he said, reaching for my arm.

"You can't do that." Maybe because Uncle Vernon was a small, bald man, the nurse thought she stood a chance against him. "I will not let you take her."

"Well, you have no choice, miss. She's my blood kin, not yours." Uncle Vernon yanked my hand, and it felt like a balloon had burst in my back. The

48

nurse caught me and lowered me to a wheelchair.

In the waiting room, there was absolute chaos. Diana was yelling at Uncle Benjamin, while the doctor mumbled unintelligibly again. Adam grabbed the handles of the wheelchair and turned me around so that my back was to the crowd, and I was just as happy to stare at nothing. Mama came and knelt beside the wheelchair. "Baby, they want to take you to a hospital."

"I know, Mama."

"We can't let them do that."

"I know."

"But I am so worried about you," she said, tears streaming down her face. "I'll see if I can reach Brother James."

"Not this time, Mama." There were already too many people there. Uncle Benjamin had bullied the nurse back behind the swinging door and held it shut against her. I saw her feet under the door, and finally she walked away. Later I figured out that she'd gone somewhere in the back to call the police.

All of them yelled out their positions, like carnival barkers. I focused on the wall, on a picture of a white stallion in midleap over a hurdle in a perfect field of poppies.

Two officers arrived, no doubt at the tail end of a peaceful Sunday afternoon shift. They were hardly prepared for the battle in the emergency room. They sent for reinforcements. One of them blew a whistle to silence the carnival. Diana and Adam stood on each side of me, but not facing the stallion, while the adults explained one by one what was going on. I sensed that Diana wanted to jump in, but Adam restrained her. I tilted my head back and saw him behind me with his arm around Diana's shoulder.

There were at least half a dozen phone calls. I couldn't keep track of them all, but finally we were told we were all to sit tight, while one of the policemen went to get something. No one spoke, but tension hung heavily in the air. I looked around at all these people fighting over me: a doctor, two nurses, two friends (did I dare to think of them as friends?), three policemen, my mother, and my two uncles.

Uncle Benjamin had flecks of sawdust in his hair. Uncle Vernon fidgeted with a key chain, sliding the keys back and forth over the chain. The faint grinding sound was like the shower curtains being ripped back in the girls' locker room or back there, in my examining room. I figured out how to turn the wheelchair around. "Please, Uncle Vernon," I said, and all the heads turned toward me. Suddenly I realized that they had all been fighting over me, but they had forgotten that I was there. I was no longer important in the battle of wills.

Then a father carried a wailing child into the emergency room. Her hand was wrapped in a white towel. "Scalding water," I heard the father say, and I felt the little girl's searing pain. The doctor and nurse snapped back into action, while the rest of us waited. Adam and Diana finally sat down.

The computer printer behind the check-in desk hummed and spun out volumes of pages from its loom. They folded in broad pleats on the floor. Someone turned on the TV, and we all pretended to be engrossed in a football game, even the receptionist.

"Yes, *yes*," one of the policemen said, as about

nine men piled on top of the one holding the ball. All of them had muddy jerseys. I wondered how they ever got them white.

"The 49ers are hot this year, eh?" Uncle Vernon said. A band played "San Francisco, Open Your Golden Gate," and six blonde women with pompons kicked their legs way up over their heads.

"Oughtn't to do that over network TV," Uncle Benjamin said, with his eyes fastened on the screen.

Some woman started to come in, nearly doubling over with a loose, wracking cough. She must have smelled the tension in the room. She looked us over, policemen and all, and turned around and left.

After what seemed like two long afternoons, one of the police officers came back with a court order to have me hospitalized, and if I'd thought there was a battle in the emergency room, it was only a border skirmish compared to the holy war that was about to begin.

I no longer belonged to my mother. I was imprisoned in a hospital bed with a needle in my arm connected to a bottle that dripped some kind of liquid into my veins. I had a police guard outside my door, a guardian *ad litem* (which is a court-appointed lawyer), a state social worker, a primary care physician, and an oncologist, for by 4:00 the next afternoon, they decided I had bone cancer.

I'd had a bone scan, which meant having some kind of dye pumped through my system, waiting around for hours, then sliding on a table through a monstrous machine that took picture upon picture of the insides of me. I tried not to watch, tried to concentrate on a stain in the ceiling, tried to name all the books of the *Book in Gold Leaf*, all the disciples, all the saints, all the martyrs, but too often my mind would wander and my eyes would stray to the screen where my body was being drawn, quarter by quarter. They explained that the dye would accumulate in those areas where a tumor was suspected. I saw the darkening ball, the size of a walnut, growing in my pelvic bone. So small, I thought. A little thing like that couldn't cause much harm, and certainly not the pain that had been waking me up four, five times a night for weeks.

"Localized," I heard the technician say. "Bet the doc'll confirm it. She's a lucky chick."

But what the doctor said was that I was to have a bone biopsy. They would put me to sleep, stick a long needle into my back and suck out something from inside that bone. The laboratory would look it over, and that would be the final word on the subject. I did not like the sound of being put to sleep. That's what veterinarians did to old dogs. I never actually thought they were planning to kill me, but neither did the dog who was lovingly led into the execution chamber. "Poetry is a bitch." I remembered Mrs. Loomis saying that and my shock at hearing it. It seemed so long ago, maybe months, since Adam Bergen and I had discussed fire and ice. But it was only a few unbearably long days.

There was nothing Mama or the men could do about the biopsy without risking arrest, but they could holler at the doctors and nurses and social workers. Only when Brother James came to my bedside were they hushed.

Brother James sent the men on to work and walked Mama down the hall to a sitting room. It was the first time I'd been alone for twenty-four hours, and I breathed the silence gratefully. A nurse had set a bunch of sunflowers in a glass by my bed, and I caught their scent like wilted summer grass. Brother James was back to fill my room with abiding comfort, and I quickly dismissed the pleasure of being alone.

"Miriam," he said, gathering me to him. I flopped onto his chest like a rag doll. His huge hands smoothed the gown over my back. "Put your life in the hands of the Lord," he said softly. "Isaiah 40: 'They who wait for the Lord shall renew their strength, they shall mount up with wings like eagles, they shall run and not be weary, they shall walk and not faint.' Remember."

"Brother James, please don't be cross with me, but I don't feel like I will ever run and not be weary."

"Remember Matthew 13. The people of Nazareth suffered for their doubt and disbelief, for we are told, 'And He did not do many mighty works there, because of their unbelief.' Let the Lord do mighty works within your body and spirit, Miriam."

"It hurts, Brother James, and I'm so scared."

"Shh, child." He smoothed my hair off my forehead and wiped a tear across my cheek with a rough finger. He laid me back down on my pillow, with the bed cranked up to a near-sitting position. He slid his chair closer to the bed and took both my hands. His voice changed, became both more personal and more distant, as if he were shouting to me from far, far away. "I shall rebuke this child's pain and disease, just as Jesus caused the fever to vanish in Peter's mother. I call the pain out where

53

I can see it, I summon it to the surface where I can smash it like a fly on the wall. What do you feel, Miriam?"

"A churning in my stomach, Brother James."

"Yes, yes. The Holy Spirit is fiercely spinning and gathering everything in its path. It is banishing Satan. It is sucking up the pain in your back, it is swallowing whole the tumor they say is in your bones. It is drawing all the evil of pain and disbelief into a tighter and tighter circle. Do you feel it?"

"Yes," I said breathlessly. The black walnut, everything, drawn out of me.

"Tighter and tighter, the circle." His voice changed pitch; it was harsher now. "When the circle can compress no smaller, it will change direction. Is it changing now, child?"

"Yes, yes!"

"Yes. It is spinning out, scattering cool sparks outside of you. You are no longer afflicted, praise God."

I wanted desperately to believe him. I believed him. He was silent for a few minutes, with his jaw locked in a determined prayer. I felt no pain, and the panic that had been just below the surface since this whole thing started settled into a serenity. The quiet after the storm, I told myself. Or was it the eye of the hurricane?

"Now that you're feeling better, we must plan," Brother James said. He still had hold of my hands. "We will not defy the law of the land, but neither will we comply," he said. I did not understand. "Oh, I could bring in half a dozen brothers and have you out of this place and back in your mama's house in no time."

"That's where I want to be, Brother James."

"Yes, but we have this court order to contend with. It says they have the legal right to keep you here. It says they can run tests on you until they have their so-called scientific answers. But it does not say they can administer any of their poisons."

I furtively glanced toward the IV dripping into my arm.

"I've checked on that. It's only sugar water, no drugs. I'll pull it out when I think it's the right time, but we'll go along with it for now. It's to our advantage, and it doesn't violate God's law. But I swear to God, and Sword and the Spirit Church will stand behind me on this, I will never let them give you drugs that they disguise as medicinal, and I will never let them pump someone else's blood into your veins. You have my word. Now, tell me about your friends."

"Are you angry with them for getting me into this?" I asked.

"No, child. They only did what their mothers and daddies taught them. Do they come to visit you here?"

"Diana's coming tonight, I think, but I haven't seen Adam yet."

"Lucifer comes disguised in plumes and finery, but is Lucifer still."

"I think he's a nice boy, Brother James."

"A very nice boy. Well-mannered, bright, fine looking boy. But remember, he doesn't follow our Lord."

"I suppose not."

"That's my girl. Now, don't worry about your mama. I'll have Sister Naomi go over and stay with her until we get this settled, so your uncles won't fret." He pulled a peppermint out of his pocket. The crinkly wrapper reminded me of green cellophane around a Christmas fruit basket. He motioned for me to open my mouth, and he slid the red and white candy onto my tongue, as if it were a communion wafer.

CHAPTER SEVEN

Told by Adam

"What is *this*? Dad, what's this mystery food she's passing off on us?" It jiggled on my plate like dead vomit-colored Jell-O.

"Tofu," my mother said. "It's healthy. It's Japanese. They eat it in California."

"Yes, but we're in Kansas, Abby. This is beef country." Dad moved the offender under a lettuce leaf, which, incidentally, was a lot greener than any lettuce we'd ever eaten in this house.

"I'm trying to make you two healthy," Mom said, pouting. She was hurt, as if she were Japanese, or even Californian.

"Speaking of healthy," my father began, "I'm up at Memorial Hospital today visiting McGorkle, that client of mine who was in the grain elevator accident, and I pass this room, you could swear a foreign potentate is staying in it. There's a sign on the door saying NO ONE ADMITTED WITHOUT PRIOR CLEARANCE, and standing outside the door's an armed guard. And who do you suppose is in the room?"

"Danny Glickman?" Mom guessed. Dan Glickman was a member of our synagogue and also our congressman.

"Not Danny Glickman. That girl, the religious nut with cancer."

"That's Miriam Pelham," I said quietly.

My mother asked, "You know this girl?"

"Sort of."

Dad squished the tofu with his fork. "So, does she really buy into all that Jesus stuff?"

"Yeah, I think so."

"God, the poor kid."

I told my parents I was going to the library after dinner, but I went to Memorial Hospital instead. Don't ask me why. I had to show my driver's license and leave it with the guard outside Miriam's door before the nurse would even go in to ask if Miriam wanted to see me. Finally, they let me in. Miriam was curled on her side with the blankets up to her ears and her back to me. She didn't say a word when I walked in.

"It's the vulture," I quipped. "You know, the thing with feathers?" Nothing. "Okay, so you're mad at me for getting you into this mess. You're freezing me out, right?"

I was feeling pretty stupid talking to her back. Maybe she was asleep, and I was really talking to myself — even stupider. So I walked around to the other side of the bed. Her eyes were wide open, and tears were dribbling down her face at this weird angle, like winter rain.

"Why are you here?" Her voice was nasally and thick, as if she had a bad cold or was me during allergy season.

"Good question. Why am I here?"

"You'll think of something. You're the debater." Those tears kept sliding down her face, soaking her hair. A wet circle was spreading on her pillow. I looked away; I was always embarrassed when my mother cried. Diana never cried, which is part of why I liked her so much. Finally — I don't know what got into me — I picked up a corner of the sheet and wiped Miriam's tears with it.

"I'b id trouble, Adam." Now she was using the sheet for a handkerchief, blowing her honker like a grieving widow.

"Can I do anything?"

"Doe."

That cut me off, clean. "Yeah, well I'll see you later, then." I was more than ready to leave. Besides, the air-conditioning was blowing spores all over the room from these big puffy flowers, and my nose was starting to run. If I stayed much longer, I'd be using the other corner of her sheet.

But when I got to the door, she eased herself onto her back. I saw the pain streak across her face like lightning. "I'b id big trouble."

Did she want to talk? I hung around a minute, but she didn't say anything else. "Listen, why don't I check in with you in a couple of days when you're feeling better, okay? I'm getting ready for a debate tournament in Dodge City on Friday and Saturday. Maybe I'll come by on Sunday."

"And baybe you won't."

That was a real possibility.

"But baybe you will?"

"Sure." Not a chance. Well, a slim chance.

* * *

59

"It's insane, Adam, clearly insane," Diana said. We were in Mr. Bennet's van, somewhere way west of Wichita. Mr. Bennet was alone in the front seat, then Diana and I had the middle section, and behind us Andy Woodman and Jeremy Schein, our sophomore novice team, were catching a nap before we pulled into Dodge. We were past the Golden Arches, the Pizza Huts, and the Taco Ticos, out into what is nostalgically called the prairie. We call it the boondocks, that wheaty flatland between Pratt and Dodge City, where Wyatt Earp is supposed to be buried, but isn't.

"I mean, the girl is stuck in the hospital with a police guard, and half the state of Kansas is arguing over what's best for her," Diana said. "I don't see what the fight's about. I know what's best for her."

"Yeah? What?" I thought about the soaked pillow.

"They should start zapping her with chemo, Adam. I know. I interviewed Dr. Miller for the *Vanguard* article." Diana, of course, was editor of the school paper. "And Dr. Miller's a cancer specialist. He's world-famous all over the greater Midwest, and he says the treatment of choice is chemotherapy. He mentioned some drug, Cytocel, that he'd probably prescribe, and he says she's got better than a fifty-percent chance of beating this thing. So what are they waiting for?"

"I don't think it's that simple." It used to be, I thought to myself, but it was getting more and more complicated every day. I was actually thinking about going back to the hospital to visit the girl.

Andy leaned forward and dug his chin into my

shoulder. "Who are you talking about, that Jesus weirdo up at Memorial?"

"They're poetry partners," Diana explained.

"Wow. She's one of the looniest space cases I ever knew."

Diana said, "You don't know everything, Andy."

"No, you're the only one who knows everything."

Diana smiled. "Well, I know what they should be doing. They should be moving posthaste into aggressive chemical treatment while the tumor is still localized. A direct quote from my *Vanguard* article. Adam? You're not talking."

"I don't have to. You talk enough for all of us."

"Well, thanks a lot. You sure depend on me to talk in debates. I'm always bailing you out."

"That's a bald-faced lie!"

"Right," Diana said, leaning over to kiss my neck.

"Stop all that slobbering. I'm sleeping," Jeremy shouted.

"But it's the evidence that's most important," whispered Diana, "and the evidence is clear that Miriam can't risk any delays."

Andy climbed over the seat and planted himself between Diana and me. "What's that crazy religion she's in? Something like Sword and Sorcery."

"Sword and the Spirit," I replied. I'd heard the name half a dozen times on TV in the past week, and my parents were always talking about it at dinner. "It's from the Bible somewhere. It means 'the word of God.'"

"Yeah, the Great Swordsman. Are they, like, nineteenth century or what?"

"All right, Woodman, let's get the facts straight,"

I said. "It's a small religious sect with about six hundred members in Kansas and Nebraska and maybe Indiana, I'm not sure. The head man is this guy about the size of Bull on *Night Court* — heavy beard, carpenter's overalls, Shepler's bargain boots — you get a clear picture? They call him Brother James. His name's probably really something like Gonzo or Howie."

"You're such a cynic, Adam. The man definitely has charisma," Diana said.

"The church gets off on the Bible, which they call the *Book in Gold Leaf.* And they're not into doctors."

"What have they got against doctors?" Andy asked. "My uncle's a urologist."

"Oh, gross," said Diana.

"Their thing about doctors is, they believe that all healing comes from God, maybe through Jesus, I'm not real clear on that, but they say it goes directly to the sick person and doesn't need an errand boy like a doctor."

"That's cool," Andy said, "only what happens if she gets sicker and sicker? I mean, like, people die of cancer."

I'd thought about this a dozen times, how she could die while she was waiting for God to cure her. Or worse, she could die while waiting for the government and the doctors to fight it out with her family and Brother James. And wasn't Brother James just like an errand boy, just like a doctor, only he didn't give drugs?

"How come you know so much about it?" Andy asked, flexing the earphones he was anxious to put on to drown out my voice.

So I kept the answer short. "I pay attention. Jesus, it's on the news forty times a day."

"I only watch CNN," Andy said. "Is it on CNN?"

No, but I had a feeling it would be soon. This thing would be huge. The prairie streaked by, and I couldn't clear my head of Miriam Pelham.

Diana slept most of the way back from Dodge. She said she was getting something and didn't think I should come over to her house. She coughed in my face to emphasize her point. I was always sneezing and snorting because of my allergies, but when Diana got a runny nose, it was like a national health crisis.

So anyway, it looked like I wasn't going to be enjoying what I'd looked forward to most that whole week — lying around on Diana's couch with the only light coming from the TV. And nothing else was going on, so after we dropped Diana off, Mr. Bennet dropped me at the hospital.

Miriam sat on her bed, dressed in her usual school clothes and with her hair pulled back over one shoulder. She was cutting words out of a magazine to make a collage or something. When I pushed her door open, the breeze made a bunch of her cut-outs fly around the room. "Hi," I said, chasing the scraps of paper around.

"How did you do in Dodge City?" she asked.

"Won."

"Of course."

"Diana's a lot better than I am."

"She couldn't be."

"Right. I lied."

She liked my grin. It made her own eyes smile,

which was a lot better than those soppy tears from the other night.

"What are you doing?" I asked.

"Oh, nothing." She gathered the words into a messy pile and stuffed them in her drawer, along with a bottle of rubber cement. On the bedside table was a small glass of some thick orange-colored juice, with its weight sunk to the bottom. I leaned forward for a whiff of it. She handed me the glass, and I drank some warm apricot stuff.

"Disgusting, isn't it?" she said.

"Then how come you gave it to me?"

"It's been here two days." She shifted around, and the magazine slid to the floor. I reached over to pick it up and felt the apricot rise in my throat. The magazine was called *Young Christian Crusader*, and it had a white basketball player on the cover, a guy who looked like he'd never sweat.

"So what are you doing with the cutouts? Making something — what — a scrapbook?"

"A sort of letter."

"About all this stuff you're going through?"

"No," she said, her eyes dimming again.

"Who's it for?" I thought maybe she was making it for me.

"This boy I know in Emporia. He's going to Greece this summer on Teen Missions International. He's going to put up buildings. It's like the Peace Corps, only Christian."

"He doesn't get paid for it either, I'll bet."

"Not a dime," Miriam said, smiling again.

"So, are you going with him?"

"To Greece?"

"No, *with* him, going out with him. Is he your boyfriend?"

"No, no, nothing like that. He's just a boy I met at a church conference. Brother James introduced us."

"Well, what's he like?" I asked. I pictured a face with pink bumps just ready to burst, and thin blond hair, and watery gray eyes. The total package came to five foot three, and maybe he sniffed a lot. But Miriam didn't realize I meant, what's he like *physically*.

"Very serious," Miriam said. "Not like you."

"I can be serious."

"I've never seen it."

"Yeah, well there's a lot you don't know about me." How do I explain why I got mad all of a sudden? Maybe because I'd had a long day, and it didn't end the way I'd expected, and now I was being asked to defend my personality, which Diana already understood so well. I was starting to fume, and sneezing about six times in a row didn't help my disposition. "Why've you got all those man-eating plants around?" I moved one plant over to the window, out of whiffing distance. Jesus, two years of allergy shots. I shoved some moldy flowers into the corner behind the chair.

"No one's keeping you here," Miriam said, handing me a couple of tissues out of the box on her tray table. It was like something your mother would do, handing you a Kleenex when you were crying at home about being called a sissy for crying about being called a sissy at school.

I hated the way my voice sounded after I'd had

a sneezing fit. "I guess you want to get back to your magazine stuff, anyway."

"Not really," she said, shrugging. "It's boring here."

"But this guy in Emporia, he's waiting anxiously for your letter."

"I doubt it. I just didn't have anybody else to write to."

She eased herself back against her pillow, with her hands behind her head and her legs crossed at the ankles. Her eyes were closed. Good thing, too, because mine were wide open as I noticed for the first time that there were definite signs of shape to this girl. For some crazy reason, her bare feet embarrassed me. Me, who's always looking for fresh flesh.

"I acted like an idiot the other night. I apologize," she said. Her eyes were still closed.

"Not exactly an idiot," I assured her. "Moron, maybe. Imbecile, possibly; cretin comes to mind. But you definitely weren't idiotic."

"Anyway, thanks for coming by, Adam."

"Am I leaving?"

"Probably," she said.

Saturday night, and here I sat beside the bed of a homely, stubborn religious fanatic. There were parties going on all over the east side, CD players and car stereos blasting, food and drink for the taking, videos, go-carts, poker games, dragging Douglas. I wanted to get going, but I couldn't take my eyes off those neat, square, faintly bluish toenails, and how the first toe gently crossed over the second, the way I used to cross my fingers as a kid to tell myself that the lie I was telling was only a white lie.

I stayed, even though we didn't talk at all for fifteen minutes. I'd never been quiet with anyone before.

At home, my father had big news.

"Adam, your mother and I have debated about this all day, and I've decided to take the case."

"What case?" I asked, with very little interest. My father was always taking unpopular cases, like he represented an abortion clinic bomber and, another time, a kid who went crazy and shot two teachers. He almost always won, but not before his name was dragged through about twelve miles of mud, and he never even made expenses on these hot cases. But my dad is the kind of man who can't resist the causes no one else would dare touch. A bleeding heart, that's what my father is.

"I'm representing the church."

"Oh, yeah?" I was thinking about the guy with the serious acne in Emporia, about buildings in Greece, about the curl of Miriam's toes.

"Your friend with the cancer? I'm representing her church against the State of Kansas. You know how I chew up these church-state issues. This one's going to be a humdinger."

CHAPTER EIGHT

Told by Miriam

Mr. Bergen came to visit me, and I could see what Adam would grow up to look like. He had a very chiseled face, with a sharp nose and cheekbones and a healthy tan, and he still had a full head of dark, unruly hair. I liked him.

"Before this is done, you will hate me," he said. "I'll make your life miserable, because I have to know absolutely everything if I am to win this case for you. I have to know every symptom you experience, no matter how personal, and I have to know every facet of your religious belief, no matter how intimate. Do you understand?"

I nodded. I was getting used to being invaded.

"Fine. We'll get along." He slid a yellow pad out of his worn briefcase and pulled the cap off his fountain pen with his teeth. "Any questions?"

"One." I wasn't sure how to ask it. He was patient with my silence. While he waited, he took off his suit coat and rolled up the sleeves of his white shirt. I did not want to be aware of the dark hair visible beneath his shirt. Uncle Benjamin and Uncle Vernon always wore white T-shirts under their dress shirts; I thought all men did. And then I thought about whether Adam's shoulders would be as broad as his father's when he was a full-grown man, or his hair as dark.

"I was wondering," I began.

"Shoot."

Should I? The man seemed so tolerant. I wondered if Diana resembled Mr. Bergen's wife, when she was seventeen, and whether Diana was Jewish. How could Adam and she go together if she wasn't Jewish? Did Mr. Bergen approve of her? All this flitted through my head as I tried to formulate my question. "What I was wondering was, you tell me that you have to know everything if you're to win the case for me. What does winning mean, exactly?"

Mr. Bergen cleared his throat. I knew I'd asked the wrong question. Questions were my downfall. But a lot depended on his reply. He answered, measuring his words very carefully. Uncle Vernon used to say, "Lawyers are famous for saying as little as possible, in the most number of words, kinda like politicians."

Mr. Bergen said, "It means we win the right for your mother to determine how your illness is to be treated."

It seemed simple enough, but I knew it wasn't. "And that means I win?"

He tilted his chair back, rocked for a while. "It means that the church wins, it means that your family wins, it means that freedom of religion, as guaranteed by the First Amendment to the Constitution, wins."

"And me?"

"I'll tell you, Miriam Pelham, you're asking the wrong person."

69

"But you're my lawyer!"

"I've got faith in the U.S. Constitution, and I've got faith in the American judicial system. But I haven't got your kind of faith."

"You mean you don't believe God will heal me?"

"I mean I haven't got your kind of faith, that's all I mean. Now let me ask the questions for a couple of minutes."

As soon as I was over the bone biopsy and all the test results were in and they were sure about their diagnosis, there wasn't anything else the doctors could legally do. They had to let me go home. Gerri Kensler, my SRS social worker, came to explain the terms.

"Okay, here's the deal. You're officially in SRS custody. That's State and Rehabilitative Services. But the state's letting you live with your mother if you do a few little things."

I snapped my suitcase shut. "Like what?"

"Well —" Gerri flipped through legal-sized pages on her clipboard. We'd only been into this a week, and there were already pages and pages about me. Gerri was pretty and black and made-up like a model in a red knit suit that would have been perfect on Diana. She said the right things, but I didn't think she cared much about me. I'd heard that she had about sixty other kids to deal with.

"Okay, I found it. You've got to take your temperature twice a day, seven a.m. and five p.m., and keep a record of it. Then, every two weeks, on Fridays, you go in to see Dr. Gregory. The hospital will do periodic blood work and bone scans, unless things turn sour before then. And don't go to Europe or Bermuda or anywhere. That about covers it."

"It's just so ridiculous, Gerri. I'm going to be fine. I'm a lot better already, thank God. And you've met my uncles. Can't you just see them bringing me to the hospital every two weeks to see Dr. Gregory?"

Gerri pressed her lips together as if she were blotting her lipstick. I'd never seen anyone with such deep, wide lips, which she outlined in a dark brown shade. "Sure, I can see it, Miriam, because you and I don't have any choice in the thing. It's like the judge is king, and he says how it's gotta be in his kingdom. We just do what he says. Ask your lawyer; he'll tell you. It's because you're what we call a CINC."

"I know, I've heard it nine hundred times this week — a Child In Need of Care, like neglected and abused children. But that's just it, Gerri. I'm seventeen and not exactly a child. In seven months I'll be voting."

"Yes, but SRS can legally maintain custody until you're twenty-one."

"Anyway, I'm not abused or neglected. I've got a good, loving family and church. They take care of me."

"Fact is, Miriam, that's not the way Judge Bonnell sees it. He says your family *is* neglecting you by not treating your disease."

I picked up my suitcase and winced in pain. Naturally, it didn't escape her.

"You're hurting, girl. What's your family doing about that? They seeing that you get some pain pills? They getting you treatment for that bone tumor? Are they even giving you vitamins to build yourself back up? If they're not, it looks like neglect to the

71

rest of us who don't have a fax machine directly to God. Now, I'll stop by your home later to see you're settled in and to tell your mother what she has to do."

Just before Uncle Benjamin was due to pick me up, Brother James came to pray with me. He put his hands on my head. Usually he smelled of strong soap or of the faintly rusty odor of outdoor labor, but there was something different this time. I couldn't place it.

"Guide this child through the days ahead," he said, in his smooth, reassuring voice. "Visit her every hour of every day and hasten her return to strength. Give her caretakers the benefit of Your wisdom and compassion. Above all, ease her doubt, sweet Jesus, ease her doubt so the pain in her body and in her heart may be lifted. A-men."

"A-men," I repeated and opened my eyes. What smelled different? A new shirt, something on his hands? "Mr. Bergen was here," I said. "I like him."

"Good, good." Brother James seemed distracted, with his hands jammed into his pockets and his shoulders hunched up. Or impatient, like someone waiting for a late bus.

"I was wondering how you picked Mr. Bergen, or did he pick us? Or did someone send him to us?"

"Someone surely sent him." Brother James took one hand out of his pocket and pointed to the ceiling, which meant beyond the ceiling. "The Lord always provides. Mr. Bergen is good, the best there is, because his specialty is civil rights. Your rights are being violated, child, and your family's rights, and your religious rights, and these Jewish lawyers, they've got some kind of conscience that's hard to figure." Brother James leaned forward and straightened a picture of Jesus on my table. "But we will use him, Miriam, as an instrument of the Lord, for our righteous purposes. We'll take the Lord's gifts, however they come to us. Mr. Bergen doesn't lose his cases. Now, you're not to worry." Brother James got up and walked back and forth across my room. With his back to me, he said, "I believe he's the father of that boy who visits you, is he not?"

"Yes, Brother James."

"Well, the Lord works in mysterious ways, sure enough." He paced some more, as we waited for my dismissal papers and Uncle Benjamin. "You all packed?" he asked.

I pointed to the suitcase in the corner, looking like an orphan at the train depot.

"Then I believe you've forgotten something, child." He came back around the bed and handed me the picture from my bedside table. "You meant to carry it with you into your home, didn't you Miriam? Right there in your two hands." There was a knock at the door, Uncle Benjamin, no doubt. Brother James lay the picture of Jesus on my lap and leaned forward to kiss my forehead. Again I sensed an unusual odor. It reminded me of an animal you come upon in the forest, an animal that's frightened at the sight of you. It must have been something he'd handled earlier that morning; I never smelled it on him again.

The closer we got to home, the stronger I felt. Uncle Benjamin turned into Old Wood Road, and I thought I'd never seen anything so lovely. That one particular day in early November, the trees were nearly bare, and a blanket of crisp orange leaves covered most of the lawns in our neighborhood. A few pumpkins still guarded the doors of my neighbors. Our house was the smallest on the block, and the prettiest, with its teal blue shutters and the awnings, like sleepy eyelids, over all the windows. I remembered when Uncle Vernon put up the awnings and taught me how to crank them open. The blue and gold stripes were as bright as a new flag. Now, after ten years, they had an easy faded look about them, as though they were proud of the weathering they'd withstood.

"We're home," said Uncle Benjamin.

Mama ran out to the driveway as soon as we pulled into the carport.

"Get out and let me see you. Why, you look wonderful, baby."

Uncle Vernon ventured out. "Looking good."

"What do you mean looking good, Vern? She's the picture of health," Uncle Benjamin said with a snort.

"The very picture." Mama pushed me just out of range to have a better look, then pulled me to her again. Uncle Vernon took the picture of Jesus from my hands and an anemic plant, while Uncle Benjamin yanked my suitcase out of the car. They let me walk into the kitchen first, as if there were a surprise party waiting for me.

I loved the sound of the screen door bouncing against the door frame. Our kitchen smelled just the same, like a cup of cooled cinnamon tea. Mama had a perky bunch of yellow-orange mums in a glass on the table. The big portrait of Jesus over the table welcomed me home, too. We sat down to talk, in our usual places, but we did not talk about what we called "the case."

Uncle Vernon began, as he always did. "So, it's back to school, hunh? You way behind?"

"Mostly in physics. But I've kept up in English and French and all."

"Are you hungry, baby?"

Suddenly I was ravenous for some real homestyle cooking, not stringy, watery, drab hospital food.

"Because I've got chicken fricasee on the stove, and mashed potatoes, and green beans with bacon, just the way you like them."

"She baked you a pumpkin pie," Uncle Vernon said. "Be sure and save me and your uncle a slice before you gobble it all up." He smiled, either at me or at the thought of Mama's pumpkin pie.

"Seems like this would be a good time to give thanks to the One who delivered Miriam back to us," Uncle Benjamin said. "Shall we bow our heads?"

We ate the chicken and made small talk. Mama's face was flushed, and her fingers danced lightly around the table as she filled our plates. Finally, the men grew tired of the conversation and picked up the paper.

Mama and I moved to the living room. I sank into the beautiful couch, remembering how I'd been tortured with pain the last time I lay on it. The afghan was folded into a neat square on the arm of the couch, as though no one had used it since Mama had tried, without much success, to warm me that day. We heard the men rustling the newspaper in the kitchen, commenting on obituaries and letters to the editor.

Mama whispered, "I guess you read a lot of poetry, those long days in the hospital."

"Oh, yes. It kept me company. There was no one much to talk to there."

Mama squeezed my hand. "There was no one much to talk to here, either."

"You need a book of poetry, Mama." I'd tried giving up the poetry, thinking that just having the book in my drawer next to the bed was enough. Just feeling the nubby binding, the cool white pages that I could almost read with my fingers as if they were printed in Braille. But those days when I felt so lonely and bewildered, lines of poetry wafted through my mind, and the sounds and words bathed my soul in warmth the way nothing else quite did. "This is Ralph Waldo Emerson, Mama: 'I heard or seemed to hear the chiding sea/say, Pilgrim, why so late and slow to come?' Isn't that purely beautiful?"

"Very nice," Mama said. Then after a few seconds, "But you musn't lose sight of the lovely verse in the *Book in Gold Leaf*."

"I never will, Mama," I swore, but for one panicky second, I couldn't recall a single line. Then I blurted out, like a baby's wail in church: " 'Love your enemies, bless them that curse you.' Matthew 5:44."

Mama was astonished at my enthusiasm for this passage. "Well, I declare! You haven't forgotten Scripture."

"Mama," I whispered, "Adam Bergen may come over. Remember him?"

"Oh . . . my . . . ," Mama hesitated just a second

and leaned over to hug me. "I'm so happy to have you home. I expect he'll just stay a short while."

Later that afternoon, Mama let him in and directed him to the rocking chair, and she and Uncle Benjamin and Uncle Vernon all hovered around. Poor Adam! He looked like a guppy in a tank full of barracudas, and the more anxious he got, the faster he rocked, until I thought he might catapult right out our front window. He ate about a pound of peanuts, tossing them way back in his mouth. I'm not sure he took time to chew them. I kept catching his eye, telegraphing him reassuring smiles. Twenty minutes was all he could tolerate, and also just about all the time I could keep from bursting out laughing. I gave him a nod that it was okay to leave, and we were all relieved when he bolted for the door.

"High-strung boy," Uncle Vernon said.

"Nervous as a cat — "

"I know, I know, Benjamin — as a cat on a hot tin roof," Uncle Vernon added.

I don't think they knew that this line came from a playwright they'd not approve of one little bit.

CHAPTER
NINE

Told by Adam

While Miriam was gone, everyone talked about her situation, but now that she was back, they treated her as if what she had, either the cancer or the religion, could spread and infect them all. Before she got sick, everyone just ignored her. Now they kept her at a safe distance. I was the closest thing to a friend she had, and the only one, as far as I know, who visited her in the hospital, except for Diana who would have visited Freddy or Orca. But what could I do? I had friends of my own.

Sitting in English, I caught Miriam out of the corner of my eye, looking pale but determined, with her elbow propped up on her desk to support her head. It honestly hurt me to look at her. I looked behind me at Diana's empty seat. Her cold had run to bronchitis, and she missed Miriam's first days back at school. I missed her, and kept looking for her, listening for her undercurrent of commentary.

"Adam, is your head on a swivel this morning?" Mrs. Loomis asked.

"He's like the girl in *The Exorcist*," Brent said. "Did you see the thing on *60 Minutes* about the exorcisms?"

"Irrelevant, Brent." Mrs. Loomis had spoken, and the bush was not consumed.

By Thursday Diana wasn't contagious anymore, and she invited me over, with all the homework assignments. She had a real set-up in the library of her modest little villa. She lay back on three pink pillows fluffed up on the arm of the circular couch. A fire sizzled in front of her and blew warm air out into the room through some black tube thing they had rigged up. The stereo played softly — Chopin, she said it was; you could have fooled me.

"Oh, Adam," Diana said, from the depths of her pillows, "I'm so glad you came. It's been incredibly boring around here." She wore a bright pink robe, the kind that doesn't button, but folds over itself, and the only thing holding it together was a tie at the waist. I considered infinite possibilities as she stretched her arms out to welcome me.

I sat on the floor beside her pillows, in the perfect spot for her to smooth my hair and trace my ears and make the hair on my neck stand straight up. In fact, everything came to attention. I was in love.

My mother had a famous saying: "Don't confuse love with lust, and if you do, keep your pants on." Diana rolled toward me, and, what luck, her robe fell open just enough to show me a hint of a brown tip I'd always suspected was there. Here at last was living proof.

I climbed on the couch. Diana scooted back to make room for me. It was a narrow, curved couch. We had no choice but to be pressed together like a grilled cheese sandwich. I was in love, I was in lust; big difference.

The door of the library opened. Diana shoved me

to the floor. Her mother, a huge woman even eye-to-eye, stood over me with one of the pokers from the fireplace in her hand. For a crazy second, I thought she might run it through my gut.

"Lucky I stopped by," Mrs. Cameron said. "The fire was a bit too intense. I'll give those logs a stir." She turned toward the fireplace and viciously jabbed at the crusty logs. "I'll be back," she threatened, this time leaving the library door open behind her.

As soon as Mrs. Cameron was gone, Diana burst out laughing. She slid to the floor beside me, tightening the sash on her robe. "A sense of humor is everything, Adam. My mother cracks me up."

"Oh, yeah? I thought buns were everything," I muttered.

"Buns, and a sense of humor. Two of the most important attributes in the human animal." She reached back for a tray of snacks, sprayed a mound of creamy jalapeño cheese on a Triscuit cracker, and stuffed it in my mouth. " 'Lucky I stopped by,' " she said, imitating her mother down to the mealy Boston accent. " 'The fire was a bit too intense.' " I chewed and laughed and sprayed crumbs all over the place. Diana brushed them under the couch and pinched my lips shut until I'd swallowed.

"You want to look at the homework?" I asked, hoping she didn't.

"Not really. They'll give me the weekend to catch up. I'd rather tell you about something revolutionary I found out this week." She sat on her knees in front of me, all seriousness now. "My mother's bridge club met here on Tuesday, and all they talked about the whole time was Miriam Pelham."

"Why her?"

"It's all anyone talks about anymore. The whole city is divided over it. One of the bridge ladies thought they should leave Miriam alone and let her family decide what to do. That's what a lot of people think, but of course they're wrong."

I felt a knot growing in my stomach. Maybe it was the crackers.

"Another lady thought the judge should get a panel of doctors to decide what's the best treatment — surgery or chemotherapy or radiation or whatever — and then the judge should order it, no matter what. That's basically my position, with subtle variations."

I was getting more and more uncomfortable with the conversation. First, I didn't really want to discuss Miriam with Diana. She'd be shocked to know I'd been spending a little time with Miriam. And second, it wasn't clear to me how the case should be handled, and I was mad that Diana was so sure of herself. Finally, I said, "My father's representing her."

"Oh, Adam, I heard that. I was just sick. I mean, how can I respect the son of a man who defends a primitive religious group that lets innocent children die?"

"Hey, listen, I'm not responsible for my father's weirdo ideas, and who's talking about dying, anyway? It's just a case of abridgment of First Amendment rights." How often had I heard that in my kitchen?

"What about 'life, liberty, and the pursuit of happiness'?" Diana asked.

I had no answer.

"I just can't believe your father would do such a thing."

"Why do I have to defend my father?" I felt this big gully grow between us, a canyon people could fall into. We didn't talk. Diana played with the fringe on her sash, and I clicked the top on and off the cheese can. I wanted to leave, but I was too stubborn to get up. I'd make Diana give in, for a change. But then I knew I'd have a white beard down to my ankles before that would happen. I thought, I'm surrounded by steel-willed Amazons. My mother's infallible like Pope John or Igor or whoever's pope this year. And Diana never compromises on anything. She's always right, right or wrong. When she was born, she probably popped out saying, "You weren't expecting me until next week, but I thought this would be a better time, so here I am."

And Miriam, wimpy and plain as vanilla in a Baskin Robbins world, was ironclad, too. She was determined as hell to believe that God would heal her, when any sane, rational person could tell it would never happen that way. Diana and my mother and Miriam were boulders; even my father was a rock. Me, I was the only one like dust in the wind.

I was startled by Diana's voice. "There was another lady at the bridge table. She's into metaphysical healing."

"Pardon me?" So polite, so formal, just like this ugly room.

"It's basically mind over matter. She says you can heal yourself by energizing your mind and applying that mental energy to the disease or pain. My mother got me the book she recommended. It's by some lady named Manice O'Rourke, who cured her own diabetes nerve damage."

"You believe this stuff?"

"Well, no," Diana admitted. "But Miriam might. As religious as she is, she's really suggestible. I was thinking that while nothing's being done for her now — "

"Something's being done. That Brother James guy we met is praying for her and so's her whole family, and she's praying, too." Okay, it sounded dumb, but Miriam believed in it, and that had to count for something.

Diana gave me the look she used on debate opponents, the one that said, "Pure bunk." "As I said, while nothing's being done for her now, maybe we can teach her some of the exercises in this book." She pulled the book out from under a pile of art books on the coffee table. "It might at least help her with the pain. What have we got to lose?"

I reluctantly agreed, which is how, on Saturday afternoon, Miriam came over to Diana's house, and we began our Twilight Zone adventure into metaphysical healing.

We settled Miriam into the center of a wicker couch on the sun porch, with her feet propped up on an ottoman and fluffy pillows all around her.

"Now, just turn yourself over to this," Diana said, thumbing through the book. In another minute, she'd be an expert. "Take a deep breath . . . exhale. Deep breath . . . exhale. The first thing to remember is that you have to relax your body, from the top of your hair to your toenails."

I remembered the toes from that night in the hospital, crossed so hopefully.

"I don't know about this. I never should have come."

I reassured Miriam: "What have you got to lose?"

"Repeat after me," Diana commanded. "My body is in harmony. I am in perfect peace."

"I can't say that because it isn't true."

"Say it, and it will become true," Diana said. "Are you self-conscious because Adam's here?"

"No," Miriam said. "He can stay." She looked like she was near tears again.

Diana flopped down beside her and took her hand. "We're doing this for your own good, Miriam. Brother James wouldn't mind."

Miriam pulled her hand away.

"Just listen. It doesn't involve any medicines, and it doesn't violate your religion, but it's guaranteed to make you feel better. Forty thousand people swear by it. It's the perfect solution. Now, say after me, 'My body is in perfect harmony.'"

"I think I'd better go home. I can't believe I came here in the first place."

"I'll take you home." I pulled out my mom's car keys.

Glaring at me, Diana said, "Wait, wait. At least check it out first. Pray about it, or whatever."

Miriam nodded. Then I watched her sort of crawl into herself, contract into a small ball, her eyes shut, her nose wrinkled up. She bit the corner of her lip and twiddled with a strand of hair.

Diana rolled her eyes and mouthed, "Oh, God!"

Finally, Miriam's eyes fluttered open. "I'll try."

"Okay, 'My body's in perfect harmony.'"

"My body's in perfect harmony," Miriam said.

"I command all stress to leave my muscles."

"I command all stress to leave my muscles."

"Good. Now say" — she read from the book — "'I am a magnificent creature. I am capable of anything.'"

"I am a magnificent — can't I just think it instead of saying it out loud?"

"If you promise you'll think it and not something else."

"I promise." I was relieved. Diana could get by with saying "I am a magnificent creature," but it would sound so ridiculously hollow coming from Miriam.

"Now, the next part is tricky. Close your eyes."

I noticed that Miriam had very long eyelashes, although she didn't wear any make-up.

"You're going to imagine a total picture of yourself healthy and strong. You took biology, didn't you? Don't talk, just nod."

Miriam nodded.

"Okay, start by picturing your circulatory system. Imagine your blood flowing all through you, carrying all that poison out of your body. Get a picture of your heart, beating in perfect rhythm like a symphony drum."

Miriam was deep in concentration, nearly hypnotized. I whispered to Diana, "I don't know if this is such a good idea."

"I'm fine," Miriam said. "Go ahead."

Diana took her through most of the major body systems, until she got Miriam to focus on her bones, and especially the one where the tumor was, and to imagine the tumor breaking into minute fragments and disappearing, like in a Nintendo game.

"How do you feel?" I asked.

"Well." She got out of the chair and walked around the porch. "Right now there's no pain."

"Of course not," Diana said, "because you are experiencing metaphysical healing. It's foolproof," she boasted, as if she had invented it or plucked it out of the cosmos.

"But that's enough for today," Miriam said. "I have to think about it."

On Monday, Miriam looked much better. I walked with her from English to physics, since Diana had to stay and get an assignment from Mrs. Loomis. Miriam's cheeks had a little more life in them, but not like the stuff girls brushed on between classes: it was real color. She clutched her books to her chest and almost bounced as we walked down the hall. She asked me, "Did you finish your physics problem set?"

"I'm finishing it in class."

"You're impossible, Adam. Don't you ever do any homework?"

"Not since we finished the poetry worksheet," I admitted, which wasn't exactly true. Lockers were slamming all around us, and we slid in and out of crowds of people who all seemed to be going in the opposite direction. It was a typical passing period. Two girls threw open the door of the lavatory and bopped me in the face. I never saw Miriam laugh so hard.

After school, the Incredible Psychics were back to do their job on Diana's sun porch. In November, the afternoons gathered enough sun to make the porch decent until about 5:00 when the chill set in that let us know Thanksgiving was coming. Diana got the scene set, mesmerizing Miriam into relaxing, opening her mind, and painting mental pictures of her healing. I was almost starting to believe it myself, as I saw the color rise in Miriam's face. Her feet were crossed at the ankles, and one foot tapped on the brick floor. She was pretty loose.

I'd just about convinced myself that we had the most incredibly simple cure for cancer, that we'd win a Nobel Prize and be fabulously wealthy. Diana, Miriam, and I would travel in our own jet all over the world, demonstrating our miracle. Miriam would do cartwheels and handsprings to show how healthy she was, while Diana and I signed autographs and passed out pamphlets that had lots of exclamation points in them. The lame and the twisted would come to us, and we'd settle them into wicker wingback chairs and work our magic with the mental paintbrush.

Diana's hypnotic voice droned on, feeding my wild fantasy. Exotic ports with topless natives of all sexes. Gorgeous but ailing women who would be eternally grateful to me and would eagerly grant my every wish, starting with a Jaguar.

"Now, repeat after me," Diana said, " 'I know no limits. My will is the strongest force in all of creation.' "

Suddenly fame and fortune and grateful women vanished.

"NO!" Miriam shouted.

"Relax. What's wrong?" asked Diana.

Miriam's eyes shot open, and she pinned first

Diana, then me with them. "Satan sent you," she hissed.

"Are you kidding?" I couldn't believe things had turned so fast.

"You fooled me into believing you, but now I know the truth about you."

"Where did things change?" Diana asked. I shrugged. It didn't make any sense.

"You both pretend to be so innocent, leading me like a lamb into the lion's den. But you failed, because you see, I will never say, and I will never even think, that my will is the strongest force in all of creation. That's pure and simple blasphemy." She grabbed the book out of Diana's hand and ripped it to pieces. Suddenly she spun around and turned her new, hateful eyes on me. "Brother James was right about you, Adam."

CHAPTER TEN

Told by Miriam

Praise be to God, it was all so simple once again. Brother James had been right all along, but he'd allowed me to discover for myself that he was the only one I could believe. Just as he promised, now I felt I could "mount up with wings like eagles, run and not be weary." I felt renewed, reborn, because I had recognized the face of Satan, disguised so well, and I had sent him away. I had been tested, and now anything was possible, even separating in my mind Mr. Bergen, my lawyer, from his dangerous son.

"I hear you had a disagreement with Adam," Mr. Bergen said. He'd just subtly dismissed Mama by saying, "Miriam and I will be fine. Don't let us keep you from your work." "You going to patch it up with him?"

"It isn't possible," I said.

"You really think he's the devil?" Mr. Bergen said, chuckling. "He's always been a pretty decent kid."

"He told you all about it? I'll bet you two had a good laugh. But it doesn't matter anymore, you see, because I've had a renewal. I'm not going to be sick anymore."

"Fine, fine," Mr. Bergen said, smoothing out the pages of his yellow pad. "But we're going to need more than a little heavenly miracle to win this case. Let's get down to business. You're required to take your temperature twice a day, and it's been showing normal for a week. Your blood test this week was also normal."

I smiled. Of course they were normal.

"Dr. Gregory says everything looks okay. You're reporting no pain?"

"None."

"And you've had no treatment other than personal and collective prayer — oh, except that excursion into la-la land with Adam and Diana?"

I hesitated for just a second, wondering how I could have believed that that hocus pocus might actually help. "Nothing but prayer," I responded.

"Okay, next week you're scheduled, by court order, to have another bone scan, so the doctors have something to compare the other one with. Then we'll know where we stand."

"I already know."

Mr. Bergen gave me a playful look, so like Adam's. "It must be nice," he said, "to have all the answers."

At first it was hard going to school after what happened with Diana and Adam. Diana, being a cheerleader type, still smiled and said hello to me every time she passed me, but she didn't call me by name. Adam didn't speak to me at all. Though I sat rows ahead of him in every class we had together, and I never turned around, I was always conscious of his eyes on the back of my head. And if I didn't get out of the classroom first, and he had to walk by me, he turned his eyes away or got busy talking to someone else. Every time I passed him in the hall, he was in animated conversation with someone, or howling with laughter. I thought of Jeremiah: "Why, O Lord, are those who deal treacherously happy?" I put a lot of my energy into ignoring him. Still, when several people were talking at the same time, I could always pick out his voice. When Mr. Moran passed out physics papers, I didn't listen for, but always heard, Adam's name toward the end of the pile.

In English, Mrs. Loomis gave back our poetry worksheets, and she called us up in our poetry pairs to get them. I fiddled with a book and pencil that kept rolling off my desk so Adam could get his paper first. Finally, he picked both papers up and dropped mine on my desk without a word. From the back side of his worksheet I saw lots of Mrs. Loomis's red scribbles, and a big red B+ at the top of the paper.

Mr. Bergen said we'd go to court before Christmas, and we'd been working on the details of my case a little each day. Meanwhile, I went to school and to church. I sang with the choir and taught the prekindergarten babies.

Mama and I had long talks while we put up cranberry sauce for the church Feast of Thanksgiving. The skins of the cranberries popped in the boiling sweet juices; tiny explosions of purple splattered the sides of the pans.

"Baby, do you ever think it's awkward living with the men like we do?"

"I sometimes wish we could have a place of our own."

"Well, but they need us. They need having us to take care of."

"Did either one of them ever think about getting married?"

"Uncle Vernon. Maybe fifteen years ago he went with a girl, a college girl, in fact. We all thought she was a fine young Christian woman."

"So what happened? Did Uncle Vernon get scared?"

"I think she did. She came home for Sunday dinner two, three times, and after a while she saw what it would be like, living not just with Vern, but with Benjamin and me and you, too."

"They could have gotten a place of their own, couldn't they?"

"And split up those two brothers? No, the girl went back to Tulsa and finished up at Oral Roberts University. She married a truck driver. Or was it a pipe fitter? I expect she's happy. Honey, turn the flame down on your kettle, or we'll have purple walls."

"And Uncle Benjamin?"

"Well," Mama said, rhythmically stirring in small circles, "he was never a ladies' man. Always hides his soft side."

"I never thought of him as having a soft side."

"Oh, honey, sure he has. When our mama and daddy died in that car crash on the way to the State Fair in Hutch, it was Uncle Benjamin who let me cry on his shoulder until I was hollowed out inside.

I was twelve, and he wasn't but seventeen or eighteen, a year or two younger than Vern, but he kept me with him day and night till I was over it. Slept on the floor beside my bed all winter long. Vernon went about his business looking after finances and such, practical things, but Benjamin was my comfort. He'd a made somebody a good husband."

"What about my father?"

Mama stopped stirring.

"Did he make 'somebody' a good husband?"

"Well, he might have," Mama said abruptly. "But he wasn't in the church, and that's that."

I can't imagine how he and Mama ever got together, except she was a pretty secretary in the cold storage business where he was junior loading foreman, and love isn't always logical. I was born a month before their first anniversary. Uncle Vernon gave my father an ultimatum: either he was to convert and witness to his faith in front of the whole church when I was baptized, or he was to get out. No one asked Mama what she wanted. My father got out.

"I forget, Mama. Was it Uncle Vernon or Uncle Benjamin who came upon Brother James?"

"Vernon, at first." Mama took up her stirring again, scraping the crystalized sugar from the crown of the pan. "Brother James was about half the age you are now, and already preaching the Word of God. The Sword and the Spirit Church came to him whole, in a glorious vision, and he got a few of his father's friends together, including your uncles, and built the church from the cement foundation clear up to the rafters.

"Oh, my word, I do remember the first time Vern

93

and Benjamin took me, and you in my arms, into that church where all the oak pews had been sanded by hand, smooth as Popsicle sticks. That day, with the sun streaming in through the small stained glass window, all pink and gold and blue, it seemed like that splendid church wasn't too much to give up your father for." Mama gazed out the kitchen window. "Smooth as Popsicle sticks. Anyway, your uncles gave us all as a gift to the church, on the very first day it was dedicated. You don't ever take back gifts, honey." Her voice was shaky: " 'Spose those cranberries are done?"

As the days passed, I felt myself growing stronger. Each fresh day I put myself in God's hands. I did my homework, my chores. I read poems, tasted them syllable by syllable, swallowed them whole; I thought about Adam barely a dozen times a day. And I waited for when Brother James would call me up in church. Finally, it came. It was a brisk day, the Sunday before the Feast of Thanksgiving: coat weather, despite the brittle sunshine. The weatherman was threatening snow by Wednesday, just in time to back things up at Mid-Continent Airport.

At breakfast, Uncle Benjamin asked, "Well, are you ready for today? Got your words all thought out?"

"I'm trusting that the Lord will help me say what I have to say."

Mama slipped a steaming waffle on my plate. "Eat up quickly, men. Brother James is especially keen to see Miriam before the service this morning, so we'll go on over early."

Uncle Vernon, his mouth full of waffle, said, "I expect there will be a lot of people in church, maybe some outsiders."

"Oh, Vern, come on."

"Louise, I'm telling you, word gets around. Even TV people. But don't let them get you nervous, girl. Just speak from your heart."

Mama leaned back against the chair, dreamily waving a piece of waffle on her fork. "Oh, we'll just be so proud to see you up there speaking out about the powers of the Almighty. Your uncles will bust their buttons, and I suspect I'll just sit there dabbing at my eyes."

Brother James had an office across from the sanctuary. It was not fine, with smooth Popsicle-stick oak; it was barely big enough for a small, overstuffed bookcase, his desk and a swivel chair, and an extra folding chair which I sat in that morning.

He wore his navy blue Sunday suit and looked broad and handsome. There were rumors that the young widow, Marylou Wadkins, who had two babies, had her eye on Brother James, and that maybe this woman, at last, was strong enough for him. I think he was nearly thirty, and they say a young, vital man needs a wife.

His chair was on casters, and he rolled over beside me. "Your simple testimony will waft up and be heard in heaven, Miriam, and it will bring comfort to others ailing in our midst. Now, tell me what you plan to say."

I stammered out a few words. I actually hadn't prepared much, because I knew that the Lord would put the right words in my mouth.

"Truly, the Lord will give you the words, Miriam, but you must be ready to let them flow through you. Let's think it through. You'll start with what?"

"Um, how I felt this pain gradually coming on?" He nodded. "And how it got worse and worse?"

"Why?"

"Because my faith was faltering. Because I'd let Satan seep into the dark cavities of my soul."

Brother James's chair squeaked as he crossed a shiny boot over his knee. "And then you called upon Jesus with all your heart — "

" — with all my soul and with all my might — "

" — to cast out unclean spirits. Remember Matthew 10:1: ' . . . to cast them out and to heal all manner of sickness and disease.' "

"And Matthew 8:16," I added. " 'He healed all that were sick,' including me."

"Praise the Lord." Brother James got up and pulled me gently to my feet. "You will do just fine, Miriam. Bless you."

"What shall I keep in mind as I'm waiting to speak, Brother James?"

"Well, I'd say these words from First Corinthians: 'I will pray with the spirit and I will pray with the mind also; I will sing with the spirit, and I will sing with the mind also.' It is meant to tell you, child, that a healthy body, mind, and spirit are one, and you are living, breathing proof of this fact."

He led me out of his office, and the heels of his black Sunday cowboy boots echoed in the empty hall. When he opened the door to the left of the altar, I nearly fainted. The meeting room was jammed with people stuffed maybe twenty to a pew, people lining the aisles, standing in the back, even sitting on the steps of the altar. Some had cameras hanging around their necks. There was even a TV news camera aimed at Brother James as he took his place behind the lectern. I sat in the front row, where Mama had saved me a place, and immediately I felt the TV lights turn toward me.

"My friends," Brother James began, "in the name of the Lord, I welcome each and every one of you here to the kingdom of Christ. Those of you who are guests at the Sword and the Spirit Church, please take your cameras from around your necks and lay them on the floor in front of you. We will have the floodlights off and the video cameras off immediately. I remind you that this is a spiritual meeting in the service of the Lord; it is not a circus, and it is not a media event." He motioned for the cameraman to fold up his tripod and be gone, which he was in no time.

My heart began to beat faster as we neared my time to speak. I sang with the choir, with my spirit and my mind, and never had the hymns sounded so sweet, so full of poetry. At last, it was time. I stepped around the people seated on the altar steps and faced the congregation, waiting for the words to come. Brother James urged me over to the lectern. He lowered the microphone for me, and, in a shaky voice, I began.

"As you can see, I walked up here on my own."

"Praise the Lord," some brothers and sisters murmured.

"A month ago, I felt a stabbing pain in my lower back, and I could not have managed these few steps without holding on to a handrail. Three weeks ago, doctors told me I had a disease that had invaded

97

my body and that might even take my life. I saw the pictures myself, I saw a black knot in one of my bones, something ugly and foreign that did not belong there. People told me, even people I dearly respect, that I should put myself in the hands of the doctors."

"Oh, Lord help us," someone cried out.

"People told me, even people I dearly respect, that nothing could cure me but the medicines and machines of the doctors. I admit, I was scared, and I started to believe them. I'm only seventeen, and I'm praying that God's not ready to take me to the next world, because I haven't had enough of this one yet. So I started to believe those people, though my mama tried to save me from them."

I looked at Mama, her face glistening with tears.

"And I'll admit, my faith was weak when the pain overcame me. I didn't always believe that I would be healed without the doctors and their medicines. Brother James stood by me and counseled me and reminded me that if the Lord meant for me to go on in this world, He would heal me. He reminded me of the place in Matthew 19:26 when Jesus says, 'With men this is impossible, but with God all things are possible.' "

"Hallelujah!"

"Brothers and sisters, I am here to tell you that the power of the Lord is awesome."

"Amen."

"And that I am not hurting anymore."

"Amen, that's right."

"And that I am healed."

"Amen! Praise the Lord."

The choir broke into "Amazing Grace," which

Brother James planned because he knew it was my favorite hymn. My face was flushed and radiant, I could feel it, and tears of joy were streaming down my cheeks as the choir sang "was blind, but now I see." I looked out over these good people who had been my family for all the life I could remember. I smiled at my uncles, at Mama's friends, at my Sunday School teachers, at my little nursery children who had been brought to the service to hear me speak in thanksgiving.

And then I saw him, sitting beside his father, and the two of them were the only ones not singing.

"A-a-a-may-zee-eee-eeeng grace, how sweet the sound," the choir sang, and I felt like a bride, like a queen, like Mary herself must have felt when she first held the Child that was promised to her.

And Adam did not lift his eyes from my face.

CHAPTER ELEVEN

Told by Adam

I knew the words to "Amazing Grace" because my mother was always playing an old Judy Collins record that it was on, but I never knew it was a church song until that day. Then I couldn't sing it, just like I couldn't say the Jesus parts of the service, and like I never could sing "Silent Night" in school Christmas programs. I'd always thought it was because when I was a kid, I was sort of embarrassed to sing about a round young virgin, but finally I figured out that there were certain things that were common in the Christian world that Jews could not do comfortably. Singing in a church full of zealous believers was one, and believing in Miriam's miraculous healing by Jesus was another.

But watching her face, I felt 100 percent sure that *she* believed, and if she believed it strongly enough, she could probably do it. Look, my parents weren't heavily into God things, but they always told me that if I believed in myself, I could accomplish almost anything. So, in order to put Miriam's faith into terms that I could live with, I assumed that she *thought* that she was trusting God, or what she believed to be the son of God, to heal her, but actually she was doing it herself. Mind over matter again.

Well, we drifted with the crowd into the fellowship hall, which doubled as a church library. Books lined one whole wall, and on another wall was a poster that said "A GOOD BOOK/THE GOOD BOOK." Underneath the poster was the punch and cookies table.

My dad and I must have stuck out like whiskers in a wart. "Good salt-of-the-earth religious types," my father muttered. "Not a suit that fits right."

I figured we were probably the only two sinners in the crowd.

An enormous lady in a flowery dress came up to us. "You're new, aren't you?" she said, as if she'd said, "You're lepers."

"I'm the lawyer," my father replied.

"Ooh, bless you. Edwin," she said, tugging at the coat of a man hanging over the punch bowl, "this is the child's lawyer." Edwin smiled broadly, with a mouth full of brown cookies.

My father said, "And this is the lawyer's son."

Edwin shook on it, his hand still wet from punch. Mine felt sticky, but I had nowhere to wipe it, except maybe down the back of Edwin's green polyester suit. Edwin said, "Say, I want you to meet Dr. Ogilvie. He's an optometrist." Dr. O. had Coke-bottle glasses and looked at you and away at the same time. At least I was glad to see that the church let people wear glasses. I wondered what they did about dentists. Were dentists instruments of the devil, like doctors? Like Miriam thought I was? Or were they just the sadists the rest of the world knew they were?

Then a hush fell over the room. Miriam came in

with Brother James. Everyone swarmed them, and Dad and I were on the fringe of the mad crowd. Miriam worked her way through it like a politician on the campaign trail, until she got to us.

"Well, Mr. Bergen?" she said, triumphantly.

"Well, Miriam. You knocked them dead."

"It was so nice of you to come, Adam." Frosty, as if she were saying, "It was nice of you to order my execution."

But it wasn't nice of me, it was imperative. I hadn't been able to get her out of my mind since that day on Diana's porch. "Can I talk to you alone?"

"I don't think that's a good idea," she said, and I felt awful that I'd caused the first frown on her day of glory. But not awful enough, I guess, because I hung right in there.

"I'll come over to your place later."

"No, Adam."

My father patted my arm, signaling me that it was time to give it up. Brother James came up to us, holding a little kid in each arm. "It's a pleasure to have you visit our humble church," he said. One of the babies pulled at his beard, and he kept yanking his face back. The other kid squirmed to the floor, with her dress stuck up over her head.

A good-looking blonde, nearly six feet tall, came over to claim the kid. She grabbed the brat with one arm and put her other hand out to Dad. She looked down at him. "How do you do, I'm Marylou Wadkins."

"Marylou, meet Samuel Bergen, Miriam's lawyer."

"Oh, I know who you are."

"And his son, Adam."

102

"It's a pleasure to meet you both." Her handshake was like a man's. "Mr. Bergen, we all appreciate what you're doing for us." She had a warm smile, like a first grade teacher, and a way of talking that said she wasn't from Kansas.

The rug rat tugged at Marylou Wadkins wine-colored dress — I guess they could wear wine, even if they couldn't drink it — and smeared wet cookie crumbs up and down her mother's curvy left flank. "Oops, we're a mess. Excuse us!" She whisked the kid off, the smaller one trailing behind like a wagon. Brother James's eyes followed them out of the social hall.

"Well, it's been quite a day," my father said, with an arm around Miriam. Miriam shifted from foot to foot.

Brother James said, "A glorious day. Did you feel the power, Mr. Bergen?"

"Clearly," replied my father, and I caught the sarcasm in his voice.

"Brother James," I said, surprising myself that I could call him by this ridiculous name. "Could you talk to Miriam for me?"

"Adam!" cried Miriam.

"About what, son?"

"Well, we sort of had a fight, and I wanted to get it cleared up today while she's feeling on top of the world. Don't you guys say 'turn the other cheek'?"

"We do," Brother James assured me.

"Well, I want another chance." I saw Miriam turn to Brother James and wait for his advice. I thought she really wanted to talk to me but wasn't sure she should.

"If you have some unfinished business, you take care of it," he said, "and be done with it." I knew he meant I was to talk to Miriam, clear it all up, and clear out of her life.

"Come by tonight at eight," she said.

My mother was curled up in the family room reading. Knowing the power of Stephen King, I hoped I could slip by her unnoticed, but no such luck. With her face buried in the book, my mother sniffed the air around her.

"You put bug spray on. Are you going out with Diana?"

"No, I'm not going out with Diana."

"Whom do you have a date with, then?"

"I don't have a date with anywhom."

"You don't drown yourself in that aftershave unless you're hot on the trail of a lady. You can tell your mother."

"Why does my mother have to be the Grand Inquisitor?"

She craned her neck to see my father, who had briefcase papers spread all over the game table. "What's going on with your son?"

"It's privileged information, Abby. You'll have to torture it out of him."

"Oh," she struck her forehead with the heel of her hand. "The light dawns. You're going to see that Pelham girl. Well, how nice of you."

What did she think, I was visiting Miriam out of pity? It was because she was driving me nuts. When I closed my eyes at night to let Diana's face fill my imagination in the eerie time before sleep, more and more there was Miriam's face butting in. I hated

104

that. I had to get things straight with her, so I could get free of her and enjoy my old fantasies.

"Poor girl, my *toochas*," Dad said. "You should have seen her today. She could have won for senator. We should all be as healthy, when we're dying of cancer."

"Wait a minute, she's not dying, Dad. I've had her in class for two years, and I never saw her look so good."

My parents exchanged one of their looks. My mother kept her finger in Stephen King and said, "It's just a matter of time, Adam."

"You guys both believe that?"

"We're realists," my father said with a sigh.

"Let me get this straight: You're defending their right to deny treatment, but you think she's going to die if the doctors don't treat her?"

"Law of averages," my father said. "People don't survive cancer any better today than they did in 1950."

"But what about this miracle healing? You were there. She had a mob of people believing it happened. She believes it."

"Aw, Adam, there are no miracles," my father said.

"You goddamned hypocrite!" I'd never talked this way to my parents before, and though my mother's face looked stricken, neither of them said a word. I had to get out of there. I grabbed my jacket and ran, slamming the door so hard that the windows rattled. My parents were both standing at the window watching when I drove away in my mother's Jeep.

Miriam was just getting back from Sunday night

church, so I parked across the street and waited. The bald-headed uncle got out and came around to open her side of the car. After five minutes or so, I went up to her porch. There was a small square of window cut into the door, but some kind of brown curtain hung behind it, and I couldn't see inside. Before I could knock, the huge uncle opened the door. Glaring at me, he rolled his belly back to let me in.

Miriam came up out of nowhere and brushed past him. "We're going out for a walk, Uncle Benjamin. Tell Mama when she gets back from the store, okay?" She started sprinting up the street.

"What's the big rush?"

"I'm avoiding you," she said.

I could hardly keep up. Damn wheezy allergies. About a half dozen houses up the block, she spun around and said, "I want this to be over."

"I just got here."

"Not you, *it*. The case. I'm sick of it. It's all so silly, because I'm fine now."

I didn't tell her that my father said it would take three months to settle the case, or about the dying part. Instead, I asked her, "What does your father say about all this?" By now she'd slowed down, and I could walk next to her without gasping for breath.

"Is this what you were so desperate to talk to me about?"

"Well, not really."

"So, what was it?"

"What, you can't guess?"

"This conversation is going nowhere, Adam."

"Kind of like when we studied poetry together."

"You got a B +," said Miriam, slowing her pace another notch. "Guess what, I got an A."

"So where is your father?"

"How's your girlfriend?"

"Okay. She's going to the Bahamas for Thanksgiving."

"Oh, mercy, the Feast of Thanksgiving's coming up," Miriam said forlornly. "I wonder if the doctors and court will let us have any kind of peaceful Thanksgiving."

Small talk; we were hurrying up the street with nowhere to go, and getting nowhere, but I was conscious of the minutes ticking away. I didn't know how to begin.

"In Portland, Maine," Miriam said. "My father."

"Your parents are divorced?"

"Oh, no. We don't believe in divorce. But they can't live together. He's not in the church. He's not a Christian. I mean, he's not *not a Christian* the way you aren't, but he doesn't practice what Brother James preaches."

"How long's he been gone?"

"I've never met him," Miriam replied. "He left before I was even baptized, and here I am."

"Listen, could we just park it somewhere?" I was gulping air like a beached whale. There was a thick log stretched across the corner of the Quik Trip parking lot. "This'll do." She sat on the log, and I straddled it, facing her profile. She had a delicate nose, round as a baby's, and very small ears. Her hair was tucked back behind one ear and gently rolled on her back.

"Satan didn't send me," I said. She sharply

glanced at me, then turned away. "Honestly, I wasn't trying to get you to do something against your religion."

"Oh Adam, I know you didn't mean to, but you couldn't help it."

"What does that mean?"

"It means, what could you do? You're of a different faith. Like my father," she said.

"So what? So that means I'm Satan's first lieutenant? I'm not exactly the serpent in the Garden of Eden, you know. I'm one of the good guys. I rest my case."

"Don't confuse me with your wit and clever debate rhetoric."

"It sure seems like you're easily confused. If you'd been Eve, you never would have gotten the serpent's message. The human race would have died of boredom in the Garden of Eden."

"You're so glib. I happen to take the Bible seriously."

"Oh, yeah, I forgot. The Gospel According to Brother James."

"It works," she said simply, and then she jumped to her feet. "Adam Bergen, in case you haven't noticed, I am perfectly well."

"Yeah, I know, I was there in the church today, remember?"

"Look!" She did jumping jacks on and off the log. "How did I get this way? I prayed about it."

"Can't we just have a normal secular conversation?"

"Oh, I know, you think it's low class and pea-brained to pray for healing, but I'm telling you, God made me well." She leaned into my face. "Read my lips, GOD MADE ME WELL. Do I sound confused?"

"I don't know."

"Oh, listen to you! You're the one who's confused. You don't know what you believe. And besides, we'll never agree on anything."

"Hey, I have strong opinions."

"Name one."

"Capital punishment. Against."

"For."

"Abortion rights. For."

"Against."

"Mrs. Loomis. Against."

"For. I rest my case." Her face radiated with satisfaction. I wanted to kiss her.

"Okay, so we don't see eye to eye on a few little things. Does that mean we can't be friends?"

"Friends?" she repeated, turning to look at me. Her hand had inched closer toward me on the log.

I covered her hand with my own and slid even closer. I could smell her shampoo, spicey-sweet. "The problem is, crazy as it sounds, I like you, Miriam."

"You shouldn't," she said, grasping my fingers and pulling them to her lips. "It isn't right."

CHAPTER TWELVE

Told by Miriam

Adam brought over a pile of newspapers, magazines, debate evidence books, rubber cement, stacks of 4x6 cards, a red marker, a ruler, a giant pair of scissors. "My weapons," he said. "Cut. Paste. Let's see if we can get a hundred cards done before the hour's up." We sat at the wobbly card table Mama had set up in front of the fireplace before she'd discreetly gone to take a nap. We knew her nap would be no more than an hour long, and after that, Adam would have to leave, because the men would be home from work.

It was a crunchy autumn day, too warm for air-conditioning, but not quite cold enough for the heater. There was just a catch in my back, nothing terrible. I had an afghan wrapped around me. The skin on my cheeks felt tight from the fire.

"I love to hear the fire crackle and pop," I said dreamily.

"Sounds like Rice Krispies." Adam tossed a scrap of paper into the fire. He had to lean way back on the rickety chair to do it. Any minute now, he'd topple back toward the fireplace.

"Adam, do you have to toss each paper scrap in?

Why don't you save them up, for one huge fire?"

"No, this is symbolic. Each piece I toss in is one more debate opponent's argument going up in flames."

"You're so incredibly competitive."

"I'm not competitive. Diana's the competitive one on the team. Hey look, I've got at least ten more cards done than you have."

"You've got a sharper pair of scissors to work with. It's not fair."

"Listen," Adam said, leaning back and tucking his hands behind his head. "I could use my Swiss army knife and work faster than you. I could use kindergarten scissors with round points. I could tear the evidence out of the paper with my bare teeth and get more cards done than you. I could — "

"It's a real pleasure working with someone who hasn't got a competitive bone in his body."

He gave me a sort of embarrassed grin and tossed the hair back off his forehead. I'm sure he washed his hair every day. It was always clean and just a bit fly-away. In the glow of the fireplace, I found red highlights in his hair, and a spot under his chin where he forgot to shave. I knew the topography of his face so well; I could see each detail even when he wasn't there.

"What did you pick as outside reading for Mrs. Loomis's class this nine weeks?" I asked. Keep it neutral.

"Some Russian thing. I think it's called *The Brothers Kalamazoo*." He was concentrating intently, his eyes flashing, color rising from his neck. Under the table, I felt his foot tap-tap-tap.

The kitchen door opened, and the men came in

111

from the garage. So soon? I prayed they'd at least be polite to Adam, or that they'd never come into the living room and find us. I heard Uncle Benjamin put on the coffeepot and Uncle Vernon open the pantry, no doubt looking for Twinkies or Ho Ho's. I knew them so well; I knew their habits and footsteps far better even than I knew Adam's face.

"Sit right there," Uncle Benjamin said. Who would he be talking to?

"And 'spose I wanted to sit over here instead," came a teasing voice. It was Brother James!

"Whelp, it's a free world," Uncle Benjamin replied. "You can sit up there on the window ledge if you want, James. Look pretty silly, if you ask me."

Adam whispered, "Oh, Jesus. Sorry. Oh, man, now we're in for it."

"You want a Twinkie?" Uncle Vernon asked in the kitchen.

"Sure, toss one." We heard the soft thud in Brother James's hand.

Adam leaned across the table. "You want me to slip out the door?"

"But that would be so dishonest," I whispered back.

"Then do we pretend we're not here? Should we slide to the floor and act like we died of carbon monoxide poisoning?"

"No, just act normal, but do it quietly."

"How can I act normal when *he's* in there?" Adam asked.

I placed my finger over his lips. "Just hush!" Partly, I wanted him quiet enough that we wouldn't be noticed, and partly I didn't want to miss a word of what was going on in the next room. I'd never

112

heard anything quite like this. The men had such an easiness about them. They could have been three buddies coming home from a football game, replaying the game over a few beers, which, of course, they would never do. All that good feeling would be spoiled if they knew we were listening, but was it right not to let them know?

"Benjamin, you make terrible coffee. A fly landing on the mug would die of the fumes," Brother James said. "You've got to get yourself a woman who can make a decent cup of coffee."

Uncle Vernon said, "Wouldn't work. You can't teach an old dog new tricks. Ever hear that?" He chuckled.

Brother James said, "You know I'm thinking about getting married. Am I too old to learn new tricks?"

"Naw, you do what comes naturally, same as dogs."

"Well, Benjamin, that's sort of a sour view of romance." Brother James had such a playful quality to his voice. Gone was the resonance, the cadence, the near-whisper that bounded off the church rafters. "Marylou Wadkins, now there's quite a girl."

"Woman," Uncle Vernon corrected him. "That's what they like to be called these days. No gal, no girl. Heck, they don't even like lady anymore." Uncle Vernon, the authority on feminism!

"But what am I going to do about those babies?" asked Brother James. "At least one's still in diapers. I'd be no good with diapers. I can't even clean up after my dog."

"Me and Benjamin learned to live with it."

Adam pointed at me and laughed soundlessly.

"Well, James, I'm telling you, you better make a move before someone else does," said Uncle Benjamin, who, as far as I knew, had never made a move toward any gal, girl, lady, or woman. "I might like to raise a couple of babies myself," he teased.

"I don't know if I'm ready, I just don't know," Brother James said. The men settled into a comfortable silence, the crinkling Twinkie wrappers filling the space left by their words.

I motioned for Adam to quietly follow me out to the porch. We couldn't risk being discovered now. We slipped out of our shoes and padded through the soft carpet. Not even a Siamese cat could have been sneakier.

Later, two things stuck with me. One, that for the first time in my life, I'd heard Brother James called by just his first name, as if all the men were close friends, equals; yet they couldn't be equals when Brother James was on a much higher plane than my workaday uncles. And when had they become such good friends without my noticing?

And then, it was the first time in my life I'd heard Brother James totally "off duty," and I realized that through the whole eavesdropping — God forgive me — I was scared he'd do something awful, that he'd cuss or say something lewd or take a drink of wine or even belch. Of course, he hadn't done anything but the most ordinary of things. But I had never expected anything ordinary of him, either. I thought of the question in Mark: "What manner of man is this?"

CHAPTER THIRTEEN

Told by Adam

So, there I was with two women in my life, and it was getting pretty complicated. B knew about A, but A didn't know about B, even though A and B knew each other. I was walking a tightrope under an electrical storm and over a pit of killer wasps, because A would eviscerate me (after she got over laughing) if she knew that I had a thing going with B.

And I couldn't tell Brent about B, because he thought B (AKA Miriam Pelham) was about as desirable as a lady mud wrestler. Not that Brent had any woman. After the poetry assignment, he even struck out with Ramona Ruiz, who would go out with an ibex.

I couldn't say much to my parents, either. I knew what they'd say. They'd tell me I wasn't thinking straight, which is what they said on my sixteenth birthday when I announced I wanted to get my ear pierced.

"You're taking pity on that girl," my father would say. "Believe me, she doesn't need it."

"You're thinking with your fly, not your noggin," my mother would add. "Men are always panting after inaccessible women. It's called the Madonna Complex or some such thing."

Like Siskel and Ebert's low-brow movie choices, Miriam was my "guilty pleasure." In a sense, she was the "other woman," the one you meet in back alleys and restaurants on the cheating side of town.

And then there was her family. The Uncles Grimm would gladly have ripped me into fajita strips if she'd said "sic!" I finally figured out which Grimm was which. The bald one was Vernon. In my rich vocabulary, he was Uncle Vermin. He was the one that almost nailed a bride, back in the days when women would marry anything that didn't wear pantyhose. The other guy, Uncle Benjamin, was the Neanderthal one — tall, semi-dangling arms, brooding face. The one who couldn't make coffee.

Both the uncles, or "the men," as Miriam and her mother called them, puttered in the garage with fix-it things, tools that Jewish men thought of as implements of the Inquisition — buzz saws, power drills, nail drivers. On Sunday afternoons, their garage sounded like a medieval dungeon. I stayed clear of the uncles. I didn't want to be one of their do-it-yourself projects.

But Miriam's mother was the mystery. I know she didn't approve of me, since I wasn't a SATS guy (Sword and the Spirit). But she was always nice to me, brought me cookies or Twinkies and milk, gave Miriam and me a few minutes alone every so often, and did not ask questions like my mother, the Grand Inquisitor, did. Come to think of it, Mother Torquemada and the uncles should have gotten together to perfect their inquisitional skills.

All of this goes to say, my whatever-you-call-it with Miriam wasn't a normal heterosexual relationship. That is, it was hetero, but not sexual, despite its back alley overtones. We went nowhere, we did nothing besides hold hands now and then. We hid out from my friends, her uncles, my parents, her preacher, and anyone else who might recognize us and say, "Hey, isn't she that religious fanatic, and isn't he going out with Diana Cameron?"

And meanwhile, with 400,000 strikes against us and all the umpires shouting YER OUT!!, we stayed in the game and got closer and closer. As my mother says, go figure.

Though we had a *prima facie* case against getting elected Homecoming King and Queen or Senior Class Couple of the Year, we were maintaining the status quo, if I can toss in some pretty impressive debate terminology.

But I wondered what would happen when the case changed. It was just a matter of time.

CHAPTER FOURTEEN

Told by Miriam

Even though everything was different now, nothing was changed. At school, Adam still had his real friends. I'd see him tearing down the hall after Brent to beg a ride home, or hanging around Diana's locker. Oh, I'd get a smile when he passed me, or a quick "Hi, Miriam," but we both knew I was to leave him alone and expect nothing at school.

Diana's locker was two away from mine, and she was always luring him over there. He was uncomfortable, I know. I really didn't want to hear what they talked about, but I couldn't help it; it's like you can't help listening when you hear people talking on the other side of a wall, even if they're saying things that make your ears burn.

Diana said, "Tomorrow night's the Thanksgiving dance. You haven't said anything about it. Oh, hi, Miriam, how are you doing? Well, Adam, are we going?"

"I'll call you," Adam said.

"No, just let me know now. If you want to go, I'll buy the tickets before the StuCo window closes. You can drive my car if you want to."

"I can borrow my mother's Jeep, it's okay."

"Oh, Adam, the Jeep? Well, we'll talk about it. My car's really comfortable." She turned coy and flirty all of a sudden. "I'm getting a new dress for the dance, something revolutionary."

"I'll call you tonight," Adam said.

"You know, Adam, I get the feeling you don't really want to go. It doesn't matter. My mom and I are flying to the Bahamas early on Thursday anyway."

"We're going," Adam mumbled.

"Not a chance," Diana said, slamming her locker.

It was almost funny, Adam squirming as he was. I shut my locker and went to catch the city bus, but I walked slowly enough that Adam could catch up with me if he wanted to.

I waved the first bus by and waited, and there he came, in those bleached jeans and holey, unlaced sneakers, with his books hooked under his left arm at his hip. My heart beat faster whenever he came near me, and I was pretty sure my cheeks were flushed.

"So, are you going?" I asked.

"Am I in a mess," Adam said with a grin.

"Well, you don't owe me anything, if that's the problem."

"You're not the problem. I really want to spend some time with you, but I've been wracking my brain trying to figure out where we could go. No dancing?"

I shook my head.

"No movies."

"No, again."

"No rock concerts, no video games. And you'd freak out at the kind of parties some of the Eisenhower kids have."

"No liquor," I said, fighting back a smile.

"So, what can we do?"

"You mean things that cost, or things that are free?"

"Let's look at free, first." Good old Adam.

"Playgrounds. It's still not too cold. Do you like swings?"

"Not since I was maybe eight."

"Well, then, Frisbee?"

"I used to be pretty good with a Frisbee, until I broke a neighbor's window," Adam said. "Also, once I fell off a curb catching a Frisbee my brother shot my way. I ended up on crutches. Eric laughed for a week."

"Oh, well, about ninety percent of my throws would probably land over your head, anyway."

"Doubt it," he said, all masculine pride.

"We could windowshop at Towne East or Clifton Square."

"I see you've got a lot of excitement in your life. How do you come down off of such highs?"

"Okay, there are lots of museums in town," I suggested, just slightly annoyed. We might never find one single thing we both liked to do.

"But we'd have to stay away from the nudes."

I blushed; how mortifying not to be able to control blushing.

"The Mid-America All Indian Center isn't a bad idea. My mother's always talking about it. They make Indian tacos or something."

"I like the Indian Center," I agreed.

120

"Saturday night?"

I shook my head. "Wednesday after school. We get out early for Thanksgiving. You don't go to museums much, do you? They're closed Saturday night." Another bus was coming. "I've got to get on the bus. I'll see you, but not see you, tomorrow," I said, and he agreed.

I twisted at a funny angle to slide into the seat and felt a pull at my back. I needed exercise. My muscles were as weak as a rag doll's. I promised myself I'd do sit-ups and bend-overs when I got home.

That night before the men came home, I told Mama that I had a nondate with Adam.

"Well, baby, is that a good idea?"

"We're just going to the Indian Center after school tomorrow. It's not like a personal-type date."

Mama sighed. She painted hamburgers with A-1 Sauce and slid them under the broiler. "I'm not easy with it, baby."

"Are you worried about what the men will say?"

"Just a bit. Aren't you?"

"They're too strict with me, Mama."

She sliced tomatoes and arranged them in a circle on a little saucer. "They give us strength, Miriam. We need men in our lives." She sighed again. "But I'll talk to them. I'll make sure they don't say anything to you about it. You'll be gone tomorrow, when till when?"

"I'll hurry home from school and he'll pick me up here. We'll be home before dark. Can Adam stay for supper?"

Mama thought a moment. "I don't believe so, baby."

When the men came in for supper, she motioned for them to follow her to the back of the house for a talking-to.

They never said a word to me about my nondate with Adam Bergen. When he picked me up Mama watched from the kitchen door, as we got into the car. I had some trouble climbing the high step of the Jeep because I was stiff from exercising. I knew that in a day or two, the sore muscles would smooth out. I was really out of shape.

Mama waved shyly. "Drive carefully," she said.

Adam drove like a madman. I was glad there was a seat belt law in Kansas. He seemed to focus a lot of his energy on his driving, since he had absolutely no sense of direction and never seemed to be in the right lane.

"Turn here, HERE!"

"Back there?"

"We'll never get there alive," I groaned.

"I always get where I'm going alive, so far. Relax."

Round-about, we found the Indian Center. How beautiful it was! It seemed to dwell so naturally in autumn, with the colors of the leaves and shedding trees outside repeated in the woven blankets and leather tools and stark paintings inside.

We followed the drum beat coming from a back room of the museum. The thin, forlorn wail of a wooden flute announced our entrance to the model Plains Indian village.

"I wouldn't mind living this way," Adam said. I could just picture it: Adam sleeping on a mat on the floor, Adam grinding his own cornmeal, Adam weaving a loincloth, Adam whittling, sewing beads, spearing game, beating drums. He'd do these things

122

while watching a TV program he'd taped on his VCR, while eating microwave popcorn, while getting the latest stock quotes on his computer modem.

"You couldn't survive twenty-four hours," I said. "How many days can you live without pizza."

"At least two."

"And then you'd break out in hives?"

"Oh, so you think you'd make a terrific Indian squaw? Going out to shoot dinner with babies strapped to the front and back of you. You'd spend all day grinding up buffalo meat and cooking meals for the menfolk. When would you have time to read poetry?"

"Well, I'd be better adapted to it than you are, because I'm used to a simpler life. Can you ride a horse?"

"Who rides a horse? I didn't even have to do it at camp. Have you ever been on a horse?"

"Maybe." I couldn't actually remember yes or no, so it wasn't, strictly speaking, a lie. "Oh, look here, it's the chief's tent." We parted the canvas flap of the tent and sat down on the dirt floor inside. A traditional chief's headdress hung on a hook, with a small plaque under it saying AUTHENTIC — PLEASE DO NOT TOUCH. Adam touched. "I knew you couldn't resist."

"I just had to know if they were soft like goose feathers or stiff as a pigeon's."

"Or maybe vulture feathers?" I teased. "Hope is the thing with feathers" — I remembered the line so well, but he'd probably forgotten about the vultures.

We wandered out of the village to look at the paintings of thin, haunted faces that gazed off into a hostile horizon or rode toward the viewer with a haughty daring; of brown mothers holding brown babies with wet, dark hair; of old chiefs' portraits showing faces etched by time and the prairie winds.

In the center arena, a crowd was gathering. Kids younger than we were and old grandmothers and grandfathers were slipping into their native dress: feathers, beads, leather slippers, woolen shawls, belts of sisal and jute. Some wore the shawls over denim skirts or jeans and T-shirts, as though the last century and the present one had come together in a colorful collage.

Adam was drawn toward the music. "Does the music bother you?" he asked.

"I have no objection to music."

"What is it then, the dancing?"

"It depends on the purpose."

"Suppose the purpose is to celebrate life," Adam said. "Don't they look like they're having a fantastic celebration of Indian life?"

"Well, I guess it's all right then."

"You want to dance?"

"We're not Native Americans, Adam," and while I was sorry at that moment that we weren't, I was glad that what we both were *not* was the same thing, for a change.

On the harrowing ride home, Adam asked, "Well, what museum do we go to next? You want to go to Cowtown?"

"I have an idea, but you'll hate it."

"The Indian Center turned out okay. Run your idea by me."

"It's not much fun, but think about it anyway.

On Friday the judge is making me have another bone scan."

The color drained out of Adam's face. "You're not — ?"

I shook my head. "No, but until your dad gets this all straightened out, I have to do what they say or they'll take me away from my mother and stick me in a foster home."

"Maybe the bone scan's a good idea."

"It's not a good idea, Adam, but what choice do I have? Anyway, I know everything's okay. So, do you want to come to a bone scan?"

"That sounds like a wild time. How do I dress, in a surgical scrub suit?"

"In pajamas. It starts at seven in the morning."

"I don't sleep in pajamas."

"Oh, good grief, I'm not going to ask what you sleep in."

"I'll dress before I come. So, what happens at seven?"

"They inject this dye stuff into me." I remembered the chilling effect of the dye and shivered. "Then I have to sit around for three hours while it spreads all over my body. That's when we could do something, to pass the time in the hospital lounge before I'm ready for the bone scan."

"What could we do, play cards?"

"No cards. I'll bring a jigsaw puzzle," I said, testing his reaction.

"How many pieces?"

"Five hundred."

"I'll bet you we can finish it in under two hours," he said. "What do you want to bet?"

"No bets."

"Oh, right, gambling is one of the seven deadly sins, along with video games and throwing crushed ice in the bleachers at football games."

"Have you got anything better to do Friday?"

"Well, my brother Eric and his girlfriend are coming home from college tonight to put some final touches on the royal wedding next month. We're stuck having Thanksgiving dinner with Eric's future in-laws, who are vegetarians. They only eat things that come from the fleshy underbelly of jungle plants. Then Saturday I'm getting fitted for a tux. So, I'll need a few thrills this weekend. I'll meet you at the hospital Friday at seven."

"Do you realize, Adam, that this holiday weekend you'll be having your first tofu turkey and also going to your first bone scan? I'm guessing no one at Dwight D. Eisenhower High School can beat that for variety."

On Friday, Mama signed me in at the hospital and nervously folded and refolded my admission papers. "Mama, with Christmas coming, it's really busy at the church. Why don't you go on in to work. I'll be fine here."

"No, no, I don't want you to be alone." She wouldn't sit down; it was as if sitting meant accepting the hospitality of the enemy.

"Adam's here, Mama." He was waiting in the lounge, his nose in an *Esquire*.

"Oh, well then. . . . Now, you call me, baby, if you need anything. I don't like hospitals, you know, not a bit. But Brother James says not to make a fuss. Morning, Adam."

Adam snapped the magazine out of Mama's vision; he must have been on a particularly awful page. "Good morning, Mrs. Pelham." His face was still wrinkled from sleep. "Would you believe I've only been up twenty-two minutes?"

"It was nice of you to come," Mama said, as she kissed me good-bye and then she was gone.

Adam fought an enormous yawn, which made his face look like a balloon blowing up. "What's that?"

I rattled the puzzle box, but kept the picture out of sight. Finally, they called my name, and people all over the waiting room turned to look at me. It seems I'd become quite a celebrity, though, heaven knows, I hadn't asked for it.

"You'll be charging for autographs next," Adam said.

A clerk snapped a plastic name bracelet onto my wrist and pointed the way to the lab. Adam grabbed my wrist. "Okay, let's see if you can get it right."

"Pelham, Miriam Berkeley, type O + ." I'd looked at a bracelet just like this one hundreds of times when I'd been in the hospital before, as if it could give me clues to why all this was happening to me.

"What kind of a middle name is Berkeley?"

"My father's. Pelham is my mother's family."

Adam read while I had the lab work-up. I peeked out the door of the bathroom and waited until he was absorbed in the magazine before I tiptoed out with my urine sample. I would have died of embarrassment if he'd seen it.

They took me into a little room and laid me on a table for the dye injection. The room smelled of refrigerated air. As the needle pricked my skin, I felt a revulsion as if I were being forced to eat raw meat. After the initial rush of heat, then cold, they said I wouldn't feel anything, but I sensed the dye spreading through me like snake venom. What came to mind was the life-size diagram in the biology lab at school of the miraculous circulatory system, with all the major and minor and hair-thin blood vessels. In place of crimson blood, I saw purple dye jetting into every blood vessel, polluting God's perfect universe of the human body.

After a while, they let me stand up, and then led me back to the lounge. I wore one of their stiff green cotton wraparounds that crinkled whenever I moved. I said nothing to Adam about my anger and revulsion. I smiled like a brave little camper. We staked out a corner of the bone scan waiting room. I'd hidden the puzzle under a chair, and now I pulled it out and turned the picture toward Adam.

"Hey, that's Vincent van Gogh."

I'd picked out the puzzle at K Mart not because he was a great painter, but because I liked the haunted face, the ripples of smoke from the pipe, the rough fabric of the coat, even the blood-red background. He struck me as a man who was forced to do something he didn't want to do.

"Yeah, that's the looney tune who cut off his ear. Look at the bandage around it. There's no ear under there."

"I thought that was just a scarf that was keeping his ears warm."

"*Ear*," Adam said. "That's the point. The other one's a goner. He sliced it off."

"Oh, that's sick!"

"And guess what he did with the hunk of ear,"

Adam said, relishing this whole perverse story. "He wrapped it up and gave it to a whore. Oops, what's a decent word you can relate to?"

"A prostitute? A harlot?"

"Yeah, a harlot. I don't know why he gave her the ear. Maybe he was short of cash, and they didn't take Visa in those days."

"Oh, Adam, that's crass." I couldn't believe I was a party to this whole rude exchange. Adam was infectious, like laughter.

We put the puzzle together quickly. It was Adam's style to start from the outside and work in, but I was drawn to the stark blue eye at the center of the puzzle. I began with the eye and built the face around it. We met at the pipe and worked up the brown stalk of it that led to the artist's lips.

"What would make a sane man cut off his ear?" Adam wondered.

"Maybe he wasn't sane."

"What did the harlot say when she opened the box?" asked Adam. "Give up? EAR-rational! Highly EAR-regular!"

"EAR-resistible!" I quipped. Me? Making jokes? Puns?

Adam pulled back my hair. To make sure I had both my ears, he said. What a weak excuse. A shiver ran down my back when he touched me. With his hands behind my neck, he pressed his lips to mine. I'd never held my breath so long, but as soon as he began to pull his lips away, I shamelessly inched toward him for more.

Then they came to get me. Adam was nervous as they led me away. I don't think he was worried about me as much as he was afraid to be in a place like a hospital, all alone. He called after me, "Don't do anything EAR-regular."

"You're getting EAR-itating, Adam. Go down and stuff your face in the cafeteria while I'm gone. I'll meet you there."

The laughter evaporated in the scan room, where everything was cold and mechanical. I climbed onto the table, feeling a slight stab in my back from those stiff muscles. Another day of sit-ups ought to take care of that. I lay immobile on the table, with just a thin gown on, shivering not just from the chill of the morguelike room, but from an unwelcome fear that stole into me. I prayed and chased it away. I was sure that nothing would show up on the bone scan. The longer Adam and I had been together, the more sure I had become. True, I knew that nothing could be hidden from the penetrating eye of the scanner, which would aim for my weak spots as surely as the nozzle of a rifle. But Brother James had said, "Remember, Jesus goes with you as your rock and your savior. Lean on that rock. Have faith in that savior." And I believed. I prayed silently while the huge drum hung above me and moved over my head, keeping me in its line of vision every second. It clicked steadily, reporting whatever it spotted in its cross hairs. The drum moved down over my neck, my shoulders, my chest, up and down each arm, taunting me as it got closer and closer to the target.

Click, click, the steady rat-a-tat-tat gave the word to the screen, as the machine moved down my left side to my toes, then up my right leg. And then the clicking picked up its pace, like a Geiger counter that's found uranium, and I willed myself to look up at the screen. There was a patch, the size of a marble, and black as the midnight sky.

What would I say to Adam, who was waiting for good news in the cafeteria? If I told him the bare truth, he would say that I'd lost valuable treatment time, that my prayers had been wasted, like the better part of an apple tossed in the trash; that Jesus had just plain let me down.

But he didn't know. He didn't know that I'd eased up on my prayers since witnessing in church and during the days I'd felt so good. Sometimes you only ask for things when you need them and only make promises for earthly rewards. I was ashamed that I hadn't been fair to Jesus. I resolved to pray with more dedication. I would be entirely faithful, and Jesus would heal me, as He had before.

And then, while I was dressing in the women's locker room, I had a frightening thought. What if Jesus were mad at me because of Adam, because in my heart of hearts, in the deep of my night, I dared to think "love" about someone who did not love Jesus? But He didn't hold grudges. He was telling me, with this knot in my bones, that He was giving me another chance. Finally, it was clear to me that I had to do two things: I had to pray constantly for my healing, pray with the spirit and pray with the mind, as Brother James had always told me to do; and I had to bring Jesus and Adam together.

And so, I told Adam, when I was done with the bone scan, that everything had tested out perfectly.

CHAPTER FIFTEEN

Told by Adam

Who did she think she was fooling, telling me everything was okay? The doctors gave the news to my father, and he told me. He figured I already knew, and because I didn't, I was even madder.

"So, are you happy now?" I shouted, pacing back and forth in our family room. "Your brilliant prediction's come true. What are you giving her, six months?"

"Sit down, Adam," my mother said quietly. "It's unfair, I know, but it's not your father's fault."

"Oh, really? He's the one who's making sure the doctors can't get to Miriam."

"I am not, Adam. What I am trying to do is preserve freedom of religion and, secondarily, family rights as guaranteed by the U.S. Constitution." He flipped to the back of a book on his desk. "The First Amendment, in the Bill of Rights, states, in part, 'Congress shall make no law respecting an establishment of religion, or prohibiting the free exercise thereof.' Then Article Ten says, 'The powers not delegated to the United States by the Constitution, nor prohibited by it to the States, are reserved to the States respectively, or to the people.' *To the people*, Adam. To Miriam's family."

"Oh, great! Miriam can die and rot in the ground, but all you care about is the First Amendment. I've heard First Amendment, Tenth Amendment, like chapters and verses of the Bible, all my life. I hate your stupid Bill of Rights, Dad, got that?"

"Stop pacing, Adam, you're driving me nuts," my mother said. I sank into a chair. "Better. It's all right, you can take your anger and frustration out on the American Constitution. It's held up more than two hundred years. It'll probably survive your attack."

Dad said calmly, "But it will not hold up if people do not struggle to keep it alive in cases like this. I realize you can't understand this just now, but preserving collective civil rights has got to be more important than one unfortunate Miriam Pelham."

"Well, Sam, maybe it's a little harsh to imply that the girl's life isn't important."

My father's head snapped up from his papers. "The girl's life is vitally important. If we win, we lose. God, Abby, how did I ever get into this business? I should have been a chicken farmer."

"You could still get out of it," I retorted.

"Don't think I haven't considered it every day since it began," Dad said. "Every day. But I just can't leave the case. I'm sorry."

"Sorry isn't enough."

"I'll get some cookies," my mother offered.

"Cookies, Abby? Now?"

"Mint deluxe brownies. I have some in the freezer. Listen, boys, I come from a long line of women who pacify their men with food. Indulge me." She left me alone with my father, who was suddenly a stranger to me, and neither of us spoke. I studied the dirt under my nails, my shoelaces, a headline on a page in the *Newsweek* magazine at my feet. My father caught me looking at the magazine.

"His top aide has resigned, did you see?"

"Whose?"

"It doesn't matter whose. What matters is that you and I can have some mutual respect for each other over this Pelham case."

"You mean, I can respect you."

"It's important to me."

"Well, it's hard for me to be as coldly analytical as you are, Dad. I like the girl."

"I like her, too," he said, with a deep sigh. "We'll pray it all comes out well, whatever the hell that means."

"Yeah, well, I never really learned how to pray. She does it just like breathing."

"So you'll start with a deep breath."

"Wow, is it ever heating up," Diana said. "It's almost too big for Wichita." It's all we ever talked about, now that Miriam was back in the hospital. Somehow, Miriam's health had become Diana's personal cause. Her Bahamas tan hadn't faded at all since she'd been back. She was golden brown and more beautiful than ever. In Nassau she'd picked up a flowery basket purse, nearly large enough to be a suitcase, and she had it stuffed full of newspaper articles on Miriam, interview notes, reprints from medical journals, and a paperback Bible she'd highlighted in yellow.

We sat on a stone bench having lunch outside Eisenhower. Diana paraded papers under my nose. "Dr. Simon Greenwood, of M.D. Anderson Tumor Institute in Houston, says that the particular form of cancer that Miriam has, localized in the pelvic bone and growing at the rate of . . ."

A wave of nausea dizzied me. "Could we just eat?"

"Oh, sure." She stuffed all the papers into her basket. "I'm ruining your appetite. I'm sorry, Adam." She leaned forward and took a bite of my. baloney sandwich, leaving her lipstick on my Wonder Bread. "It could use Grey Poupon," she announced, like a TV gourmet cook. She wore a knockout red and purple and orange sweater that I'd never seen before and that she filled to distraction. I pictured the sweater on Miriam, and it didn't translate well. The sleeves would be too long, the shoulders too broad, the colors too flashy. Now Diana propped her feet up on the bench and pulled the sweater over the mountain of her knees. "The thing is, Adam, this is a time bomb right in our community. Journalists from all over the country have their eye on us. Doesn't that titilate you just a little?"

"Not really."

Diana pouted. "Nothing does, anymore. Are we still boyfriend and girlfriend, or did someone forget to mention that it was over? That would be rotten for my ego, Adam, because I've never actually been dumped before."

"I'm not dumping you."

"Then what's the deal?"

"I'm just preoccupied, I guess."

135

"Twenty-four hours a day? How do you have time to shower? You haven't phoned me in nine days; I've been calling you. And in case you didn't notice, we never made it to the Thanksgiving dance."

"Yeah, well."

"Oh, but I'm giving you another chance," Diana said, raking her long, bright pink nails down my chest. "But only because I'm crazy enough to be crazy about you." Her fingers slipped in between two buttons of my shirt, and when she touched my skin, I shivered.

"That's better." She leaned forward and kissed my ear.

"No PDA's," snapped Coach Ortega, who appeared out of nowhere, on bush patrol. "That's Public Displays of Affection, kiddos. Save it for Saturday night."

Diana pulled back. "Right, Coach," she said, flirting like crazy.

Coach Ortega grinned, patting his hard belly. "Hormones," he muttered, moving on to the next group of offenders.

"But as I was saying, Adam, things are really heating up. I'm doing this massive, supercomprehensive article for the *Vantage*, and I think the city paper will even want it. It's a big, impassioned plea for medical attention for Miriam. I've got stats on life expectancy, specs on drug dosage, case histories, the works. I'm talking Pulitzer quality, Adam. I'm blowing this story out of the water."

She would, I knew, and I was scared to be around for the tidal wave that would follow. I couldn't stop her, any more than I could stop Miriam from be-lieving her God would cure her.

If only I could stop wishing Diana's fingers were still under my shirt.

In every class, the same seat, Miriam's, was vacant, and I think it unnerved some of the teachers. Mrs. Loomis made us all change seats. No one wanted Miriam's desk, but Mrs. Loomis made up this ridiculous rule that all the front rows had to be filled before the back rows. This really hurt Tyrone Boyles, who made a career of sleeping in the back row on Monday mornings after every football weekend. No one bothered him much, because he was a terrific linebacker and smart enough to get his work done even if he snored through English, and either way he was sure of a juicy scholarship.

Reluctantly, Bailey Mathews inherited Miriam's seat. She gave fresh new meaning to the term "hang-over" when we were treated to the vision of her jeans pouring over and out of Miriam's desk chair.

Just after Thanksgiving, Mrs. Loomis sprang a new surprise on us. "How many of you clever students are going to college?" Since Senior Honors English was an advanced placement class, one hundred percent of us put our hands up.

"Well, we haven't failed the future entirely," the Big Bang said. "Now, how many of you are applying to state colleges?" About nineteen of the twenty-six kids raised their hands, including Brent. Someone nudged Tyrone, who also raised his hand. "So, I'm assuming that the world has not changed radically since last November, and the state colleges are still not requiring tricky essays for admission, correct?"

"That's right," Tyrone said, shaking the sleep out of his eyes.

"Good morning, Mr. Boyles. Now, may I assume that the rest of you are applying to private colleges?"

"You may," said Diana. "And you wouldn't believe the essays they're asking for."

"Oh, yes, I would," Mrs. Loomis said, coming out from behind the barricade of her desk. I hoped she would pull one of her most spectacular circus acts, backing herself up to her desk and tempting fate by daring the desk corner to support her. It was our lucky day. She inched back, hoisted one cheek up, then the other, and commandeered the corner of the desk. Between her and Bailey Mathews, you would have thought the entire classroom would tilt to the north. I guess Tyrone, weighing in at 230, balanced the room.

Mrs. Loomis said, "Those little essays are the topic of our discourse this morning, ladies and gentlemen." Her legs dangled like giant salamis in the delicatessen. "I want to see your essays," she thundered.

Well, this was news, because I hadn't written any of them yet. My parents convinced me to apply to all these small colleges for underachievers, like Grinnell and Carlton, where you got in on potential, but once you did, you had to try really hard to flunk out. All the essays were due before January 1, and I wasn't going to worry about them until December 30, at the earliest. But here was Mrs. Loomis taking control of my destiny.

"You seven, I expect to see all your essays by Monday, December seventeen."

"Aw, Mrs. Loomis. Let us turn them in after Christmas," Arnita whined.

"Before winter break, ladies and gents. It won't do you a bit of good if I peruse them after you've sent them off to the colleges." There was a lot of gloating, of course, from the nineteen students who thought they were off the hook. But they'd underestimated the Big Bang. "For the rest of you, I shall be handing out a sheet with six devilishly difficult topics, and you are to write on two of them by next Monday." She shifted on the desk, and its back left leg wobbled. We expected a real show any minute. But to our disappointment, she slid off the desk and didn't even seem to notice when it jumped in relief.

Diana raised her hand. "Mrs. Loomis, I have my essay ready for Yale. Would you like to see it tomorrow?"

"I would be delighted. Perhaps you could read it to the class as an example of how such a thought-provoking essay ought to be researched and written."

"Oh, I couldn't," Diana said, and we all knew she could.

I caught up with her after class. "What am I going to turn in? I'm not writing these stupid essays before winter break."

"That's my Adam, always planning ahead. You know what, Adam? You have problems with decision-making. You have problems with commitment. I can't understand how you even figure out what you're going to have for lunch."

Lately, Diana was always picking scraps with me, but I was in no mood for an argument. "Give me a break. Grinnell wants a thousand words on a significant event that changed the course of history. The only thing I remember about history is that in seventh grade, Mrs. Thorensen had a heart attack during Egypt, and we got that sub who was a shop teacher, and that was the last we ever heard of the Great Pyramids."

"Come on, you must have learned something in a year of world history," Diana said.

"There was something about Mesopotamia. That's about it. I remember that, because it's one of my favorite bands." I flashed her my most adorable grin.

"You know, Adam, you're not as stupid as you pretend to be."

"Sure I am."

She looked me over more deeply than usual. "Maybe you are. Okay, you can use one of my extra essays. The question for Swarthmore was something like Grinnell's. You can adapt it."

"You'd do that for me?"

She shrugged. "It's no different from letting you use my car." We'd come to physics class and were passing Miriam's empty seat when Diana said, "Let's say I'm doing it for old time's sake."

The hospital filed a suit against Miriam's mother, demanding that Miriam be evaluated for aggressive treatment. Judge Bonnell was persuaded by the sheer numbers of doctors and nurses who signed the petition that went with the suit: every doctor on staff, and 92 percent of the nurses and lab techs signed. Miriam had a police guard outside her room again. I was there right after school, and her eyes were ringed with red. I tried to make a stupid joke.

"What? On top of everything else, you've got pink eye?"

"No," she replied, in a baby voice. "I read Diana's article in the *Wichita Eagle* today. You must really be proud of her."

"Listen, I'm not her journalism teacher." What could I say?

Miriam obviously decided not to say what was on her mind. "Well then, her journalism teacher should be proud of her. She presents a very persuasive argument." Miriam's voice waivered. "But why is she against me? I never did anything to her."

Again, what could I say? If I defended Diana, it would look bad, and if I sided with Miriam, it would look worse.

Miriam quickly composed herself. "Well, we all do what we're called to do, right?"

"I guess so."

"Hold my hand, okay?"

I took her small hand, soft as feathers, and noticed the sensible white half-moons of her nails. There was a Band-Aid at the tip of one finger, maybe where they'd taken blood. She wore a hospital-issue green cotton robe, drab as a prison uniform. They'd taken her shoes and clothes, she said, so she couldn't escape.

I had this crazy idea of kidnapping her and taking her to the Bahamas where she would get some color into that pale, pale face. I'd hide her out in a thatched hut with a dirt floor, or in an Indian tent, and I'd surround her and hold her so tight that nothing else could get in to invade her bones.

"What happens next?" I asked.

She shrugged. "They don't tell me. They're afraid I'll tell Brother James, and he'll make a fuss."

"You want me to see what I can find out from my father?"

"If you can. But, I'm not sure you should even come here any more."

"Why not?" I lifted her hand to my cheek, and she moved her fingers to my lips, then drew her small hand into a fist.

"Because I'm just making trouble for you, with Diana."

"I'm making my own trouble, Miriam. Let me handle it." She opened her hand again. I kissed her fingers one by one. "Hey, I'll bring a puzzle. I don't know if I can get a guy who cut off his ear or any other appendages, but would you settle for a baseball card puzzle? I've got one in the back of my closet. I'll bring it after school tomorrow, okay?"

"Tomorrow," she said, smiling through her tears.

But by the next day, the pain was back worse than ever. The court order had said that the doctors could evaluate and recommend action, but they'd have to go back to court for permission to start any specific treatment. And anyway, the court order didn't say a thing about pain control. So there was nothing they could do when Miriam could barely sit up in that cold vinyl chair in her room.

I laid out the pieces of the puzzle, and Miriam struggled with it. "That's the Mick," I said, aiming for a light tone. "Mickey Mantle, probably the greatest baseball player of all time." Her face was like ash, twisting with pain every time she shifted in the chair. "His best average was .317."

"Is that a fact?" She didn't care, but I had to fill

the room with sound, just like infield chatter was supposed to distract the man at bat.

Suddenly I was having brilliant baseball insights. "Yeah, really. His all-time homerun record was fifty-four, in 1961, but Roger Maris, who batted right after him on the Yankees, he hit sixty-one homeruns that year. Too bad. I still think Mickey was the greatest. He was a switch hitter."

"What's that?" she whispered.

"Could hit just as well with his left or right hand."

"I guess that would be convenient," Miriam said, without much enthusiasm.

I was nervous. The canned heat in the room and the thick strands of pain were closing in on me. I couldn't stop talking. "No one's ever been able to do it like the Mick. Lou Gehrig was great, too. Here, here's Gehrig's face." I held up a jagged piece of the puzzle. "Did you know he played in 2,130 consecutive games? The guy never got a cold!"

"So what happened to the 2,131st game?"

"He got sick. Couldn't play anymore."

"And then?"

"He died." Wrong thing. We weren't supposed to talk about sickness and dying. "I'm really sorry."

"It's all right, Adam. Listen, I think we'll finish the puzzle some other time. I'd like to lay down on my left side; that sometimes helps. But keep talking."

I did a monologue, my best Jay Leno and Robin Williams material, for a couple of minutes, but then I was worn out from the effort of trying to translate it all into clean language. So I just sat there quietly, rubbing her shoulders, her neck, her cheek, while she hid the pain by keeping her back to me.

CHAPTER SIXTEEN

Told by Miriam

Back in the same room of the hospital, with the guard outside my door again, my faith was sorely tested. The days drifted by like storm clouds: slow, dark, and threatening. I prayed when I was awake and slept as much as I could, because I wasn't aware of any pain when I slept. Even when I wasn't asleep, I'd pretend I was, whenever anyone, except Adam, came into the room. Then, I'd lay awake in the shrill quiet of the hospital night, longing for company. The Jeremiah passage came to mind in those desolate hours — "Why is my pain perpetual?" — and also the words of Christ at his hour of agony — "My God, my God, why hast Thou forsaken me?"

When I thought I couldn't endure another minute of despair, I would fall asleep and wake up to discover two or three hours had mercifully passed, and it was nearly dawn, and the pain had lessened.

Dr. Gregory was often there when I woke up and so was Brother James, who would be kneeling beside my bed as my eyes opened. His soothing voice was my corridor back to dawn. "God has given you the gift of another day, child. Isaiah 58:8: 'Then shall thy light break forth as morning and thy healing shall spring forth speedily.' "

"The miracle of a new morning," said Dr. Gregory, who'd been reading the nurse's notes on how my night had gone. "The night has healing powers."

"Only because she gives herself over into Christ's hands when she sleeps," added Brother James. In subtle ways, they fought over me, as if I were the testament to each one's brand of faith.

But each morning I believed them both, and my faith was renewed. I would get up to eat breakfast in the little dining room down the hall. Then I'd take a shower and wash my hair, rinse out a few things in the bathroom sink, rearrange things on my bedside table, pull off dead leaves, and pray. By 10:00, I would feel the pain seeping back in like a low fog. By 11:00, the pain would be nearly unbearable again, and I would be grateful that Brother James had gone on about his day and wasn't there to see my weakness and tears of frustration.

Mr. Bergen usually came around 11:30, when lunches were delivered, so they'd let me eat in the room with him instead of the dining room, where sick people made me nauseous. Mr. Bergen would pull out thick sandwiches of dark bread with deep green lettuce spilling over the edges like the dust ruffles on my bed at home, and two or three pieces of fruit, and a wide-mouthed thermos of soup or chili. It all looked delicious. I pictured Mrs. Bergen lovingly preparing it in the mornings. But I was never hungry. I picked at the food on my tray. The best I could do was a few spoonfuls of tapioca.

As December began, Mr. Bergen grew more and more restless. He paced my little shoebox of a room, jiggling the coins in his pocket and tapping the wall with his pen. He drank my milk in two or three greedy gulps, slamming the empty carton back on my tray. At least the nurses would think I drank the milk and not nag me so much about eating.

"I've been thinking," Mr. Bergen began on one of those tense days.

Sometimes these are the most dangerous words in the language, because they usually signal cracks in one's steadfastness. I found myself trembling.

"And I've been talking to Adam. For just a minute, I'm taking off my lawyer hat and putting on my good friend hat." He doffed an imaginary derby toward me as I had seen Charlie Chaplin do in movie clips on TV.

He said, "What do you want?"

The question startled me. Of course I wanted to be well, and I wanted God to answer my prayers, and I wanted not to disappoint Brother James or Mama, or disgrace myself with cowardice and infidelity. But I could not tell him any of this.

He continued, "Because I know what the church wants, what Brother James wants, what the hospital wants, what Adam wants, what I want. But my God, Miriam, what do *you* want?"

It was a question I had never expected to hear, and at the same time had been dreading all along. And I thought about Mama, when she talked about my father: "No one ever asked me what I wanted."

"I want the pain to be over with."

"What's it worth to you?"

"I don't understand."

"How far are you willing to go to be pain-free?"

It was unfair of him to ask; he wasn't a believer.

146

"Well, I'm not willing to denounce God."

"But are you willing to take legal measures open to you? You could petition the Court to let you give informed consent for your own treatment. If you knew what you wanted."

"I could never do that."

"Wait, wait, consider it at least. Admittedly, it's stacked against you, because you're only seventeen, and you have one accessible parent who has already denied treatment. But I ran across a 1970 Kansas case where a seventeen-year-old-girl gave consent for a skin graft from her arm to patch the end of a finger that got cut off in a car door. That wasn't even a life-threatening case, and they accepted her consent. We could use this as a precedent, if you wanted to."

I shook my head.

"Don't reject it yet. Think about it."

"I don't think it's right, Mr. Bergen, for you to suggest such an idea when you're representing not just me, but Mama and the church, too."

"You're too smart." He slumped back in the chair, looking troubled. I felt a pang of guilt. My being sick was causing everyone I liked so much anguish.

"Here's the thing," Mr. Bergen said. "I've got Adam biting at my heels on this case, and he's not as whipped up over the Constitution or freedom of religion as I am. All he wants is to have you up and well. The truth is, I want that too, Miriam. Believe me, it's no fun to come here at lunchtime and see you cringing with pain and turning away this beautiful gray hospital grub." To punctuate his point, he got up and lifted the aluminum hood that hid something stewlike on my plate. He was right: the meat,

147

the potatoes, and the green beans were all gray. He quickly covered the dismal mess up again. "If you want to pursue this informed consent thing, you're right, I can't ethically represent you on that, but I can ask some of your court-appointed people to check it out and advise you on it. Just say the word."

Again, I shook my head. "The subject is closed tight."

He cleared his throat and sat down again, fumbled for a plastic bag of apple slices in his lunch, and offered me a slice. I turned it down with the same determination, as if accepting it meant accepting his blasphemous idea. I knew I could never go against Mama and Brother James and the church. I just would not allow myself to think of this in terms of my comfort alone. I had to think about what God had in mind for me. Never for an instant did I doubt that God would heal me with remedies far stronger and long-lasting than those of the doctors. Where I waivered was in wondering when. How soon? Would my strength hold out until He saw fit to relieve my pain? I wasn't afraid of dying. I was terrified of pain and what it told about the weakness of my soul.

Mr. Bergen said, "I'll bet you think if you did this consent thing, you'd be betraying your mother and Brother James, right?"

"Yes," I admitted. "That's part of it. The other part is I'm not honestly sure I know what I want anymore. I am praying for a clear sign from God. I know it will come soon. Be patient."

"Well, there's another alternative, Miriam." He blew up his empty sack and popped it, just as Adam would have done. "Gerri Kensler, your social worker, could track down your father and appeal to him to give consent for treatment. The Court would go with his consent, and you could be returned to your mother's custody, and both you and Mom would be off the hook. How about it?"

"That's impossible. He can't be found."

"He's in Portland, Maine. Sandstone Street. Everyone is findable," Mr. Bergen said.

"Not this one, not now. I think you'd better switch to your lawyer hat."

He put his hand up, signaling "halt." "Okay, okay. We never had this conversation."

Something bizarre happened. I think I was hallucinating. It wasn't frightening; no devilish monsters appeared to taunt me, but I wasn't tracking at all. The nurse came in to take my blood pressure, and she talked to me from the deep, wide end of a tunnel, of a funnel. Sound poured like liquid through the cone. I became aware of the ticking of the clock, which seemed as loud as a drumbeat. I itched, but my efforts to scratch my arm were clumsy, as though I had to reach through whipped cream.

MEER-EE-AHM, TAKE UP THY TIMBREL . . .
I didn't exactly hear the words, nor did I see them. They seemed to be formed in the beige sand of my mind, etched by eddies of swirling waters, and when the waters parted, the words were clear as sound. MEER-EE-AHM, TAKE UP THY TIMBREL . . .

"Whazza timbrel?" I asked the nurse.

"A what?" She had my right arm propped on the shelf of her slung hip, and she pumped air into the blood pressure cuff.

"Tim-b-rel."

"Never heard of it." She let the pump go, and it hissed like air from a tire. "You've got company." She signaled for Adam to come in.

"Hi." He flopped on the end of my bed. "How're you feeling?"

"Fuzzy." My tongue was thick and stuck to my teeth. I know I talked far too loud. My voice bounded back to me off the walls, but I didn't hear it inside my head at all. "Whazza timbrel?"

"Your guess is as good as mine." I sensed Adam pulling away. I struggled to keep him in focus. Then he was on his feet, backing toward the door, blocks away, maybe a mile, and then he was gone, way off down the beach. He must have alerted the nurse to my crazy condition, because she hurried in and put a cold washcloth on my forehead, hung an IV bag, and waited by my phone for the duty resident to call back. As soon as she had the doctor's approval, she called for a lab tech to draw blood. "Analyze it stat," she said.

I drifted in and out of sleep, surprised to see her still standing there. "What timezit?" I bellowed.

"It's 4:15."

"What timezit?"

"It's 4:18."

"What timezit?" And on it went until the lab results came back, and she stuck me with the IV.

The next morning my breakfast tray came without milk or butter. I wouldn't have used either one, but hospitals have a way of snatching away your major privileges, leaving you to indignantly demand the silliest ones back. I commanded Dr. Gregory to my bedside, and he explained everything.

"Your calcium climbed right off the charts, Miriam. It made you incoherent and muddled. Did you feel slightly out of control?"

"Yes, it was awful. I probably did something terribly embarrassing. Was I cackling like the three witches in *Macbeth*?"

He snickered. "I've seen worse."

"But why did my calcium leap so high?"

He wrinkled up his brow before answering. "Well, that's a symptom of tumor activity in the bones. I'm ordering another bone scan."

"Not again!"

"It alarms me, kid, I'll admit it. We know what you've got, and we know how to treat it aggressively, but we're not treating it."

"You think it'll get a lot worse?"

"No question, the longer we delay."

"Well, I won't allow it to get worse."

He patted my hand. "You do your best to stop it. Everything helps."

With the calcium regulated, I was back to my old self in a day, but I still had the IV in when Adam came to visit me after school. "Did I look totally stupid yesterday?" I asked.

"Let's put it this way. On a scale of one to ten, with one being stone cold dead and face down in the river, and ten being Joan Rivers doing a two-minute monologue, you'd be a twelve. If I didn't know about Brother James and the church and all, I'd have thought you were stoned."

"Thanks for getting the nurse in right away. I

feel more like a regular person now."

"Can we go for a walk? I hear the scenery's beautiful down by the elevator."

I yanked at the tether of the IV. "Too complicated. We'd have to roll the IV stand down the hall, too, as a chaperone."

"Aw, forget it," he said, pouncing on the foot of my bed.

"Anyway, I wanted to talk to you about this odd conversation I had with your father. He's really confused about my case. Do you think he'll resign?"

"Not him. He's always preaching about long-term commitments and sticking it out and hanging in there. I guarantee, he's in it till the end."

The end? But I was relieved. I was also afraid for Mr. Bergen, because it was wrong for him to be talking about bypassing Mama and the men, or hunting down the man who was just barely, by scientific definition, my father. I thought about telling Brother James that our lawyer was practically defecting, but I liked Adam's father so much. I really wanted him on my side. What I wasn't sure about was exactly which side Adam was on.

"Adam, I know you're a friend I can trust and I know you wouldn't intentionally do anything to hurt me, so please tell me something."

"Anything. My locker combination?"

"It's 30-18-9. I already know it. I knew it before."

"Before what?"

"Before *before*. I mean, before things got hysterical and I started fainting in class."

"You spied on my locker combination?" He pretended to be horrendously shocked. "Don't you realize you could get suspended from school for that?"

"Too late. I'm already out. Actually, I knew everything about you. I knew your birthday, I knew your home address. I passed your house every chance I got. How humiliating to admit this." I covered my face with my hands, but peeked at Adam through my fingers. How would he react to such a corny disclosure?

"Wait a minute, hold it. Now I've got this figured out. This whole incurable disease thing was just a trick to trap me?"

"Yes! Has it worked?"

"And you got Mrs. Loomis, you got the Great Wall of China, to assign us as poetry mates as part of your diabolical plot?"

"Worse. I got Emily Dickinson to write the poem about the thing with feathers, so you could look idiotic trying to interpret it, and I could save you from idiocy."

"I didn't look idiotic."

"Yes, you did. Bickering over words and telling me that Emily's frail little bird was a vulture. That's got to be the least poetic of all birds."

"What about a falcon? Or a bald eagle?"

"Bald eagle!" Suddenly the mood shifted. "Adam, I'm having another bone scan, and if that — thing — is bigger, the doctor will ask the judge for me to have chemotherapy, drugs. Dr. Gregory says I could lose — "

"Your lunch?" Adam went into a violent wretching act.

"My hair."

That sobered him, but old Adam, I really had to hand it to him, made a fast recovery. "Okay, from now on your nickname is Indian Squaw Bald Eagle." He leaned across the hump of my knees, ruffled my hair, and shook it all over my head. I saw his sad eyes through straggles of hair. He drew a strand of hair to his face. "I like the way it smells," he said. "Head and Shoulders?"

"No, Simon and Garfunkel." It felt so good to laugh with him. You can't hurt and laugh at the same time. And I forgot about the question I was going to ask him, until he was gone, and I was alone again.

After the bone scan, Dr. Gregory asked the Court to order treatment without delay: the tumor was growing and spreading. What I had was called Blanding's sarcoma. I wondered who Blanding was and how his children felt about having a cancer named after them. Dr. Gregory's big concern with the Blanding thing was that it would leap to my lungs.

Adam's father went to court to argue for me. I suspected, when Mama didn't come to the hospital that afternoon, how the decision had gone. Mr. Bergen came to tell me about it, Adam with him. "Dr. Gregory asked to administer a drug called Cytocel. It's very effective against your type of cancer."

"Has a terrific track record," Adam said. They sat at either side of my bed, and I turned my head from side to side as if I were watching a tennis match. Finally Adam came around and sat on the bed between his father and me.

Mr. Bergen said, "I argued before the judge about the possible side effects."

"Like what?"

"Oh, nothing important. I just had to make it sound as bleak as possible, to appeal to the judge's weak stomach."

"Like what?" I asked again.

"A few intestinal problems, nausea, occasional hair loss, canker sores. In rare, rare cases, and, hardly ever in kids your age, kidney complications. There have been a few incidents of congestive heart failure, two or three cases maybe, but nothing you'd need to worry about. Other than the tumor, you're as healthy as an Amazon."

"So," I asked quietly, but I already knew the decision, "did you persuade the squeamish judge?"

Adam took my non-IV'd hand, even in front of his father. I would never have dared do such a thing in front of my mother. We locked fingers as Mr. Bergen delivered the treacherous news: "The judge ordered that, beginning tomorrow, you're to start on Cytocel, in the dose prescribed by Dr. Gregory."

"Any other drugs?" I asked. I tried to sound calm, but my heart was racing.

"The hospital has to go to court for any other treatment, like combinations of drugs or immuno-therapy or radiation. This is a one-trick pony, Miriam. But, once the judge has allowed one, the hospital won't have any trouble convincing him of others. I'm sorry." I thought he might cry. Adam looked positively jubilant, which was the answer to the question I hadn't asked him.

I felt the tears welling up but refusing to spill. I wanted to cry for the injustice of it all, for how they were violating my body and soul, for the nausea and hair loss I'd have, for the two or three people before me who'd gone into congestive heart failure, for Blanding's children. But I couldn't cry, because I knew that, come morning, I would have to face the sagging disappointment of Brother James, who had had such faith in me. I would save my tears until after Brother James left my side.

CHAPTER SEVENTEEN

Told by Adam

Eric and Karen were home for winter break and were in the final stages of planning the wedding. They'd reached the point where they were mad at each other all the time, and both families were feuding. As my mother said, things were progressing normally.

But with Miriam, things were a long way from normal as we waited for the side effects to hit her during those first few days of chemo. I'd leave the hospital worn out from trying to make conversation when the only thing that really mattered was the one thing we couldn't talk about. I really needed a break from the weight of her silence. It came in the form of a Christmas party, on the third night of Chanukah.

Diana gave the party, with a DJ from T-95 and the spinning lights, the whole works. The Grande Room of the Olive Tree was decked out for Christmas, with a nine-foot flocked tree (fir, not olive) and ropes of evergreen with red bows scalloping the walls and tables. It was what my mother called High Goy.

The week before the party, Diana asked, "You're

coming, aren't you, Adam? Or am I supposed to invite someone else as my date? The rules are a little unclear these days."

"No, I'll be there."

"Wow, what a prince. Well, I haven't got time to develop a new relationship now anyway, because I'm working on the party and college applications and papers that are due right after Christmas. So, let's stay together, okay? Adam and Diana forever? Or at least till after the pictures are taken at my party. Come and have dinner at the Olive Tree before the party. I've ordered a rack of lamb for the six of us. I'll just put it on my father's tab."

I wasn't looking forward to the party, and I didn't mention it to Miriam, since it made me feel like a worm, but once I got to the Olive Tree and the Grande Room, my hedonistic nature took over, and I had a great time. It was about 4:00 a.m. before I actually felt my first twinge of guilt.

What a night. First there was the incredible spectacle of the rack of lamb.

Brent said, "That's disgusting. It looks like the king lost his head, with the crown still on. We're gonna eat that?"

"Poor little lamby," said Monica Bliss, Brent's date. "It never knew its life would end this way."

Terra, who was Diana's best friend, had brought a date from The Academy. That's not one of the public high schools, so they're colossal snobs over there. They have cheers at their basketball games that go, PRIVATE SCHOOL, STATE SCHOOL, WE'RE SMART, YOU'RE DUMB! Also, YOU MAY HAVE MORE POINTS THAN US, BUT SOMEDAY YOU WILL WORK FOR US! Anyway, this Academy guy Mike had actually seen a rack of lamb before, and he took us on a guided tour.

"They send somebody who's into gourmet stuff to the farm. These aren't Kansas sheep, you know. They're from back east. Anyway, the guy picks out the cutest little lamb he can find, one with big, soft eyes."

"Omygod," Terra groaned.

"Wait, that's not all. And the lamb's still wobbly on its legs, but it's got a plump gut. You see, this part comes from the central gut portion of the lamb." The Professor of Sheep pointed with his fork, while the waiter cut the cord that held the crown on.

"*Excusez-moi*," the waited said, elbowing his way in between Terra and Mike.

"Okay, so when they've got the cutest little fat lamb they can find, they kill it. Blood's flying everywhere, they skin it for a lamb's wool coat, and they chop off its head, but they're real careful with the legs, because leg of lamb is a big treat, if you know how to carve it."

"This is fascinating, Mike. Do you guys have a course in butchering over at The Academy?" I asked.

"Stop, I'm going to throw up," Terra threatened, holding the stiff white napkin to her mouth.

The waiter interrupted the happy banter as he slaughtered the remains of the poor little lamby and gave us each a jiggly slice. Thin pink juices ran from it.

"Delicious," Mike declared. The rest of us just sat and stared at the flesh that was brown and crusty on the outside, but a mooshy pink inside. The lamb came with vegetables that looked like toys, like corn on the cobs no bigger than my thumb but soft enough that you were supposed to eat the whole cob. It was all pretty sickening, but at least we had a good dessert. Diana had ordered Baked Alaska, and a whole tribe of waiters marched in with it, warming its little buns over a can of blazing Sterno.

"Isn't that the stuff that winos drink?" Brent asked.

"Control yourself and be awed by this creation. Baked Alaska is one of the seven wonders of the world," Diana proclaimed. She was glowing in the candlelight. "It's paradoxical. It stays frozen inside and hot on the outside. Kind of like Adam." I laughed along with the others.

We got to the Grande Room just as the DJs were setting up. Diana was like the director of a TV show, telling them where to stand, how loud to talk, where to put everything, including the giant screen that would continuously show the videotape of every move we made.

"Look, miss, we do this two, three times a week. We can figure it out for ourselves," the Velcro Voice of T-95 said.

"You don't understand." Diana nodded her head furiously and loosened a strand of hair from her high-rise hairdo created for this occasion. "I'm going to be an architect. I have an inherent spatial sense. Also good taste."

"Well, I'm going to be a DJ," the Velcro Voice oozed, "and you're not. So get outta our way."

"I'm paying the bill," said Diana.

The Velcro Voice turned to the guy behind him,

who was on his hands and knees, laying cable. "Hey, Grotto, did you hear that? They're gonna pay us for tonight."

Grotto, who was not a recognizable on-air personality, said, "Wow, now my kids won't have to sleep in doorways at Douglas and Broadway."

"Shake it off, shake it off," Diana said quietly. "I'm determined to have a good time tonight."

Kids from Eisenhower started coming in, followed by the expected crashers from Southeast and The Academy. Except for those tightwads who slipped by, they each paid a dollar toward the DJ's kids, but Mr. Cameron would still have a whopping bill, because the food wasn't cheap.

I wouldn't call it real food. It was art pretending to be food, things like puffed up mushrooms filled with mystery vegetable products, and chicken drumsticks no bigger than the legs of a rat, and hotdog bites rolled in bacon, and celery stuffed with cream cheese that had suspicious red flecks in it, flecks that lodged in your teeth and that I could feel under my retainer the next morning. Then there were the meatballs that disintegrated when tortured by fancy toothpicks, and pizzas the size of a silver dollar, and about as hard and dry. But what could we do, after the disgusting rack of lamb? Brent popped in the hors d'oeuvres by the handful. "I hear these suckers cost a buck a piece. I guess I've had my money's worth."

"Oh, yeah, you paid your dollar," I said.

The DJs started spinning some discs, and before I knew it, the whole dance floor was full. Diana was circulating, she said, performing her duties as a hostess, but she found me for the first slow dance. With

161

her hands locked behind my neck, she pulled herself close to me. Her dress was some shiny bronze fabric that itched me right through my shirt. I also discovered that I was allergic to it, and my eyes started getting watery. Diana put her head on my shoulder; we couldn't have been much closer if we'd been Siamese twins joined at the navel. Tears ran down my face and landed in her hair, but her hair was in such a bird's nest of curls, she didn't feel the tears until she turned her face up toward me, and one dripped onto her forehead.

"Why, Adam, you're crying."

"No, no," I protested. A sneeze would have helped the whole situation, but I couldn't force one up.

"Is it the music?" she asked softly.

I grunted something unintelligible. I wasn't a terrific slow dancer; we mostly moved in a tight circle. If her feet had been on top of mine, we could have corkscrewed ourselves right into the floor. Then my nose began to run, and I lifted the back of my hand off her waist to catch the drip. Finally I was forced to reach into my pocket for a tissue and to feel around to make sure my little nose spray bottle was there, in case things got desperate.

Diana pulled herself away from me. "It's your allergies, isn't it? How predictable. I actually believed the music and the nearness of me had moved you to tears. I'm going to remember, in my next life, not to go out with a guy who has allergies."

"I'm taking shots," I said feebly.

"What is it, my hairspray you're allergic to?"

"I think it's the dress."

"It was nearly two hundred dollars, Adam. I

guess I'm going to have to find hypo-allergenic clothes. Maybe I can order them from a hospital supply catalog."

The music changed to something fiercer, and once I wasn't close enough to breathe the fumes of her dress, my eyes dried up. "I'm okay now," I shouted over the music.

The party got wild. Of course, no liquor was served on Mr. Cameron's tab, but a lot of people had bottles stashed around the room. Diana got officially crocked and draped herself across my lap. I had to pull my head back as far as I could to avoid her dress. "I don' wan' you to think I have a drinking problem," she said. "I'm jes unner a lotta pressure. Iss tough being perfec."

"Yeah," I said.

"But I'll get uze to it."

I gave her coffee to drink. She hates coffee, but she gulped it down. "Jes fer you," she said, scrunching up her nose with the bitter taste. She picked up a fondue fork and scratched through the nest of her curls. "I feel mush bedder now." I took the fork, ditched it into a potted plant, and led Diana to a couch out in the hall. She fell asleep with her head hanging on the offending bronze dress.

The rest of the party went really well. Diana slept through the best part of it, while I danced, I ate, I drank Dr Pepper, I mugged for the photographer, and checked every so often to make sure Diana was still breathing. I hadn't had such a good time since Mrs. Loomis turned my life upside down over poetry partners.

I didn't even go to the hospital on Saturday or Sunday. My excuse was that I had to finish my college application essay to turn in to Mrs. Loomis. That involved retyping Diana's paper, changing a few semicolons to periods, and looking up synonyms for some of Diana's more exotic words, such as avuncular and peripatetic. I was very satisfied with the finished product, which I turned in on Monday, so satisfied that Brent and I cut out at lunch period and snuck up to Burger King.

"How did you like the party?" I asked him, while we waited for our Whoppers.

"Great. Diana was bombed. Too bad she missed it."

"A lot of people were bombed."

"That's a sign of a good party." We took our orders to a table under an obnoxious hanging plant. "You kept your head up," Brent said. "It must be from hanging around with the Holy Roller. What does she do for kicks?"

"Puzzles," I said, stuffing an onion ring into my mouth.

"Gimme one."

"No." It was already going down his throat.

"Puzzles. Say, there's an exciting woman. Listen, I read in the *National Enquirer* that over in Salt Lake, where it's about eighty-five percent Mormon, kids don't drink or dance or anything, so you know what they do to pass the time?"

"Puzzles?"

"Screw. Fornicate, copulate, you name it. Everybody gets pregnant. You gotta do something on Friday nights. So, what's the deal with Miriam? Are you getting anywhere with her?"

"She's in the hospital, for Christ's sake."

"In bed?" He waggled his eyebrows like Groucho Marx.

"Jesus, what a pervert."

"Okay, okay. Lemme have another onion ring."

I shoved the whole bag toward him. Suddenly I was getting nervous about being AWOL from school, like Coach Ortega might come into Burger King at any moment and catch us, and I'd have detention, and they'd call my parents, and my mother would ground me until I was forty, or went to college, whichever came first. "Let's get back. I've got to return a book to the library before the bell rings."

"I read a book once," Brent said, "but not recently. If you're smart enough, you don't have to. My sister left me a whole library of Cliff Notes when she went to college. Hawthorne, Shakespeare, Melville, Tolstoy, you name it. I'll rent any of them out to you if you need one. A buck a book a day. Hey, what are friends for?"

"Forget it. I hear the Cliff Notes are out on video now."

CHAPTER
EIGHTEEN

Told by Miriam

After ten days on Cytocel, I'd had very few bad effects, but neither had there been any evidence of the tumor shrinking. The hospital went back to Judge Bonnell and asked him to approve radiation along with the chemotherapy.

Radiation. I was to have mysterious invisible X rays, thinner than a fine stream of boiled syrup, burned into my body. Brother James was furious. But he had a way of turning his fury into a compressed knot of quiet rage. He would never explode; he would implode.

"These people are barbarians," he said, and a muscle throbbed just above the hollow of his cheek. His fingers on my arms felt like taut ship ropes.

Uncle Benjamin was tired of waiting around. "Well, what are you gonna do, James?"

My window overlooked the parking lot, and Brother James looked down at the little Matchbox cars. He jiggled peppermint wrappers in the pocket of his overalls. He took a deep breath that caused his plaid flannel shirt to pull across the back of his shoulders. " 'To everything there is a season, and a time for every purpose under heaven.' It's time we took things in our own hands, with God's help."

"Me and Vernon are ready. Just give us the word." Uncle Benjamin jammed his fist into his other hand, eager for action.

"I swear, Brother Benjamin Pelham, the child will not spend Christmas in this Godless place."

"And meanwhile, what am I to do, Brother James?" I asked.

He turned from the window, and I had the familiar sensation that he was surprised to find me still there. "Nothing, child. Leave it all to us."

"Shall I cooperate with the doctors and nurses?"

"By all means. You're not to let on that anything's up." He came over and patted my head.

"You mean I have to go to radiation?" I was shocked that he'd let it go so far.

He pulled a chair up beside my bed and waved Uncle Benjamin away. "Listen." He cocked his head.

I listened for the still, small voice beyond his.

"Your strength is vital, Miriam. You are not to let them do anything to you."

"You mean *not* go to radiation?"

"Go, but you shall close yourself to their machines and poisons. They can do what they will, and none of it shall penetrate your flesh. You will lock them out, do you understand?"

"I think so." I did not understand at all.

"Fine."

"But how will I do it?"

"With all your power, child. With all the horses of the kingdom of Christ pulling you, with chariots of fire rushing you away from their needles and rays." He engaged my eyes; I almost felt that I was

167

being hypnotized. "You . . . will . . . not . . . feel . . . anything . . . they . . . do to you."

I yanked my eyes away from his, as though my head were being tugged from behind. "Yes, Brother James."

There was Adam — how much had he heard? — standing at my door with a pizza in the flat of his hands. "Adam," Brother James said, with a gesture not unlike the tipping of a hat. "There's no pork on that pizza, I reckon."

"No, sir." Adam flattened himself as Brother James brushed past him. There was an eeriness in the room that I was glad Adam was there to dispel.

"Good thing you brought the pizza tonight. Tomorrow I go to radiation, and I'll probably be throwing up all over the place after that."

Adam flipped the Pizza Hut box open, like a jeweler displaying his wares. "Ta-duh! Half black olive, and half mushroom. You look better today."

"It's so dumb about the pain. It comes and goes unexpectedly."

"It goes when Brother James comes," Adam said.

"Yes."

"Well, I wish I had that effect on women."

Dr. Gregory poked his head in, on evening rounds. "Oh, you've got a gentleman caller," he said merrily. "I'll come back. I just heard that the Reverend asked to talk to me."

"You mean Brother James?" I giggled to think of him as the Reverend. Didn't he know that reverend was an adjective? "You just missed him. You can call him at the Sword and the Spirit Church in a little while, though. He practically lives there."

"Well, you seem to be spiffy tonight. I'll check

on you tomorrow, kid. I've got *sick* people to see tonight."

That night I lay in the dark, trying to block out the laugh track from the TV in the next room and waiting for sleep.

MEER-EE-AHM, TAKE UP THY TIMBREL . . .

I heard it, or saw it, or sensed it again, and this time I wasn't hallucinating on a calcium high. I sprang to my feet and buzzed for the nurse: "Could you please find me a dictionary?"

Her voice came over the tinny intercom: "Well, I'll try, but I doubt it. Are you doing a crossword, hon?"

The dictionary never came, and eventually I fell asleep. I don't remember dreaming at all; maybe they drugged me. In the morning, Brother James was there when they were due to take me to radiation.

"I'm scared, Brother James."

" 'The Lord is my shepherd,' Miriam, say it."

"The Lord is my — "

"He would not lead you where He does not want you to go."

I was impatient for him to be done, and I all but interrupted him. "Brother James, do you know what a timbrel is?"

"A musical instrument, I believe. A kind of tambourine."

"Is it in the *Book in Gold Leaf*?"

"It surely is. It's in one of the psalms." He reached into his pocket for his Book, which was bloated and dog-earred from loving use. "Here, right at the end, Psalm 150." He mumbled through a few lines.

"Here it is. 'Praise Him with the blast of the trumpet; praise Him with the psaltery and harp. Praise Him with the timbrel — ' And it mentions a few other instruments. Has the Lord spoken to you, Miriam?"

"I think so."

Brother James's sober face ignited with a smile. "Praise Jesus," he cried, sounding like a boy who's just found a red tricycle under the Christmas tree. "You listen to every word carefully, Miriam, and to the words that aren't spoken. You listen and do what He says."

"Yes, Brother James."

Dr. Gregory poked his head in. "Ready, kid?"

"Before the child goes, Doctor, I'd like a word with you," Brother James said. "There was a petition from this hospital that went to Judge Thaddeus Bonnell, and it was about getting medical treatment for Miriam."

"Yes?"

"You signed this petition, sir?"

"I did, yes."

"And are you a Christian?"

"I believe I am."

"Are you, or are you not?" Brother James's voice was rising, as it did when he warmed to a sermon.

"About as good as the next guy," said Dr. Gregory.

"You believe in the body and blood of Christ, you believe that Christ died for your sins?"

"Well, now, Reverend, I don't think this is the proper forum to discuss such things."

"God is appropriate at any time and place, is He not, Miriam?" There was the muscle in his cheek, beating like a heart just under his skin.

"Yes, Brother James."

"Why not, then, in a so-called house of healing, I ask you? Has it passed through your mind that you are interfering in God's work, Dr. Gregory?"

"I believe I am doing God's work."

"Interfering in God's work, sir. There are consequences."

Dr. Gregory opened the door and called for the security guard. "I'm taking Miss Pelham down to radiation. Will you please escort the Reverend to the elevator?"

"Think about it, Doctor. Think about the price," Brother James said, dwarfing the security guard who led him out of the room.

Dr. Gregory's jaw was locked tight, and his hands were shaking when he put the stethoscope to my chest. Just then the radiation technician appeared.

True to Brother James's word, I felt nothing from the radiation, and it was over in seconds. How much harm could it have done? Dr. Gregory had assured me that it would shrink the tumor and also reduce pain, but I knew better. I knew that they could take me down to radiation each morning at 8:00 and bombard the same dot on my back with their unseen rays for one week, two weeks, and it would make no difference at all, but that when the tumor shrank, and my pain receded like the sea at ebb tide, it would be because God had seen fit to purify me.

Dr. Gregory stopped in on his lunch hour, but he said nothing about Brother James. "You may get sick to your stomach from the combined chemotherapy and radiation."

"I don't think so." I knew I wouldn't. In fact, I couldn't, if I refused to let their rays penetrate my body. Neither would my skin be burned, nor would I lose a strand of my hair.

Dr. Gregory said, "I've asked a professor from the nursing school to stop in and see you today. She does a noninvasive therapy that I think will help. I assure you, it's nothing weird or anti-Christian, no matter what your preacher thinks of us here. Give it a try, kid, okay?"

The new nurse's name tag read Alberta Chin, R.N., Ph.D. "You're a doctor nurse," I said. Any new face was a treat. The hospital boredom was draining me of energy.

"I teach in the nursing school, which is why I'm a doctor nurse." She had the shiniest black hair, curled under gently, and it dangled in front of her face as she leaned over me to listen to my heart. Huge pink glasses dominated her small face and made her Asian eyes seem enormous. "Dr. Gregory thinks my specialty will help in your overall treatment program. I teach a new course for nurses, called Therapeutic Touch."

She ran her hands down the length of my body, about four inches above my skin, pausing here and there to concentrate intensely. She spoke sparingly, but with kindness. "Sit up, please." She helped me sit at the edge of the bed and ran her hand down the back of me, never touching my skin.

"What's Therapeutic Touch?" I asked.

"What I'm doing. I'll explain later. Don't talk, please. How long have you had this pain in your abdomen?"

172

"Only today. But I never told anyone. How did you know?"

"Don't talk, please." She squatted at my feet, running her hands down my legs, never touching, but I felt the hair on my legs stand up. Dr. Chin got very busy with my feet, as if she were pulling something out of me. She seemed to be listening at my feet. What possible sound could they be making? "Yes, yes. Tomorrow we will begin."

"If we're beginning tomorrow, what happened today?"

"Today was only a diagnostic, like when you take your car to the mechanic. I can help you. I can use Therapeutic Touch to ease your pain, and for this we don't give you any medicine, and we don't cut into your skin, and we don't blast you with anything. Just like today."

"Is it like metaphysical healing?" I asked, remembering the terrifying time on Diana's porch.

"Not at all," she said, and her eyes were lost in a huge smile. "If it's like anything, it's like the old time laying on of hands, but I do not lay a hand on you."

"How does it work?"

"Who knows?" She shrugged. "It just works. We don't know how any kind of healing really works. I will be back at nine-thirty tomorrow. You'll be here?"

"I have no choice."

"This will be the best thing that's happened to you in this hospital, I promise."

Dr. Chin came back the next day, just after my shower. Her big round glasses were tinted blue this

173

time, to match her blouse. She carried a plain wooden stool, and she plunked a straight-backed chair in the center of the room, across from her stool. "Wait, please." She flashed me a DO NOT DISTURB sign that said HILTON HOTELS, and she hung it outside my door. "Sit down, please," she said guiding me to the chair. I wished there were arms to lean on, to relieve the pressure on my back.

"First we will breathe very deeply." Dr. Chin put my hand up under her breasts so that I could feel where the breathing was to start from. She sat down on the stool and we breathed together, in through the nose, slow and deep, until I felt a cool draft inside my nose, and out through the lips with a faint hissing sound; in . . . out. "Now we will think very deeply."

"About what?"

"About nothing. About the vast void of the universe. Or you may think of a scene that brings you serene pleasure. A meadow. A babbling brook. I like an ocean breeze, because you can hear it and feel it on your skin."

"Would a rainbow do? 'My heart leaps up when I behold a rainbow in the sky.' William Wordsworth."

"Lovely, but don't speak, please. Think."

I thought deeply and wholly of the rainbow, glimmering, shimmering through the haze of a summer rain, but at the same time I was conscious of Dr. Chin's hands. She began with both hands held like a benediction above my head, then slowly she brought her hands down past my ears, over my face, to my neck. "There is tightness here, heat." She waved her hands over my neck as if she were ironing out wrinkles, stopping to shake her hands into the air like Mama does when she shakes off dishwater to answer the phone.

"There, much better," Dr. Chin said, and it was true, my neck did feel more relaxed. Down her hands moved, over my shoulders, my back, my chest. "Some congestion in the lungs," she whispered. "Cough, please." Though I hadn't really noticed before, now my lungs did feel tight, the way I usually felt when I was coming down with a cold. Dr. Chin worked her hands over me, smoothing and ironing the wrinkles, but never touching. "Cough again, please." This time the cough was looser. She reached behind her for a tissue, and I coughed up something thick and bitter. "Drop the tissue, please. Relax your fingers."

Down, down she moved, as if she were petting the fur of a fluffy collie. She would stop to shake off whatever had accumulated on her hands, sometimes frowning. She seemed to be concentrating very hard, her breathing slow and even.

"Lean, please." I leaned forward and put my chin to my chest. I felt loose enough to touch my toes, as her hands glided down and hovered above my back. She finally came to the black spot. "Much heat. Much energy bunched up here." She worked and worked over the spot which the bone scan had betrayed. "Breathe in, breathe out. In, out." Her motions became more jerky, and she shook the heat or energy, or whatever it was, out of her hands every few seconds now. She cocked her ear, as if she were listening for a distant train whistle, then nodded slowly, faster, faster still. "Yes, yes, better. You feel something?"

"I'm not sure."

"Soon." Her movements became more rhythmic as she worked down my flanks. Finally she sat on the stool and held my feet in her lap. Massaging gently, she said, "I have begun at your head and have evened out the energy all over your body. I have shaken off what I could of the negative energy, but now I must pull the rest of it out through your feet." She ran her hands above the tops of my feet, and it looked like she was squeezing the last of the toothpaste down the tube and out through the small hole. She squeezed and shook her hands rapidly, but smoothly, not a gesture or a second wasted.

At last, maybe thirty minutes after she'd begun, she said, "We will both breathe very deeply." I saw that her eyes were closed, and I closed my own. "Think rainbows, please." I did. After maybe two minutes of silence, she gently lowered my feet to the floor and stood up. "We are through. How do you feel?"

"Like I've had a long soak in the tub, with bubble bath up to my ears."

"Good, good. I like that." Perched on the stool again, she smoothed her denim skirt over her knees.

"Can I ask you a question, Dr. Chin?"

"You may ask me a question, yes. But first, stand up, please."

I stood up, stood on my tiptoes as she requested, stretched, reached way above my head to the channel switch on the TV that hung from the wall. It felt wonderful!

"The question?"

"Are you a Christian?"

"Buddhist."

"Are there a lot of Buddhists in Wichita?" I'd lived here all my life and never met one.

"Not so many. Who will my son marry? But now, I go to teach a class. You will walk around, not stay in bed. Tomorrow we will work together again," she called to me gaily from the door, where she plucked up the DO NOT DISTURB sign. "Think rainbows through the day."

CHAPTER NINETEEN

Told by Adam

"Dismissed," Mrs. Loomis said, a full two minutes after the bell rang. "Not you, Adam." I told Brent to explain to Moron, and I hung around until everyone had left. Mrs. Loomis's next period class was already straggling in, so she took me into a work area between her classroom and the next one. "I've read your essay," she said.

"Oh, yeah?" I shifted from foot to foot.

"It was quite polished."

"History's always been a special interest of mine."

"The style was reminiscent of another student's."

If I stayed cool, she'd never be able to prove anything.

"I want to see both your parents and you tomorrow after school."

"What do you think, I couldn't write a paper like that?"

"That is not what I think. I only think that you *didn't* write the paper. Tomorrow at three-thirty," she said. "Now, my sophomore class is waiting." She dashed off a pass for Mr. Moran and thrust it at me without even looking at my face.

I called my parents during lunch, then cut out to

the hospital and told Miriam about my latest brush with Mrs. Loomis. Since Miriam had been having the Chinese lady's touch treatments, she'd been feeling pretty good, so they let us go down to the cafeteria for something to eat.

"That wasn't too smart, Adam. Do you think Mrs. Loomis can keep you from getting into college?"

"Are you kidding? It's not her business anyway, it's Grinnell College's business, and they're never going to read anything Diana Cameron wrote. So what's the difference?"

"It's cheating, that's all."

"Oh, yeah, swell, I should have known better than to tell Miss Goody Two-Shoes." She looked hurt, and I felt a little sorry, but she wasn't helping me feel any better either.

"And did you think of how Diana could get in trouble for this?"

"Naw, not Diana. She always comes out a winner."

"I guess so. She won you," Miriam said.

"Well, there wasn't much of a competition. Like the girls were waiting in line, taking numbers."

"I never even got a number."

"Yeah, but the weird thing is, I'm around here a lot more than I'm at home, or out with my friends."

"I certainly wouldn't want to keep you from your friends." She'd come to the bottom of her Coke and was poking ice cubes with her straw.

"There really isn't anybody I'd rather be with, to tell you the truth." She had the good sense not to say a word. She just kept on sucking air at the bottom of her glass.

* * *

The Loomis thing wasn't so bad for my father, because all he had to do was mark off the hour on his schedule, but my mother had to arrange to leave work at the college bookstore, which meant she'd have to make it up later. They weren't thrilled to be called for this conference with Mrs. Loomis anyway.

"Let's get the facts straight," my father had said, when I dropped the bomb at lunchtime. "Did Diana write the essay, or not?"

"Not exactly."

"Not exactly? Well, what percentage did she write? Would you say your input was in the range of two-to-five percent? Um-hmm. Very honorable."

"Good grief, Adam, I thought you had better sense," my mother had groaned. "When are you going to pull yourself together and be a real student? You're only cheating yourself, Adam, don't you see that?"

Oh, I could tell we were in for a great time with Mrs. Loomis.

There were chairs arranged in a semicircle around her desk. I took the hot seat, in the middle. My mother's eyes shifted nervously, while my father sprawled in his chair with a yellow pad open on his knees, his Mark Cross pen ready for action. I pulled a paper clip into shapes previously unknown to humankind.

"I am disappointed in you, Adam," Mrs. Loomis said, lowering herself into her chair behind the desk. The chair squeaked and groaned. My mother shot a glance my way, and I wondered if she remembered that Mrs. Loomis was the one I called the Big Bang and the Great Wall of China. My mother's eyes crinkled slightly; yes, she remembered. Never mind. I had to start taking this seriously.

Mrs. Loomis said, "The offense is contemptible."

My father nodded and wrote a couple of words on his yellow pad.

"Contemptible for two reasons. One, Adam is passing someone else's work off as his own, and two, he is capable of something quite as good as this, but he doesn't bother producing it. That is not only contemptible, but inconsolably sad. Do you see the gravity of the situation, Adam?"

To me, it looked like she was blowing the whole thing out of proportion. But there was my father, feeding her just what she wanted to hear.

"We are deeply concerned over Adam's performance at Eisenhower," he said, "because we have seen his IQ scores and aptitude tests, and we acknowledge that his work does not measure up to his potential."

"I'm terribly sorry, Mrs. Loomis," said my mother.

That made Loomis mad. She leaned toward my mother. "You do not owe me an apology nor should you apologize for your son." She seemed to be having trouble breathing. I heard a faint rattle in her chest, which I recognized because of my own allergies. She was pretty upset. I wondered if she'd have an asthma attack.

"All I can say," my father promised, "is that my wife and I will talk with Adam about this privately, and nothing like this will ever happen again."

Mrs. Loomis reared back in her chair. "I understand that you're under a great deal of pressure, Adam. The Pelham case has taken its toll on many of our students, and I've heard that you've become a friend of hers. She needs friends. Perhaps I'm to blame for this grave situation, pairing you two on the poetry assignment."

"Oh, no, no," my mother protested. "You only did what — "

I'd had it. "You know something, Mrs. Loomis?"

"Adam," my father warned, but I ignored him.

"You talk about the 'gravity of the situation,' but let me tell you what's really grave. It's having this disease that's probably going to kill you. It's having your family fight it out in court." I looked at my father, and he turned his eyes away. "You think I'm going to worry about a stupid thing like some event that changed history a million years ago? Grinnell College doesn't care, but personally, what's going on with Miriam Pelham is the most important event in history right now."

"Adam, I understand the nature of your concern."

"No you don't, Mrs. Loomis." I felt my mother's hand on my arm, but I shrugged it off. "You understand verbs and thesis sentences and foreshadowing. Well, let me tell you about foreshadowing. The doctors, the preachers, the journalists, the lawyers, they're all dropping hints that a good reader wouldn't miss. Death. Dark shadows, the Grim Reaper, heavy organ music, the whole works.

"See, the doctors want Miriam to die so they can prove that the preachers are crazy. The preachers want her to die so they can say the doctors are the Antichrist, and besides, she's headed for greater glory in the next world."

"Adam, let's go home," my mother said gently.

"No, wait, I'm just getting to the point in this brilliant essay. Okay, what about the journalists? Well, they don't care if Miriam lives *or* dies. They just want to sell papers, and hey, death sells better than just about anything except celebrity sex scandals."

"And the lawyers?" my father asked. I saw my mother shake her head, and I wasn't sure whether she was trying to stop him, or me.

"Oh, the lawyers are the heroes in this thing. They're willing to let Miriam die because it preserves our good old American civil rights."

I'd said it all so calmly, though my head was pounding. I saw my mother wipe a tear from the corner of her eye. Then I added, "It was cheating. I screwed up. I'm sorry."

"The situation is behind us now," Mrs. Loomis said. "I will expect your essay by tomorrow, Adam. If it is at least ninety percent quality, I shall not penalize you for turning it in late. And thank you, Mr. and Mrs. Bergen, for coming to discuss this matter."

"You know, Mrs. Loomis, I'm directly involved in the Pelham case myself," my father explained.

"Yes," she said, with a strong note of disapproval in her voice. "But my concern is with Adam's learning to be a literate and honest person, not with the legal ramifications of the Pelham melee. I'm certain these two can be kept separate."

Well, maybe she was sure, but I wasn't. The neat little compartments of my life were spilling over into one another. For some dumb reason I thought about second grade, when we each had cubbyholes for our books and crayons and those impossible round-tipped scissors. Mrs. Jackson used to say, "Ladies and gentlemen, your cubbies are a mess, but look at Adam's. On the count of three, see if you can all get your cubbies to look just like Adam's." Mine was always neat because I never used it. I was always borrowing everyone else's paper and crayons. *Some things never change.*

The truth is, they changed a lot. Until my tirade in Mrs. Loomis's room, I hadn't understood just how furious I was about Miriam's crummy situation, or how much she meant to me. Then it suddenly felt like I had to write the best possible essay as a sort of tribute to Miriam. Grimly, I thought, it could end up as her eulogy. I worked on the essay all afternoon and most of the night, taking my ideas to the hospital to discuss with her.

"I could write about the fall of the Roman Empire," I said. Talk about irrelevant. "Or I could dip way back and write about when Moses received the Law. I'm not sure you'd actually call that history."

"Of course it is; it's in the Bible," Miriam said.

"Well, I'm not convinced that Bible and history are the same thing."

Although she didn't agree, she listened intently. Finally she said, "I know what I'd write about. The birth of Christ. I mean, even if you're not a Christian, Adam, you have to admit it's changed everything for the last two thousand years."

"No," I said, picking my words carefully. "It wasn't the birth that changed everything, it was the death. I guess I'll write about that."

"The death of Christ?" she asked, wide-eyed.

"The death of Jesus," I said. "There's a difference."

I got up at 4:30 on Friday morning to type the paper. Usually my mother typed for me, but this time it seemed important that I do it all myself, even with only two fingers flying over the keys of the computer. I finished with just enough time to grab a quick shower and run my hair under the water without shampoo. With the hot steam clearing my eyes, and the water dribbling down my back, I thought about the strange twenty-four hours I'd had, not a day I'd want to live through too often. No video games, no basketball, no 10 o'clock trip to Godfather's Pizza. I'd read at the library, I'd taken notes and discussed my ideas with Miriam. I'd even stopped in at the synagogue to run a couple of thoughts by Rabbi Fein, worrying now and then about whether it was cheating to bounce ideas off other people. It wasn't, I decided. It was a good way to sharpen fuzzy thinking, and I was a world class expert on fuzzy thinking. Even in debate, where clear reasoning was the big goal, while I wowed the judges with fast, slippery words, Diana was always clarifying my evidence.

Ferociously drying my hair with a beach towel, I suddenly realized that the only person I hadn't talked to about the essay was Diana.

I met her at her locker before lunch that day. My belly flip-flopped because she looked so damn beautiful in a pumpkin colored blouse with puffy sleeves and white slacks.

"Oh, hi, Adam," she said brightly. "Have you heard the news?"

185

"What news?"

"We broke up. We're still debate partners, of course. Don't forget the regionals coming up in two weeks. Other than that, there's no Adam and Diana."

But there had always been an Adam and Diana. We'd been together at practically every dance, every party, every concert, and every debate tournament since the beginning of our junior year. "Who says we broke up?" I whispered. This was not a conversation for the P.A. system.

But Diana was broadcasting. "You did. Actions speak louder than words," she yelled. "Everyone knows you're going out with Miriam Pelham."

"Out? We went to a stupid museum one day after school."

"Oh, face it, Adam. You just about live at the hospital. They might as well put a cot in her room for you. Now really, how can I compete with a deathbed case?" She slammed her locker so hard that it sprang back against the wall and cracked the plaster. "Oh, it's too bad about the history essay. I hear Mrs. Loomis was breathing fire. You'll be happy to know she flunked me on it, too. But I wrote a better essay on the death of romanticism in Western culture, or at least in Wichita, Kansas."

I was supposed to have a snappy retort ready, but all I could think about was, If Diana's leaving me, where does that leave me? But she answered the question clearly: "Listen, I've got to run, and your little Miriam's waiting." She stood on her tiptoes and kissed my cheek. "Have a great Christmas vacation." She backed away. "The thing is, I just never thought of you as a martyr, you know?"

186

CHAPTER TWENTY

Told by Miriam

Adam had good news that, typical of Adam Bergen, he tossed off casually. "Oh, by the way, I'm not going out with Diana anymore."

My heart leapt up, as if I were William Wordsworth! But then I got this panicky feeling in the pit of my stomach. If Diana had no claim on him, and he spent just about all his spare time with me, I guess that meant we were going out together. Going out — what a joke. We never went anywhere, of course, since the judge was so paranoid about losing me. A major trip was down to the cafeteria for thirty minutes or down the hall to the lounge where the cigarette smoke was thick enough to kick up Adam's allergies. We could only stay there until his eyes were running so badly that he looked like he'd been peeling onions.

But if Diana wasn't in our way anymore, and we were sort of "going (nowhere) together," I was in real trouble. It's a fact: we weren't supposed to like each other. I wasn't supposed to feel the soaring elation at 3:00 when I knew the bell would be letting Adam out of school. And I wasn't supposed to be watching the door as the long minutes ticked by until 3:25, when he'd fill my doorway, and I wasn't supposed to feel the joyous sickness in my stomach when he did. And to be sure, I wasn't supposed to have the overwhelming wish that he'd kiss me, that he'd hold me, that he'd push me to the side of that lumpy, egg-crate mattress and climb in beside me. With our clothes on, of course. I wouldn't dream of anything else. I just wanted to have him warm and close.

But I wasn't supposed to feel any of this.

"Yep," he said. "It's a clean cut with Diana. We decided today."

The words were light and casual, but I saw the hurt in his eyes, and I knew *she'd* broken up with *him*.

"The funny thing is, I barely felt anything when it happened. I mean, I didn't bleed."

"I'm sorry, Adam." I tried to sound sincere.

He grabbed my big toe in a fierce hammerlock. "No, you're not. I'm not releasing your toe until you admit it."

I tried wrestling it away, but he only grabbed the big toe on my other foot. I yanked and pulled, like a fisherman with a soggy boot on the end of the line. I did manage to upset his balance — a small victory — so that he flopped onto the bed on top of my feet, still holding on to my toes for dear life.

"You're pretty strong today, Schwarzenegger. Admit it, you're not sorry," he growled, milking both toes.

"Okay, I'm glad."

Immediately he let go of me and jumped to his feet. "Let's get out of here." He grabbed my robe from the closet and sent the wire hanger clattering to the floor. He pressed the nurse call button, and this grainy voice came over the speaker: "Nurse's station."

"Nurse, we're going out for a couple of hours," Adam shouted. "Hold all calls." We heard the intercom click off, then the shuffling of rubber-soled shoes. By the time the nurse and the security guard got into the room, we were flattened against the wall behind the door.

"Oh, good grief, she's gone," the nurse cried.

Officer Baylor, the plump little guard, kept a cooler head. She said, "Whoa, whoa. We'll just have a look around."

"Surprise!" we yelled and watched them practically leap into the air.

"You like to give me a heart attack." The nurse clutched her considerable chest.

"We're desperate," Adam explained. "We've got to get out of here."

Officer Baylor closed in on us. "You mean go AWOL?"

"No, Baylor, nothing like that. We just want to go to another floor. Any other floor. You can follow us, if you want, just let us *out* for a few minutes," Adam pleaded.

"Hold on." Officer Baylor phoned for Dr. Gregory. The one advantage of my being such a celebrity was that any call concerning me was put through immediately. Soon Dr. Gregory was on the line, giving permission for our journey into Worlds Beyond, as Adam said, but Officer Baylor was to trail us closely.

No one wanted to see sick people, so the three of us agreed to go to the nursery on the fourth floor.

As soon as we came out of the elevator, we heard muffled crying from behind the thick glass, as some of the babies let the world know they were good and mad. Life seemed pretty easy for them.

Adam said, "They all look the same, like Winston Churchill."

"They're not all alike. See? Some have pink blankets, and some have blue blankets."

"This is clearly sexism in the nursery," Adam said, huffing in indignation. "That bald pink one over there is probably going to sue the hospital."

"Oh, look at little Sangit Singh. He's the picture of Gandhi, but with a little more hair." I glanced back to see the guard, holding her distance to give us space, but craning to see the babies, too.

Adam liked the one with black hair hanging over her wrinkly forehead. She lay on her back with her eyes wide open, following every move we made. "Look, she's the Night Watchwoman, keeping the vigil so no one snatches any of the Churchills or Gandhis."

"Oh, look at that one," I said, pointing to a round blue bundle with its rump in the air.

The elevator behind us opened, and Officer Baylor snapped to attention. A harmless-looking older man in a gray business suit came over to the window. When the baby nurse spotted him, she rolled maybe the ugliest baby in the nursery right up to the window. He was red-faced and pimply and had not one strand of hair anywhere on his head, but he had a fairly thick patch between his eyes.

"That's my grandson, Roger Comiston III," the man boasted. "Which one's yours?"

"Oh, we're — "

"That one," Adam said, pointing to the Night Watchwoman.

"No kidding? Well, they change a lot in just a few days. Young Roger, he'll have hair before long. Well, you two take care of that little princess." Mr. Comiston pulled a business card out of his breast pocket. "It's not a minute too soon to buy her life insurance. Say, give me a jingle when you get the little squirt home."

Officer Baylor moved in closer to read the card, and Mr. Comiston backed off a bit and looked me over a little more carefully. "Say, aren't you that girl? Well, I'll be. They sure never told anything in the paper about you having a baby."

"Oh, no, I'm not that girl," I said, amazed at how easily I could let a lie roll off my tongue when it was all for pure fun.

"Um-hmm. Well, give me a call when you're ready to make an investment in your kid's life. It's not a minute too soon. The Third's already got a thirty-thou term policy on his life." Mr. Comiston backed into the open mouth of the elevator and was swallowed up.

Christmas was coming, and everyone around me had turned nervous. I felt like a hot wire, a conductor for their tension. I gave them excuses. Maybe it was because Christmas was close and the nurses were overwrought, trying to shop and bake and decorate along with their work at the hospital. I knew Adam tensed up whenever the subject of Christmas came around. I wasn't exactly sure what Jewish people did for Christmas, but I thought they must at least have a tree and exchange gifts. Even

Dr. Chin, the Buddhist, said their family each got a special gift on Christmas morning. But when I asked, "Adam, what does your family do on Christmas?," he said, "Nothing. Sometimes we go to a movie." "No tree? No presents?" "No," he replied, "it's not our holiday." So, he was really tense, bristling every time he tried to set his schoolbooks under a small tree with red snow-flocked balls on my night table. He'd started dropping his books to the floor, and the echoing slam they made against the tile felt like an insult to me.

Dr. Gregory, too, was as tense as a caged rat. Brother James had been working on him, encouraging him to stop being a sinner. Sometimes, when he came by to see me, the longing in his face made me feel like he was just itching to return to Jesus. I prayed for him every night; I prayed that by Christmas, he'd be reborn.

When Brother James stopped in, I was feeling pretty good. He pulled my pillow to the floor for me to kneel on. We knelt together, our elbows on my bed, our shoulders touching, and he confided, "I feel something about to happen, Miriam, just like you can tell a train's coming by the vibration on the tracks. Do you feel it, child? Bow your head." Brother James's voice was a smooth, rumbling sound from the depths of his chest.

I laid my forehead on the soft weave of the blanket and felt Brother James's words come through me, shoulder to shoulder, as if I were picking up his vibrations: "Isaiah 58:11,
And the Lord will guide thee continually,
And satisfy thy soul in drought,
And make strong thy bones;

And thou shalt be like a watered garden,
And like a spring of water, whose waters fail not.
A-men. Say it with me, Miriam."

"A-men." Our voices were in perfect symphony, one voice.

In the middle of the deep hospital night, with everything as still as a canyon, it came again.

MEER-EE-AHM, TAKE UP THY TIMBREL . . .

I lay absolutely motionless, waiting for more. Minutes of silence passed. And then, as if way off in the distance, I heard music. It sounded like drums and cymbals, lyres and lutes, tambourines with their sweet, brassy jangling, and the mournful blast of a ram's horn. The music grew louder, as if a parade were rounding a corner toward me.

PRAISE HIM WITH CYMBALS SOUNDING; PRAISE HIM WITH CYMBALS RESOUND-ING . . .

Then the parade turned another corner and faded away, leaving only a dimming memory of music.

I lay there breathlessly, straining to catch gossamer wisps of notes in the air. Silence. There was only my own rhythmic thumping, as if I were the drummer who had set the pace.

There was perfect harmony in that ancient symphony, and I knew, at last, that God meant this as a sign that I had been healed.

And then it was just a matter of waiting patiently for whatever would happen to get me home for Christmas.

In the morning, I told Brother James, "I've had another sign."

"My prayers have been answered, child." I saw

the hint of tears in his eyes. "Now, you must be ready, for your time is at hand. Be vigilant, Miriam."

I was vigilant. Hours crept past. Finally, Brother James brought me some clothes and shoes in a grocery sack and told me to put them on, with the robe as cover on top. "Just move quick as lightning, and do whatever I say."

Hadn't I always? In my little bathroom, I slipped into the familiar blouse and skirt that smelled of Mama's iron, glorying in the freedom of something as simple as having street clothes to wear. Someone down the hall — Uncle Vernon, as Brother James explained hurriedly — was creating a hullabaloo.

"You can't do that!" a nurse yelled. "Dr. Gregory, this man's going into everyone's room and pumping up these poor unfortunates with Jesus talk. My God, they're going to be pouring out into the halls hollering out hallelujahs and hosannas!"

I heard Dr. Gregory's voice clearly, though he was way off down the hall. "Officer Baylor, give me a hand here. We've got to remove this man before he upsets our patients." Officer Baylor ran down the hall; I heard her keys jangling. At that moment, Brother James whisked me out the door and down the stairs to the loading dock of the hospital, where Uncle Benjamin was waiting with his car running. We drove off into the blinding snowstorm, the blue norther that the weatherman had warned of. Cars were stalled all over, but Uncle Benjamin had put chains on his tires, and we tore recklessly through the streets. He took the most roundabout route to avoid stoplights, though driving down the side streets, even with our chains clanging, was like gliding across glass.

I didn't believe I'd survive the trip. Brother James murmured prayers for us all. We spun into a driveway, narrow as a panel truck, in front of an unfamiliar little house with cement steps leading up to it. "Can't I go home?" I cried.

"Well, Miriam, I'd sure like to be taking you home to your mama, but that's the first place they'll look for you," Brother James explained. "I'm hiding you out here, where you'll be safe and where we can have a nice old-time Christmas together."

"What is this place?" I asked, trying to dispel the feeling that I'd been kidnapped and taken to a hideaway where Adam would never find me.

"Trust, child," Brother James admonished. I was shivering, for I had nothing but the robe over my thin clothes to keep me warm. With his gloved hand, he clutched my arm, and my shivering stopped for a second. He opened the car door and shepherded me up the cement steps. The front door opened just a crack, then was closed so the chain could be slipped off.

The room was blazing with warmth that I was greedy for, though it smelled faintly of gas. I was afraid to breathe deeply. Two little girls peeked out from behind their mother, and Marylou Wadkins said, "Praise the Lord!"

Marylou was with me every minute. I slept with her in her big double bed, remembering that her husband had died there no more than a year before. His picture was the first thing I noticed when I awoke, or maybe I hadn't slept at all. I lay there with my head on a hard, foam rubber pillow, staring at the yellow spot on the ceiling where there'd been a leak. The little girls were singing in the next room. Thin walls separated us.

Marylou made some babylike sounds as she was waking up, too. "Are you up already?" she asked.

"I couldn't sleep."

She shot up in bed and felt my forehead. "You're not sick again, are you?"

I laughed. "I thought sick was something we didn't get."

"Purely a reflex action. I used to be a nurse, you know, before Brother James found me. Big hospital emergency room. I worked the graveyard shift, when all the night action took place. I saw enough people stabbed, babies burned or kicked down stairs, drug overdoses — sweet Jesus, it just about made me crazy."

"And that's when you came to the church?"

Marylou sat on the bed with her long legs tucked under her. Even though the corners of her eyes were crusted with sleep, her face glowed at the thought. "One day, after my shift ended? Brother James found me in the park, just down from St. Francis Hospital. It was about seven-fifteen in the morning. I was sobbing and carrying on because I thought no one else was in the park. He appeared out of no-where. Put his arms around me. Imagine, I cried on the shoulder of this total stranger in a city park. But I knew he was good. He said, 'God woke me this morning before the sun came up and sent me here to this park.' Well, I was saved, in more ways than one."

"What would we do without Brother James?" I said, forgetting for just a moment how angry I was about being here.

"A-men. Anyway, he found me a job at Boeing, in personnel, and that's where I met Billy. I hired him, in fact. He was a machinist. Darlene came along, then Annie, and then Billy, well, he died, he went on to the next world." Tears filled the corners of her sandy eyes. "Well, I can't mope about it, can I?" She swung her legs over her side of the bed. I wondered which side had been Billy's.

The room was way overheated. I longed for a crack of fresh air, even though the snow was swirling around outside the bedroom window.

"It's awful hot in here, isn't it?"

"Why not? Utilities are included."

"After breakfast I'm going to call my friend."

Marylou shook her head firmly.

"Anyway, I have to call Mr. Bergen. He's my lawyer."

"Brother James says no phone calls. We can't take the risk, not just yet. You want to get in the bathroom before I go?"

I wanted to get *out*. If this was my rescue, I wanted out.

There was a loud thumping on the other side of the wall. "That's Annie, working her crib across the room. You should see what it does to that wood floor. My word!"

Marylou went into the girls' room and brought Annie back to our bed. The older girl, Darlene, peered at me from behind the thumb she was sucking. "Go to the pot, go on," Marylou urged her.

I'd watch for an opportunity, when Marylou was busy bathing the girls, maybe, and I'd get to the phone then. I could be patient just a while longer.

Annie smelled. Marylou held the diaper pins in

her mouth, while yanking a sopping wet yellow thing out from under Annie's bottom.

"Besides," Marylou said, "until I get a little bit ahead on my bills, I'm not going to be able to afford a phone. We haven't had one since a month or two after Billy died. It's a good thing Brother James stops by now and then, to see if we're hurting for anything."

CHAPTER
TWENTY-ONE

Told by Adam

The University of Colorado Buffs were trying to work the ball down K.U.'s field in a blinding snowstorm, while my father and I crunched popcorn in front of a fire and watched the uniforms gets blacker. The phone rang, and the call shot a lazy afternoon of football all to hell. I only heard his end of the conversation.

"How long ago? What's left in the room? Who was on the floor at the time? Where was Security? All right. Call my service if you need to reach me." He slammed the receiver down. "I could have predicted it would all turn to bilge water before Christmas. Those goddamn fanatics. Haven't they ever heard of the season of peace and goodwill?"

I turned off the Buffs. "What happened?"

"Your little girlfriend flew the coop. Or, more precisely, Brother James put a ring in her nose and led her out to pasture."

"Where is she now?"

"Who the hell knows? We've got a blizzard raging out there. She could be under nine feet of snow, or she could be clear down to the Oklahoma border, if they're stupid enough to drive in this stuff and

199

take her across state lines. And they are. They've got brains the size of chick-peas. These are my clients I'm talking about. Trust in the Lord. Jesus will provide. All you got is fish? No problem, he'll turn 'em into loaves. Water in the way? He'll just walk across it. He'll cure the blind and the lame; he'll cleanse the lepers. I'm telling you, he's better than the Wizard of Oz."

"I hope she's okay." What else was there to say, with my father ranting like that? He must have said ten times that he never should have gotten into the case. It wasn't the time to tell him how much I agreed. "What do we do now?"

"Feel like freezing your butt off?" He tossed me a pair of gloves from the front hall chest. "Grab a coat and something to cover your ears, and let's go." I guess it didn't matter that I was still grounded for the essay felony.

Our first stop was the hospital, where my father scanned every inch of Miriam's room with his professional eye. She'd left a few things behind, but no clues. No addresses, no phone numbers, no notes or photographs, except the picture of *Him*, which had taken a temporary backseat to the Christmas tree.

Our next stop was Miriam's house. The snow had drifted almost as high as the doorknob, and we beat it off with our gloves just as Miriam's Uncle Vernon opened the door.

Squinting to recognize us in the blowing snow, he said, "She's not here." Mrs. Pelham huddled behind him, and Uncle Benjamin behind her, with his massive hands on her shoulders.

My father said, "I know she's not here. But your

church is paying me a pretty hefty sum of money to represent her, so doesn't it make sense to let me know where she is?"

"I can't do that," Uncle Vernon said. "I thought Brother James told you we're not needing a lawyer anymore."

"Listen, Mr. Pelham, you're going to need a lawyer worse than ever now. Kidnapping's a serious offense, and if they've taken her across to Oklahoma or Missouri, it's an FBI matter. Look, it's freezing out here. Can't we come in and talk?"

Uncle Vernon didn't budge an inch.

"Mrs. Pelham, you've got a mother's heart. You must be worried sick over the girl. The weather's vicious, the roads are impassable. Wouldn't it comfort you to know she was somewhere safe and warm?"

"She is. She's in the Lord's hands. Now please, go and leave us. At least give us Christmas."

Uncle Vernon began inching the door shut, until I felt only a thin strip of warmth.

My father shoved his foot in the door. "Will I hear from you after Christmas? If you make me a promise, maybe I can keep the police off her trail until then."

" 'The Lord is my shepherd,' " Uncle Vernon said, and, as the door closed, we heard the voices swell like a church choir inside, " 'I shall not want. He maketh me to lie down in green pastures. . . .' "

In the car, my father hung his head on the steering wheel. "Think, THINK!" he commanded himself. "Can you name any of her friends?"

"She doesn't have any, besides me." I thought about that guy she wrote to, the missionary she met at church camp. Did he live in Emporia? Abilene? Was he even from Kansas? And if she ever mentioned his name, I sure didn't remember it.

"Brother James has got to be hiding her at the home of someone in the church," I said. My teeth were chattering; my father probably couldn't understand a word I said. "Let's head home, Dad." He started up the car, and for one sickening moment we felt the wheels spinning in the ice. My father jerked the car from one gear to the other, until he loosened it from its rut. "You gotta be more careful, Dad." Ironic. Every time I walked out of the house, one of my parents said, "Be careful, drive safely." Here I was telling my father the same thing.

As Dad pulled into our driveway, I struggled to pick out faces and names among the church people in my memory. There was the polyester guy over the punchbowl. Edwin, Elvin, something like that.

The automatic garage door opener was sluggish in the subzero temperature, but finally we were out of the snow. The door from the garage into the kitchen stuck, as usual. I thrust my weight against it, and it finally gave. The house was warm and hazy with soft winter light. My mother wasn't home from work yet. We'd have to go through the whole explanation with her.

Edwin, Edgar? No last name, of course. In fact, people who called each other brother and sister wouldn't bother much with last names.

Except one. One woman was introduced as if her first and last names went together like beer and pretzels. Brother James was standing there. He had something heavy in his arms at the time; the picture

202

was coming to me. She was somebody special, judging by the way his eyes followed her. And Miriam had told me later that she thought Brother James might marry her after Christmas. Mary; Mary Lou. Marylou Wadkins, yes, the one with the pesky, cookie-crumb kids.

Then I was sure Miriam was at Marylou Wadkins's house. I ran to the phone book, looked up Wadkins; no listing. I tried Watkins, which was in the books, but didn't show a Mary, Mary Lou, or even an M. I tried every possible variation on the spelling and finally had to slam the book shut.

I flipped on my radio, tuned to the best classic rock station, and got "Jingle Bell Rock." A fake cheerful voice warned of zero visibility and noted the travel advisories. The DJ would be spending the night at the studio, I guessed. Where was Miriam spending the night? And why didn't she call me?

The sun woke me up. It was the kind of day when the sun bursts out after a threatening night of snow, and the rickety trees are coated with ice that melts in the sun, and you just know that by lunchtime the snow will be wet enough to hold together for a snowball fight. A perfect Kansas day to teach Miriam the aerodynamics of killer snowballs. Then I remembered: she was gone.

It was Sunday, December 23. The bells of St. Thomas were calling Catholics in our neighborhood to mass. Suddenly I had a brilliant idea and sat up in bed. She'd go to church!

But in a cooler second, I realized that was a dumb idea. If I'd thought of it, half the state of Kansas would, too. I plopped my head back down. But why not go to her church and see if I could find out anything about the Marylou Wadkins person?

The last time, it was standing room only, but that was for Miriam's great performance. This time there were only about sixty people in the church, maybe half of them small, noisy children. Marylou Wadkins was not there. That was a sure sign. I waited in the back where no one could see me. Mrs. Pelham and the uncles sat in the second row, with their backs to me.

The door behind the altar opened, and Brother James appeared. The whole atmosphere became charged. What power this guy had. The mothers tucked their sons' shirts in and hushed the girls, and the men slid into the pews beside their families. I quickly walked down the side aisle and joined a family of people with dark hair, so I could blend in.

Brother James's voice was a low rumble. He caressed the microphone and delivered his words into it as if he were — I swear — seducing a beautiful woman. "The Holy Spirit is here this morning. Can you feel it, brothers and sisters?"

"It's here!" someone cried out.

"I feel it!"

I didn't.

"The Holy Spirit is strongly with us this morning, because we have come through the valley of the shadow of death, we have come through the dark night. Our Lord Jesus Christ said, 'The foxes have holes, and the birds of the air have nests; but the Son of man hath nowhere to lay his head.' But I tell you, the daughter of this church laid her head down in a place of safe harbor last night."

"Praise the Lord!"

"Paul himself said, 'For God is my witness, whom I serve with my spirit in the gospel of the Son.' " Brother James's voice rose and fell like ocean waves. "The key word here is witness, brothers and sisters. The Holy Spirit is with us this morning. Who will bear witness to its awesome power to move and heal us? Who among us?"

Brother James stopped, caught sight of me. "We have a guest, my friends. God led him into our simple tabernacle this morning to witness. Yes, I feel it. Do you feel it, brothers and sisters? There is an important message seething under the skin of this boy."

I looked for the nearest exit; there was nothing between the altar and the back door of the sanctuary. Suddenly the family around me was urging me to my feet. A thin woman with a flowered hat smiled, pressed a Bible into my hand, and motioned for me to go forward. Her sons each took me by the arm and steered me to the altar, like prison guards to the electric chair. I stood where Miriam had stood that day, on the steps facing the congregation, holding the Bible to my chest the way she used to hold her schoolbooks.

Brother James said, nearly whispering into his microphone, "This is Adam Bergen. This is not his first time to visit Sword and the Spirit Church. Tell us, son, what moved you to return?"

"He's comin' back to Jesus!"

"Thank the bountiful Lord!"

What was I supposed to say? There was a certain

frenzy in the air that was unmistakable. For a minute I understood fully how kids could be sucked into a cult — swamped with love and attention, they were given an airtight system of belief that appeared to explain away everything they'd ever wondered or worried about.

"A-dam, A-dam, A-dam," the people chanted. Someone shouted, "The first man God created. Tell us what's in your heart, Adam."

"It says somewhere," I stammered, with no clear idea of where I was going. It worked in debate, I kept thinking, maybe it would work here. I tried to avoid Mrs. Pelham's gaze. "It says that God takes care of widows and orphans. Doesn't it say that in" — what did they call the Bible? miraculously, it came to me — "in the *Book in Gold Leaf*?"

"Many times, in many ways," Brother James said.

"Well, I want to do something for the widows and orphans of this church."

"The Holy Spirit is in the boy this very morning," an old lady cried.

"So, uh, last time I was here, I met a young widow with two little children." (Oh, I was warming to this performance. It was worth a nomination, if not an Oscar.) "Two precious orphans. And I sensed the poor woman's, the poor young sister's struggle."

"A-men!" someone said, in a throaty whisper, which was echoed by people all around her.

"Wadkins, her name was. Can anybody tell me how I can find the widow, Sister Marylou Wadkins?" I saw Mrs. Pelham go pale and fumble around in her purse for something.

"Well, Adam Bergen," Brother James said, taking me by the shoulder. "Our little family here surely appreciates your sense of Christian charity and duty. We'll see what we can do. You may step down, son." His eyes burrowed into me, and I stepped down. I heard at my back, "Who else will witness on this beautiful winter morning? Who has been healed of a deep hurt this week? Who walks straighter, or bends easier? Come forward and tell us. Come, come, don't be shy. God's miracles are to be broadcast from the highest mountain."

I wanted to walk right up the aisle to the back door of the church and be out of there, but a little kid patted the bench as I passed his pew; they'd made a space on the aisle for me. Just then everyone stood up to sing, and a girl with a mouthful of braces handed me a blue hymnal, open to one of those songs with eighteen or twenty identical verses. I held the book up to my face, glancing over it to see what Brother James was doing. His arms were waving in rhythm to the dreary song, while he whispered to some young guy, who then left through a door by the altar.

After that, Brother James's voice chimed in and, as if he were a cheerleader, the pace of the song picked up.

When the hymn was finally over, I sat down in my row of the solemn faithful, ready to make a dash for the exit as soon as I dared. If they say anything about Jesus healing anybody, I promised myself, I'll bolt. If they say anything about Jesus dying for my sins. If they say anything about Jesus.

"Brothers and sisters, before we bow our heads. . . ." Even with the microphone behind his back, Brother James's voice caressed the congregation.

The girl who'd given me the hymnal leaned around the kid between us. Never taking her eyes off Brother James, she whispered, "That was purely beautiful, Adam Bergen. I babysit Miz Wadkins's kids sometimes. She lives over on the corner of Gilbert and Elpyco. It's the pink house with white shutters. Those babies are darling. Do whatever you can for them, praise the Lord."

"Thanks," I whispered, with my heart racing, then forced out an unfamiliar benediction that was used around my house only when someone sneezed: "God bless you."

CHAPTER TWENTY-TWO

Told by Miriam

Sunday morning, and we weren't in church. Marylou and I sat on her divan trying to comprise a small congregation, while Darlene sprawled on her belly on top of the comics.

I glanced around the room, which didn't smell like Christmas, like wrapping paper and cranberry-orange relish and evergreen. Yes, there was a small tree on a table in front of the window. Gingerbread doll ornaments hung heavily from its frail branches. I had the feeling Marylou had no history, that she'd sprung up full-grown with two children of her own. Then I remembered the day in the park when she'd been saved, and Billy.

"Odd, isn't it," she said, in a dreamy sort of voice. "It doesn't seem right not to be in church this morning." She sighed and looked so forlorn.

I couldn't tell whether she missed church or Brother James. So I asked, "Are you and Brother James going to get married?"

"Well, the truth is, he's not exactly asked me yet."

"Do you want to marry him?"

Marylou drew her knees up to her chin, pointing her pink-fluff slippers toward the floor. "I've been lonely this year without Billy. But I'm not sure. I've had so many changes in my life."

"Not sure of what? That you love Brother James?"

Annie toddled in from the kitchen and flopped down on Darlene's back.

"I'm reading the comics," Darlene said, "and you can't read."

"Snoopy!" Annie pointed to the little house with the familiar dog staring up at the stars. "Snoopy-poopy-poopy."

Marylou signaled for the girls to hush as she opened the *Book in Gold Leaf* to just any page. "We all love Brother James — you, me, everybody."

"But do you love him the way you have to love him to marry him?"

"Well, I don't know that I'm worthy of a man like Brother James. My Billy was just a plain man, nothing special except to me." She wrinkled her forehead and began to read in earnest. I think she needed glasses. She seemed to be looking for a particular passage. I held my copy of the *Book in Gold Leaf*, and it felt as comfortable as a kitten nesting there in my lap. I stroked its soft leather skin. But I didn't open the book.

Adam told me that they read only the Old Testament in their church. No, they didn't call it a church; they called it a synagogue. And they didn't even say "Old Testament." They said "Hebrew Scriptures." I liked the sound of the name. It sounded so dignified, so . . . Christian.

"I heard something," Marylou said, dashing to the front door. She parted the tiny curtain over the diamond-shaped window on the door. "Oh, my heavens, it's Brother Timothy, coming right this way, and us in our nighties!" We both pulled our robes tighter and pushed our hair into some sort of shape before Marylou opened the door to Brother Timothy.

"Good morning, sisters," he said, all shy around us. "Brother James sent me to take all of you out of here as quick as can be. He said pack an overnight bag and whatever you need for the babies, and your Christmas packages, and any food you can spare, and come."

"Bye-bye!" Annie cried, and she ran for her coat.

"Where are we going?" I was thinking that maybe I'd be home for Christmas after all.

"To my parents' farm, over past Whitewater. Your mama's coming, and Brother Vernon and Brother Benjamin. We'll all be there."

"Anybody else?" Marylou asked.

Brother Timothy gave us a wide grin that made his eyes all but vanish. "Me and my mama and daddy, Miriam and her folks, you and your kids, oh, and Brother James. Is that what you were waiting to hear?"

"I'll pack directly," Marylou said.

It wasn't twenty minutes later that we had the little girls bundled into their snowsuits and were out in the car.

A car carved a path slowly in the ice on Gilbert Street. The driver hunched down to read numbers or names. Just as we passed him, I got a clear look: Adam! I rolled down my window to wave at him, and Brother Timothy took off like a rocket.

"Don't kill us all, Brother Timothy," Marylou said, clutching one child in each arm.

211

Had Adam seen me? I couldn't tell. In any case, he wasn't behind us. I guessed that he hadn't been able to turn around fast enough on the ice to follow us, and now we were blending in with the heavy Christmas traffic on Oliver Street. I prayed he would catch up to us, follow us to the farm. But even if he did, what then?

All the way to Whitewater I twisted toward the back window to search for Adam. Two weeks before, I wouldn't have been able to move my body so easily. Now there was no pain; I would have no pain for Christmas.

And then the light snow flurries turned to thick, angry-looking flakes that stuck to the back window, and I couldn't see a thing.

"Might as well turn around, Miriam," Marylou said quietly. "It's no use."

We were powerless, she and I, in the hands of someone as wondrous as Brother James. I nearly believed he had caused the snow to fall, to give us all a beautiful white Christmas. But in doing so, he'd hidden Adam from me.

All my life I'd lived in Kansas, but I'd never been in a farmhouse. Yet, if I'd pictured one in my mind, it would have been exactly like this one. Mrs. Hobart, Brother Timothy's mother, opened the door wide to us and revealed a room warm with a honey glow. Her kitchen, where, as it turned out, we all spent most of the next two days, was a big homey room. Along one wall a fireplace crackled with smoldering pinecones among the thick logs. A great round table, its curled feet and legs as thick as a piano's, as thick as Mrs. Loomis's, sat in the middle of the room, inviting us to help ourselves to the

212

apples, oranges, and pears piled high in a basket at its center.

The Hobarts hugged us quickly, then gathered up Darlene and Annie as their own. Mrs. Hobart led them to a wooden wagon loaded with old toys, and the girls were busy all morning.

In some ways, those days on the farm were the most peaceful days of my life, and, even as I scanned the snowy horizon for signs of Adam, I prayed that I'd never be found.

Mama and the men arrived just after us. "Let me have a look at you," Mama cried. "Benjamin, I don't believe I've ever seen her look healthier, do you?"

Uncle Vernon carried in suitcases and a Coleman Cooler full of the treats Mama had cooked for Christmas. "I'll have a wrenched back, hauling all this stuff in," he grumbled, but I think he was proud to be able to provide so much food.

"Where's Brother Timothy?" Mama asked. "I want to thank him for going after Miriam on such short notice."

"Oh, he's out back seeing to the dog," Mr. Hobart said, sucking on an unlit pipe.

Annie and Darlene were locked in a fight over a wooden doll, and Marylou yanked them apart. She seemed jittery to me, more impatient than usual with the girls.

But of course, she was like an animal that knows beforehand when a tornado is going to hit, or an earthquake, because not a minute later there was a thunderous knock at the door, and Brother James was among us. Because it was Christmas, he wore a navy blue suit and a white shirt with a starched collar. We all felt his strength — the men were silenced, Mama smiled meekly, Marylou fidgeted with a tissue and hovered behind me. "I ironed his shirt," she whispered into my back.

I felt like a queen. After all, wasn't I the one they were all there for? I bit my finger; what happened to humility? When had I become so prideful? My cheeks burned with shame.

"Have a seat, Reverend. We're proud to have you in our home," said Mr. Hobart, while Mrs. Hobart fussed at the stove to fix him a cup of hot cider.

Darlene said, "I never heard nobody call Bruver James that."

Marylou looked mortified and clapped her hand over Darlene's mouth.

Brother James smiled the smile that fills your body with warmth. "In our church," he said, "we call each other brother and sister, but you folks haven't seen fit to join us yet. Well, we'll wait till the Lord lights the way to our door for you. Remember, the door's always open. Meantime, you're good Christian souls to take us all in this way. Brothers and sisters, shall we all bow our heads and thank the Lord for these kindly people?"

As I bowed my head, I saw Marylou gently shove Darlene's chin to her chest.

"Sweet Jesus, we gather in Your name in this humble household to celebrate Miriam's renewal at the season of Your birth, so many long years ago. . . ."

I heard the words, but the words were not what counted. What was important was the spell Brother James cast upon us all. Ordinary people a minute ago, now we were transformed into beings little less than angels.

I remembered how Brother James had been called

to the pulpit when he was not very much older than Darlene, how he'd quoted Scripture from memory before he could even read, how he'd let the power of God surge through his hands to heal a woman whose eyesight was nearly gone. That day he'd had to stand on a step stool to reach her shoulders for the blessing. When he was half my age, he founded our church.

Marylou stood guard over the little girls. I glanced over at her, and saw her face in the harsh country lamplight, and felt that she was asking herself, at that moment, whether she loved Brother James enough to dedicate her life to him.

The women cooked and laid the table for dinner, while the men talked of manly things — cars, pheasant hunting, Senator Dole. I had no place in the second group and wasn't needed in the first. I went outside and was amazed to see blackbirds filling the front yard, all of them foraging for a crumb or a berry, as the storm grew into a blizzard. I hurried back inside, pushing the door against the heavy wind.

In the blinding snow, one of the birds flew right into the window. The bird lay among shards of glass on the kitchen floor, battered. We saw its tiny chest heaving with every breath. By the time Brother James got to it, it was dead, either from the impact or from bleeding to death. How much blood does a small bird have to spare?

Mr. Hobart offered to toss the blackbird out back, but Brother James wouldn't hear of it. "This bird is one of God's noble creatures, and we will give it a proper burial."

Mrs. Hobart went for a shoe box, which she lined with soft patchwork fabric and the few twigs and leaves Brother Timothy could find in the yard. We all put on our coats and stood around as the storm subsided and the sun began to set on Christmas Eve. Uncle Benjamin and Uncle Vernon dug a shallow grave in the hard earth.

The grave dug, Brother James lowered the box, and Darlene was allowed to throw the first handful of dirt and snow over the bird's small coffin. Each of us followed, as Brother James spoke soothing words about the bird and the sacred night we shared.

Brother Timothy stood with his arm around his mother's shoulder. Both of them had tears freezing on their cheeks.

Afterwards, when we were inside huddled around the fire, Mrs. Hobart said, "Brother James, I want to join the church."

My heart was filled with thanksgiving, and I fully felt the words of the Twenty-third Psalm, "my cup runneth over."

Some time in the middle of the night, when I thanked God for using me to bring Mrs. Hobart to Jesus, it occurred to me that I no longer thought of myself as the instrument of Adam's salvation, and I wasn't sure whether that meant he was lost, or found.

CHAPTER
TWENTY-THREE

Told by Adam

Brent made himself a baloney and sweet pickle sandwich, with a few other specimens from the animal and vegetable kingdoms. The sandwich was piled dangerously high. If it had been summer, and the ceiling fan had been on, meat and tomatoes would have been flying all over the kitchen. He pressed the tower down so he could wrap his mouth around it, and after his first bite, it popped back up, like a foam pillow. "Want some?"

"You make it look disgusting. I wouldn't eat that stuff."

Brent shrugged, wiping mustard off his mouth with the shoulder of his T-shirt. "It's my dinner."

"You're having dinner at four in the afternoon?"

"Hey, it's Christmas Eve. We don't officially eat on Christmas. We just eat all day and all night. So, go on. You're tearing down this dirt road, and there's nothing around you but frozen cows."

"Okay, I'm going way too fast. My mother would have a seizure if she knew I was hitting fifty on an icy road. My windshield wipers and defroster are cranking like crazy, but I'm keeping the Chevy station wagon in sight all the way out there. Suddenly

I check out the gas meter, and it's twitching just above empty. There's not a gas station in sight. I'm gonna run out of gas. I'm gonna have to walk eight miles to the nearest pay phone; then I won't be able to call because my fingers will be frostbitten, and they'll snap off in the holes of the dial, and besides, I don't have a quarter."

"Is this girl worth it?" Brent asked, curling an extra slice of baloney and sliding it whole into his mouth. "Isn't she gonna croak anyway?"

How could I answer that? I wanted to sock him in the gut for saying something so insensitive and so true, but a part of me knew that as little as a month before, I would have said the same thing.

"Okay, so what happened? Did you follow the station wagon all the way?"

"Probably ten minutes have passed since I've seen an actual building that isn't just a silo or barn. Then, out of nowhere, I spot chimney smoke blackening the sky. That has to be where they're going. Finally the Chevy stops, a girl gets out — not Miriam, some lady from the church. Anyway, she gets out, opens the iron gate by the mailbox, closes it after the car's pulled through, then jumps back in. The car's gone, disappears up a winding road before I even reach the gate.

"I get out to open the gate. I'm telling you, it's *cold* out there. No trees for windbreakers. I'm reaching for the gate, when I hear my mother's voice, as clear as sonar: 'That's private property, Adam Bergen. Open that gate, and you'll pull back a bloody stump.' I just can't make myself open it. I'm trying to convince myself it's electrified, even though that girl just opened it without frying. I just can't do it. I can't go up that driveway."

"Pluck-pluck-pluck," Brent said. "Chick-*en*."

"Anyway, what would I have done when I got to the house? Storm it with machine guns?"

"You jerk, you went about nine hundred miles down a dirt road, in a snowstorm, and now you're telling me you just turned around and came home, with your tail between your legs like a little puppy dog?"

"Well, I've always been famous for wasted potential," I muttered. "Anyway, I'm going back there tomorrow morning. Between now and then, I'm coming up with a plan. You want to go with me?"

"Oh, wow, that's really tempting. But, it's Christmas, and I gotta do family crap." His cheeks stuffed with a cold, greasy potato pancake, he said, "I think I'm getting a car stereo for Christmas. What are you getting?" While all this was going on, we were both standing there in front of the refrigerator like we were worshipping at the Holy Ark. Brent dove in for a handful of black olives. "I mean, what are you getting for your own kind of Jewish Christmas, whatever you call it."

"Chanukah, got that? CHA, as in gargling with salt water; NOO, as in nude; and KUH, as in duh, as in dumb. CHA-NOO-KUH. And it's not the Jewish Christmas. It's about freedom, not about a messiah, or *the* messiah. And it was over on December 19 this year. So I'm not getting anything for Christmas." I slammed the refrigerator shut, making those bottles on the door stand up and pay attention. They must have been shaking and rattling on their shelves, wondering what act of terrorism I'd perform next.

"You didn't get much this year, hunh? Okay, okay," he said, backing off with a gallon of milk hanging from his thumb. The sandwich was history now, and the olives, too. He splashed the milk into a tall glass.

"The milk's expired," I said. "It's December 23 milk."

"Smells okay." Brent took the next step of his feast to our pantry, for a Hostess apple pie. "Lighten up, Bergen. It's just a holiday. So now, the cops are out looking for the girl?"

"I guess so. I've got to call and tell them where she is."

"You're holding out on the cops? Jesus, Adam."

I knew I should have called an hour ago, but somewhere in the heroic pit of my stomach, I wanted to be the one to rescue Miriam. Dumb. I wasn't even sure she wanted to be rescued.

"What are you gonna do after you go out to Whitewater tomorrow, big shot?"

The conversation was turning as sour as old milk, and I wasn't sorry when Brent stuffed the last half of the Hostess pie into his mouth and mumbled, "Well, I gotta go. We're putting out our *luminarias* as soon as my dad gets home. Me and my brother have to fill up about a hundred lunch bags with sand. But it sure looks beautiful when the whole neighborhood's lit up at dusk. It just isn't Christmas without *luminarias*. How come you guys don't put them out? Every other house on the block does. It doesn't mean anything, just candle lights."

"I'll take it under advisement," I said. It was an

expression I'd learned from Diana, in debate. For a second I missed Diana deep in my belly, the way you feel after your first dog croaks.

"Well, let me know how it turns out with the big rescue mission *mañana*," he said. Suddenly, inspired by the *luminarias*, he was sliding into fourth-grade Spanish.

"Yeah, right."

I pulled my arms up inside my T-shirt, fuming about what a crappy friend Brent had turned out to be. Or maybe I was having a severe case of the yellow-stripe-down-the-back Bah Humbugs. Or maybe I was missing Diana's TV room and being pressed up against her on that curvy couch. Anyway, I was completely miserable as I followed Brent to the front door.

A dribble of apple pie sat on his shirt collar. What a slob. How come I'd never noticed before? He put on his ski jacket and trudged through the snow, digging deep Nike trenches between my house and his. As sort of a last tribute to our friendship, he shouted from his porch, "*Feliz Navidad*," and someone shoveling a driveway across the street yelled back, "Merry Christmas to you, too!"

I shut the front door. The air was hot inside. The furnace roared its way through probably its last winter. "Merry Christmas," I muttered to myself. "Happy Chanukah. Happy Winter Solstice, Happy Holiday-of-Choice."

I flashed on a picture: Diana in Acapulco, sunning on a beach. Bronze-chested beach boys would be bringing her frosty drinks with Christmas bows and a sprig of mistletoe tied to the straws. She'd be wearing a suit that was — what did she say? —

revolutionary. I wasn't in the picture.

I sat in front of the window, watching my neighbors put out the sacks of sand, carry in packages, rearrange a string of lights on a pine tree on the front lawn. I turned on the radio. Perry Como's smarmy voice promised, "I'll be home for Christmas. . . ."

Lights were coming on all over the neighborhood, as darkness hit with December suddenness. ". . . If only in my dreams," Perry promised. And that got me wondering, What did Diana dream about for Christmas that she didn't already have three of?

And wherever *she* was, what was Miriam's dream? That she'd be around for one more Christmas?

CHAPTER
TWENTY-FOUR

Told by Miriam

What a glorious night! I had never, not even in church, felt such an outpouring of love as I felt on that Christmas at the farm. After we buried the blackbird, we went back to the kitchen. Brother Timothy sat a little apart from the rest of us, listening, thinking. Mr. and Mrs. Hobart swayed to and fro in their maple rockers on opposite sides of the fireplace, their outstretched toes nearly touching. Mrs. Hobart's face glowed like a bride's. Across the table from me, Mama looked like she'd come home at last, and Uncle Benjamin and Uncle Vernon seemed relaxed and jovial and full of Christmas spirit.

Brother James held one little girl on each knee, and Marylou sat on the floor, leaning against his legs ever so lightly.

The image of the small bird in its soft, patchwork nest came to me: Dear God, help me to remember that hope is the thing with feathers that perches in the soul. In that moment I almost believed that the words had come from Scripture.

Then Brother James led us all in prayer, and we asked for peace on earth, goodwill toward all men, as He would have wanted. "Silent night, holy night," we sang, with only candles and the fireplace aglow. Brother James spoke barely above a whisper, and we all reached for every word. I thought he looked so blissful, with Marylou at his feet and the little girls' heads resting on his shoulders. I envied how they fell asleep to the humming of his body as he spoke.

One by one, people went off to bed. The unmarried men were to sleep in the front parlor, and Uncle Vernon and Uncle Benjamin went off to lay out their bedrolls. Brother James carried the little girls upstairs to the bed I would share with them later. I knew he meant for me to stay downstairs after the others had gone, and so I waited.

When he came back, there were only small fingers of fire left. Brother James stirred the embers and threw on another log, and I knew it was to be a long talk. He motioned for me to take the rocking chair opposite him.

"This is a Christmas I will always treasure, Miriam."

"Me, too, Brother James."

"Might have been more appropriate for Easter, though, because I see that you have been renewed, just like the buds that burst forth on the trees of spring."

"I feel stronger than ever," I told him.

"I don't doubt it." We rocked quietly, as I wondered what would come next.

"About the boy," Brother James began.

My heart sped up. "Yes?"

"It won't work, child. You're fish, and he's fowl."

I blurted out what was on my mind: "Do we have to hate people who aren't like us, Brother James?"

"No, child. We don't hate them, any more than we hate the snow that made that poor bird hit our window. Remember, God said, 'This I command you, that you love one another.' But we surely worry about them."

I did not think Adam and his father needed our worrying. But then I thought, Not in this life, maybe, but what will become of them in the next life?

"You see, we love them so much that we want to bring them along with us, but it troubles us that they haven't found Jesus yet. Miriam, you know the church teaches that we have a God-given obligation to save them. 'Go into all the world and preach the gospel to the whole of creation.' You've been tied up in your own problems so long, maybe you've forgotten what God expects of you."

I wasn't entirely sure what he meant, but I felt myself tensing up as I waited for the next words.

"I want you to make this Adam Bergen boy your personal mission, Miriam. Saving a thousand strangers isn't as precious as saving one troubled soul you know only too well."

"I've meant to, Brother James. I've promised Jesus, and I've thought and prayed about it. I can't get any kind of a foothold. Adam's not very religious, but anyway he seems pretty comfortable with his own faith."

"Comfort? What's comfort got to do with God's word? We're talking souls here, child."

I'd thought comfort had everything to do with God, but perhaps Brother James meant something else.

"If you like the boy, bring him around to our door. Look at the joy in the face of Brother Timothy's mother. Don't you want the same for Adam?"

I wanted to tell him that I'd brought Mrs. Hobart to Jesus, just by causing all these people to be together on Christmas, and wasn't that enough? But of course I could not boast that way, and I didn't want him to think I was trading Mrs. Hobart's salvation for Adam's.

Brother James said, "I want the boy's soul for Jesus. As it says in the *Book in Gold Leaf,* 'Be a fisher of men.' Reel him in to us, child, and that's how you can thank the Lord for the miracle He's performed for you. And let me remind you about First Corinthians, 'For as in Adam all die, even so in Christ shall all be made alive.' Is he worth it to you?"

I was reminded of Adam's father asking, "How much is it worth to you to be pain-free?"

I couldn't answer right away; I don't think Brother James expected me to. His words hung in the air, gradually trailing off like the scent of vanilla in Mama's kitchen.

"I'll think about it," I promised, and he reached across and patted my hand which was clutching the arm of the rocker.

"That's all I ask, Miriam. Just give it some thought. Now, *I've* given some thought to Marylou Wadkins and me getting married." There was a thick pause. I wasn't sure how I was supposed to respond. It was inconceivable that he was asking my advice. I rather thought he was measuring my reaction.

"She's a kind woman," I said.

"She needs someone to look after her. We could build a home together — Marylou, her little ones, and me."

Yes, but did he love her? Did she love him? If comfort had nothing to do with God, was it also true that love had nothing to do with marriage?

"Do you think she's put Billy Wadkins behind her?"

Why was he asking me this? Surely he had a friend, someone in the church he could discuss all this with, even Uncle Vernon.

"You must have some idea. You spent the night at her house. Does she keep a picture of him beside her bed?"

"I — I don't know what to say."

He turned his face away, staring into the fire. All at once it came to me: Brother James was lonely.

"I think she likes you a lot," I said tentatively.

"At times, she does seem to."

"And the little girls adore you." As I had adored him, when I was a little girl.

"I'll be thirty come April. It's time I had a wife and family." He rocked, I rocked; the only sound in the room besides the crackling fire was the thumping of our chairs on the worn linoleum.

"Well, I expect I'll be asking her before long," he said quietly.

I moved Annie over closer to Darlene and slipped in between the cool, crisp country sheets. I knew they'd been starched and ironed by Mrs. Hobart, maybe weeks ago, just in case someone stopped for the night. Little did she know she'd have a house full of strangers for Christmas. I thought about the passage in Hebrews that said, "Be not forgetful to entertain strangers; for thereby some have entertained angels unawares." Brother James, of course, was the only one of us who came close to that description, but who knew what the Lord had in mind for Annie and Darlene? I tucked the covers tight around them.

"Has Santa been here?" Darlene asked, her voice still slurry with sleep.

"Not till you and everyone else goes to sleep," I whispered. But I could not sleep. I lay there, watching the thin organdy curtains billow in the breeze from the heater, watching a crack in the high ceiling, counting the lilacs on the wallpaper, and thinking.

I had made a promise that I would try to convert Adam. It was what Brother James wanted. It was what God wanted of me. After all, wasn't I supremely grateful? It was the least I could do.

There was a gentle knock at the door, and Mama came in.

"Baby, are you awake? Marylou's fast asleep, and I've been waiting up for you." Mama, wrapped in an afghan, lay her pillow across the foot of my bed, and we whispered, so as not to wake the little girls. "What did you and Brother James talk about so long?"

"About Adam," I said. It was partly true; I couldn't tell her about the Marylou part, because it would have been a betrayal of Brother James's confidence in me. "He wants me to bring Adam into the church."

"That would be the answer to my daily prayer," Mama said. "I know how much you like the boy."

"I feel like I'm starting over, Mama. I know I'm healed. It's like having a second chance. I have to live my life the way God intends me to."

Mama said, "If only we always knew what God intended."

Then we sort of drifted back and forth from conversation to sleep, like slumber party girls, and before I knew it, the sun was coming in through the curtains on Christmas morning.

Somehow, there were presents for everyone. The uncles gave me a pink leather billfold with lots of pockets and slots for pictures, and Mama's present to me was a thin volume of American poems. "I never heard of any one of these people," she admitted, "but I know how you dearly love verses." She'd given me the book earlier that morning, while Brother James and Marylou were taking a walk out in the brittle morning. Of course Brother James wouldn't have approved.

The little girls were showered with gifts from everyone — crayons, and clothes for their dolls, and Wedgwood-type teacups, and, for Darlene, her first pair of roller skates, with thick plastic wheels. Mrs. Hobart gave each family a jar of preserves and a jar of green beans, corn, or beets she'd put up herself; each jar was tied with a crisp red bow.

And after we were done oo-ing and ah-ing over everybody's gifts, Brother James made an announcement:

229

"This is a fine day, brothers and sisters, to share some wonderful news with you. Annie, Darlene, come stand by me. Marylou?" He extended his arm, and she, tall as she was, fit right under it, as if he were her umbrella. "Sister Marylou Wadkins and I are going to become man and wife."

Oh, everyone went wild! All the men pumped Brother James's hand, and we women hugged Marylou and each other. Darlene and Annie danced on Brother James's feet.

"When? When?" we all cried.

"When is after we get everything settled with Miriam and the doctors, maybe February. Does February sound good to you, Marylou?"

"Just fine," she said, beaming. I wondered if she'd go home and pack away the picture of Billy now.

"And who will perform the ceremony?" Mama asked.

"Well, I don't know. Mr. Hobart, you think your preacher might do the honors?"

"We'll just ask him, Reverend. We'll just call him up and ask him," Mr. Hobart said, as if he were proud to be an instrument of the Lord. "He's a Baptist, though."

"We'll not hold that against him," Uncle Benjamin said, sounding much more jolly than usual. "Vernon and me, we were Baptists once, but we got over it."

Then everyone was laughing and clucking about wedding colors and bridesmaids and, of course, flower girls. And while I was just as happy as everyone else, every few minutes it flashed across my mind that Brother James didn't know that Marylou Wadkins was still in love with Billy. And, I'll admit it, some moments I resented that all the attention had shifted to Marylou. I had come to expect to be the center of attention. I remembered the words from Proverbs: "Pride goeth before destruction, and a haughty spirit before a fall."

CHAPTER
TWENTY-FIVE

Told by Adam

"Are you sure we're doing the right thing, Dad?" It was maybe the twentieth time I'd asked, as the Jeep crawled along the snow-packed road to the house out in Whitewater. I'd insanely flown over this road the day before, and I wondered if a person could suddenly develop an adult sensibility or if it came on slowly like a crippling disease.

"You have to notify the police," Dad said. "It's the law, because she's under court jurisdiction and she's been abducted. But since you never said anything to me about this until this morning — "

"I couldn't. You're her lawyer."

"Anyway, the police have already lost about twenty-four hours in the search, so what's another couple of minutes?"

It was a fantastic day, like so many Kansas mornings after a vicious blizzard. The snow hunkered in peaceful banks along the road, and the sunlight made it glitter with rainbow colors. Even to someone like me, who only thinks of weather for its entertainment value, it was a day designed to take your breath away.

Though we both wore shades, we squinted; that's

how dazzling the morning was. "There's the Quik Trip you told me about," Dad said. "What is it, about six or eight miles from the house?" We slowed up. "It looks locked up tight."

"Well, it's Christmas, Dad. Even McDonald's closes."

"Yeah, but there's a pay phone outside, so you can make your call there. Remember, Adam, the truth."

I dialed the number I'd repeated over and over in my head through the ride out into the country. "Can I talk to someone who's working on the Miriam Pelham case."

"The who? We've got a lot of cases," the cop said. He sounded as though he'd have preferred to be someplace other than the Wichita Police Department for Christmas.

"Pelham," I said. "The girl who was kidnapped."

"The church case, you mean?"

"That's the one." People didn't think of Miriam as a real person anymore. She was the cancer patient, the kidnap victim, the church case.

"I can take the information," the cop said, sounding bored by the whole thing.

I gave him directions and the description of the house outside Whitewater. He seemed to be writing everything down, only grunting during my pauses. Finally he said, "Well, that's not WPD jurisdiction. That's Butler County Sheriff. Jesus Christ, it's Christmas."

"Aw, too bad," I said, but the sarcasm was lost on him.

"Who are you, some kid? How old are you? I need your name, your address, and your phone number. What's your connection to this case?" I answered all his questions, offering as little information as I could. I was standing in a foot of snow that had drifted into the phone booth, and I hopped from foot to foot for some warmth. There were long pauses while the officer wrote everything down. A wobbly heart had been carved on the wall of the phone booth:

BECKY JASON
Always and Forever

I traced the heart, wondering if Becky and Jason were debaters I'd met at a tournament. Suddenly I thought about Diana and how she'd love an adventure like this one. Her eyes would be fiery, her eyelashes would be jumping like windshield wipers to keep every detail clear. She'd be wound up and ready to spring.

"Okay, I got it down. I'll get someone out there," the cop said. "Butler County or us, one or the other. Stay where we can reach you." Then, like it was out of a different throat, came the cheery, "Merry Christmas."

When we reached the driveway, I had no problem opening the gate this time. As my dad drove through, it felt like a scene from a World War II movie in which the Allies storm a Nazi compound — one of those spooky old houses with attics and dungeons — and victory was in sight.

We drove up the winding road to the front door of the house. All the drapes were shut; there were no lights showing. The house looked empty, as though the family who lived there had gone away for Christmas. Not even a mangy mutt barked. Later I found out that the deserted look at the front of the house was because all the people — and there were a lot of them — were around back, in the kitchen.

We'd just about given up, when someone came to the door. A man in his fifties, sucking on a dead pipe, greeted us with typical country hospitality: "Yep?"

Dad said, "We're looking for Miriam Pelham."

There was just the faintest pause before he said, "She ain't here." That told me two things: (1) she was, and (2) as a liar, he wasn't a member of Sword and the Spirit Church.

"Well, sir," Dad said, trying to sound down home and not city lawyer, "whether she is or isn't, the Butler County Sheriff's on his way over here, and I suspect he'll have a search warrant."

"Who are you, anyway?" the man shoved the pipe into his pocket and picked a fleck of something off his tongue.

Then Brother James appeared out of the shadows. "God bless you brothers, come in."

"This is pure insane," the other man said. "Haven't understood one thang since it commenced."

Brother James smiled at the man and led us through the house into the kitchen.

"Adam!" Miriam jumped to her feet. I hadn't seen her move so quickly and easily in weeks. I thought she was about to run right to me, but her two uncles flanked her, and each took an arm.

"Brothers and sisters," Brother James said, dripping charm, "you all remember Mr. Samuel Bergen, our lawyer, and this is his boy, Adam."

Dad said, "Listen, we can cut the formalities, because you haven't got a minute to lose. The police are on their way, and they will take Miriam back and arrest you, Brother James, for kidnapping and all the rest of you for conspiracy to kidnap and for obstructing justice. They'll have a whole laundry list of charges against you, but I think we can — "

"No, they won't be filing any charges," Brother James said, "because I am personally taking Miriam back to the hospital."

There was a small flutter of surprise, and I saw Miriam's face turn gray.

"Look at the child," Brother James said. As all eyes turned to Miriam, she seemed to shrink back into her uncles. Her mother sidestepped subtly across the room to stand by her. I had the feeling no one in the room moved without Brother James's approval. "Look at her," he said. "Miriam, come to me."

Miriam took a few tentative steps toward Brother James. Her mother's arms were outstretched toward her, as if she were giving her to Brother James, whose arms were stretched out to receive her. Miriam stood in the middle of the room, facing him.

"Touch your toes, child." She did. "Twist this way and that." I was embarrassed for Miriam, performing as if she were a trained seal. But she could *move*. "You see," Brother James continued, "the pain has left the child."

"Praise Jesus," some young guy said. I remembered him from my last visit to the church.

Brother James was warming up to his subject: "She's come through the long night of her travails.

She's been tested like Job, like Jonah, like Abraham, and as God is my witness, I tell you, she's been healed. She's been healed, body and spirit, as surely as God healed Miriam of leprosy in the desert a thousand years before He sent His son Jesus to us. On that day in the parched desert, Moses cried unto the Lord, saying, 'Heal her now, O God, I beseech Thee.' For seven days she suffered, just as our Miriam has suffered these many weeks, before God saw fit to lift His hand to heal her." I saw his outstretched hands trembling. The room was charged with electricity. A cat by the fireplace arched its back, and Miriam had tears streaming down her face. I wanted to hold her face, wipe the tears away with my two thumbs.

Brother James dropped his hands and folded them across his belly. Now he spoke barely above a whisper: "So, I will take Miriam back to the hospital, and I will insist that they run all their tests on her first thing tomorrow. And I am confident, just as I know that Lord Jesus rose up after His ordeal and death on the cross, that the doctors will find no sign, no sign at all, of the disease that inflicted the child, because she is whole again. A-men. Now, let's get going."

Suddenly everyone was bustling around, like stagehands between acts. Mrs. Pelham came back into the room with a small suitcase, an older woman packed up a sack lunch. Someone helped Miriam into a coat that hung too loose to be her own, and they were ready to go.

The young guy said, "Brother James, y'all go out the back road, hear? It's narrow, and it's covered over with snow, but the Lord will guide you. Anyways, it winds down to Route Ten. That way, you don't come eye to eye with — anybody on the main road."

Miriam hugged all the women and Marylou Wadkins's two children, who'd been coloring in a corner of the kitchen. The uncles stood like soldiers with their arms at their sides, following Miriam with their eyes. As for her eyes, they rested on me and said a silent good-bye, or was it a thank you? And then she was gone.

With Brother James out of the house, the whole atmosphere changed. The pipe chewer said, "I reckon you better be going, too." He herded us toward the front door.

I was more than glad to get out of there and feel the fresh sting of cold on my face. But Dad was furious. He walked ahead of me. I saw the anger and resolve in his shoulders.

We climbed into the Jeep to wait for the cops, rubbing our arms and stinging-cold faces and blowing into our gloves for a little warmth.

CHAPTER
TWENTY-SIX

Told by Miriam

"Name?"

"Miriam Pelham."

"Pel-um, Pel-um," the hospital volunteer repeated. She was thin and twiggy. Her bony fingers flipped through cards on her Rolodex. "Pel-um. Oh!" Her face turned the color of her smock. "Just hold on." She spun around in her swivel chair and cupped her hand over the phone.

Brother James rested his hand on my shoulder. I wondered how he could be so calm, especially when two security guards headed right for us.

"This way, please," the taller guard said, and the other fell into formation behind Brother James. They took us to a hospital administrator, not the chief administrator, I guessed, because he'd be off for Christmas. We heard the disembodied voice of the intercom: "Dr. Gregory, please report to Mr. Finelli's office. Dr. Gregory to Mr. Finelli's office."

Mr. Finelli looked very uneasy as Brother James, towering over him, shook his hand and then motioned for him to sit down behind his own desk.

"I've brought the child back," Brother James said, "because I believe in the law of the land."

"Well and good, Mr., uh, Reverend Davies, but you realize that you abducted a patient who was under court order to remain in this hospital."

Brother James sat back in the round chair. He had a way of making every chair fit his contours. He crossed his ankle over the opposite knee, so cool, so relaxed, while my stomach turned somersaults.

"Well now, Mr. Finelli, I only took Miriam home for Christmas. Will you be with your family today for Christmas dinner? The wife, the children, the little grandchildren all around your table? Think of their faces, sir, and tell me you would have denied Miriam Pelham a Christmas with her family."

"That's not the point, Reverend."

"Then I don't know what is. No, I sure don't." Brother James leaned forward, and I saw Mr. Finelli sort of pull back.

Then Dr. Gregory arrived. He fluttered around me, looking me over closely, feeling my neck and throat with two soft, cool hands. "You don't look bad, kid."

"She's healed." Brother James stood up and slid his fingers into the back pockets of his overalls. "Tomorrow morning, first thing, I want you to run every test in your arsenal — the blood tests, the computer tests, all of it." He looked upward, toward places most of us could only imagine. "And God Almighty, strike me dead in this very spot tomorrow if those tests turn up any sign of the sickness that once sorely oppressed poor Miriam Pelham." He came up behind me and placed his hands on my shoulders.

It was a gesture meant to calm me, I know, but I was terrified that something, anything, would show up on the bone scan, and God would strike Brother James dead. Yet he seemed so confident. His fingers were like cloth of great woven strength that would swath me through the tests.

No charges were filed, and I was returned to my old room. But this time I was well and strong and couldn't stay in bed. I walked every inch of the room until I was dizzy. I sat on the window seat, counting the cars in the parking lot below. I invented stories for the families going to and from the cars.

A father held two small boys by the hand, then seemed to have quite a struggle getting them buckled into their car seats. I imagined that they'd just been up to visit their mother and new baby sister, and one of the boys would have to grow out of the car seat before the baby was ready for it.

There were other stories, too: a woman sneaking a pizza in to her husband; a priest coming to give the last rites to a nun; a man hidden behind a sunburst of red and green balloons meant for a boy in Pediatrics. At the end of afternoon visiting hours, people poured out too fast for me to conjure up their stories.

The afternoon dragged on, until Dr. Chin came in, wearing a pretty orange shirtwaist dress and carrying her stool.

"Merry Christmas," she said, her voice as tinkly as ever. "You are back. I'm so glad." She moved a chair to the center of the room. "Sit, please." She sat on the stool in front of me, hands on her knees. I had the sense that she was focusing deeply, for her eyes, behind those absurd huge glasses, never moved. Finally she said, "Very well. We start. Breathe very deeply, in, out, in, out. In through the nose, out through the mouth." Her hands passed over me, like a Hovercraft looking for a landing site.

"How do I feel?" I asked, half teasingly.

"Do not talk, please. Clear, very clear." When she'd been all over me, she sat back down on her stool. "You feel fine. No tight spots, no hot spots. Your body is harmonious. Dr. Gregory will claim the miracle, and so will your church. But you and I know what did it."

"You mean Therapeutic Touch?"

Dr. Chin rolled her head from side to side. 'No, no, no. Harmony. Your body is in harmony with the cosmos."

"Do you really believe this?"

Dr. Chin shrugged and plunged her hands into her deep orange pockets. "I believe in everything that works. Tomorrow the tests will confirm my findings, and you must be very relaxed and centered and balanced for the tests. Now, rest, please." She hustled me along to the bed and pulled from her pocket a downy white feather. "Hold this, stroke this. Brush it against your cheek. It will help to center you. Think of the bird."

Adam came by. He poked his head in the door and asked, "Are you speaking to me?"

I was sitting in the center of the bed, thumbing through an old copy of *Good Housekeeping*. I pinched my cheeks to get some extra color in them and pulled my hair out from behind my ears. "You can come all the way in. I won't throw a bedpan at you."

Adam stood shyly beside the bed, twiddling with his car keys. How many times had we met this way, with me in or on the bed and him beside it? Normal

242

couples didn't have their dates in hospital rooms. But we weren't a normal couple. In fact, I wasn't even sure we were a couple.

"I'm not mad at you."

"That's a relief." He dropped the keys on the bedside table and took over the bottom half of my bed. He leaned forward as if to kiss me, then I guess he changed his mind. The rules were so confusing. He asked, "So what happens next?"

"Tomorrow they're testing all the motors and gears, but they won't find anything wrong."

"You're really — what would you say? — not sick anymore?"

"I'd say healed."

"Heavy."

"I don't expect you to understand it." It was awkward for a moment. I pretended to be absorbed in the magazine, and he tried reading the article upside down. I said, not daring to look at him, "You were brave to go out there to the farmhouse."

"I could have been shot," Adam teased. "Those guy are NRA types. How's your Christmas been, considering?"

"In some ways, it was the nicest time of my life, out there at the farm. I wish you could have been there, for the good parts." I told him about the blackbird and his funeral.

"I get this picture of you all standing around in the snow storm, saying *kaddish* for the bird."

"What's cottish?"

"It's a Jewish prayer to remember dead people. Animals, too, I guess. But it doesn't say anything about dying. It's about life, not death. Weird, isn't it?"

"Do you believe in life eternal?" Maybe this would be my foothold on Adam's soul.

"Yeah. That's an hour in Mrs. Loomis's class."

I smiled in spite of myself and wondered who but Adam could joke about heaven and hell. Or did all Jewish people take eternity so lightly?

"I'm sorry I can't be here for your bone scan tomorrow. It was such a great time last time. But I've got to finish my college essays. I've got this dynamic paragraph I'm trying to work into all of them. No, it's okay. I wrote the whole thing myself. I'm a debater. I can tie any two things together."

God and Jesus? Despite that part of me saying Leave him be, it isn't right, you can't do it, I still thought I had to try to win Adam to Jesus. But how? If not through his soul, through his heart? I asked, "How's Diana?"

"Who knows? She's in Mexico. Listen, I'll come over tomorrow afternoon to hear the big report." He actually tweaked my nose. "You look fantastic, Miriam. I'm not kidding."

"You're always kidding, Adam Bergen."

He grinned. "I guess so. Well, I've got to go and figure out what Carleton College expects me to bluff my way through. Don't run off. Remember, I can always find you."

"That was a good piece of detective work. How did you do it?"

"Professional secret." He grabbed a forkful of cherry pie that was left over from lunch. "This is awful. Can I have it?"

"You're taking nourishment from a poor sick girl? Look at me, I'm skin and bones." Actually, I'd gained some weight and looked fuller and healthier than ever. He looked closely, with those roguish eyes. I had to say something, I had to. But I couldn't get the words out of my mouth. Instead, I said, "Eat the pie. You need it worse than I do."

"So, what happens next in your soap opera?"

"I think the judge will send me home. We go to court on Thursday, and they won't be able to keep me past then."

"Well, if you're out by Saturday night, do you want to go to my brother's wedding?"

A wedding! The perfect place to get my work done. "Sure, I'd love to go." At that point, after practically being imprisoned for so long, I would have gone anywhere, even to the city dump, just to be going. Mama wouldn't be wild about the idea, and certainly the men would have a fit, but I would tell them that a wedding was the right place to begin the Lord's work on Adam. Saturday night I would begin showing God how grateful I was.

The hospital vampire sucked blood from my veins and filled half a dozen tiny glass vials. For the fifth time, the drum of the bone scanner rolled over me. Once again I was strapped to the sliding table of the scanner, like a damsel tied to the railroad tracks in an old time melodrama.

Where was the hero to rescue me, I wondered, then reminded myself that I wouldn't need rescuing, because I was well. More important, Brother James was safe.

I watched the computer draw its pictures of my inner workings. I prayed that there would be no sign of the black walnut that had intruded on my body before.

"Well?" I said, when all was done.

The technician replied blandly, "Your doctor will interpret the results," but when no one was looking, he gave me a "thumbs up" signal. Anyway, after so many go-rounds, I knew what to look for, and I knew it wasn't there. The blood tests would be back in the morning, and then they would have no reason to keep me.

It wasn't that simple, of course. In the morning, when everything came back clear, we had to go to court. Mama and Brother James came for me at 8:00.

Judge Bonnell's desk was up high, like an altar, and he looked down on us with an uncompromising expression. Mr. Bergen and I sat at a long table with our heads tilted back to look up at him. It reminded me of the scene in the movie *The Ten Command-ments*, when Moses came down from the mountain with the tablets and addressed the multitude of people below, and *that* reminded me of a joke Adam told me when he realized that my name was the same as Moses's sister. "What did God say when Moses complained of a headache? 'Take two tablets and call me in the morning.'" Typical Adamism.

In the courtroom, Brother James, Mama, and the uncles sat in the gallery behind our counsel table. Mama sat perfectly still with her ankles crossed, and Brother James wore his Sunday suit and black boots.

The judge mumbled, "In the interest of Miriam Pelham, Case Number 96JC48, Sedgwick County, State of Kansas, who are the interested parties present for this case?"

Several state-appointed people identified themselves, including Gerri Kensler, my social worker, and the guardian *ad litem* who was supposed to be representing my best interests. I'd never met her.

Mr. Bergen stood up to introduce himself. "Your Honor, I am Samuel Bergen, counsel for Miriam Pelham, who is sitting to my left."

The judge lifted his glasses to peer at us, then replaced them while he flipped through some papers. We all waited tensely. I stroked Dr. Chin's white feather in my lap. Finally Judge Bonnell said, "How are you feeling, Miss Pelham?"

"Fine." Mr. Bergen elbowed me, and I stood up. "I feel fine, Your Honor."

"These reports from the Secretary of Social and Rehabilitative Services and from the medical personnel involved in your case all indicate that there is no sign of the cancer that, until recently, afflicted you.

"Miss Pelham, off the record, to what do you attribute your astonishing cure?"

I felt the eyes of Brother James at the back of my head. "The Lord," I said meekly.

"Hogwash," replied the judge.

"Well, sir, you asked me."

"I did indeed. Counsel, is it true that Miss Pelham has received aggressive therapy for her tumor?"

"Yes, Your Honor, a full cycle of the drug Cytocel and ten radiation treatments."

I felt Brother James stir behind me and was afraid he would rise to confront the judge.

"Did you receive any other forms of therapy, Miss Pelham?"

"A nurse practiced Therapeutic Touch, but I'm not sure — "

"Well, for the record I want it made clear that the young woman received a variety of conventional and alternative forms of treatment, and at this time there is no sign of disease. I will ask that Miss Pelham undergo a full battery of diagnostic tests at six-month intervals for the next four years, at which time she becomes twenty-one. If nothing turns up, the case will be dismissed. If there's evidence that the disease has recurred, I want the principals back in court immediately. Miss Pelham's to be returned to her family. Any questions?"

Brother James stood up. "One question, Your Honor. Might you concede that Miriam Pelham has been healed by the hand of God?"

"You are?"

"Brother James Davies, sir, preacher of Sword and the Spirit Church."

"Well, Reverend Davies, I would say to you that it is not up to this court to make that judgment. I will leave that to a higher court, and I do not mean the Supreme Court, sir, I mean the Highest Court, and that's all I can say if I intend to uphold the First Amendment of the United States Constitution. Next case."

CHAPTER TWENTY-SEVEN

Told by Adam

They'd gone together since high school and had been engaged for a year, but now that Eric and Karen were getting married, my mother couldn't stop crying.

"Is this the thanks I get for marking all his clothes when he went to camp? He goes off with another woman?"

My dad said, "It just isn't kosher for a person to marry her own son, Abby." I think he was losing patience with my mother and with his tux that didn't button the way it had when we were all fitted after Thanksgiving. Yanking at his cuffs, he said, "Please, Abby, pull yourself together."

"I'll be all right. I'll be fine." My mother blew a juicy one into a tissue. "I promise you won't have to carry me out of the synagogue on a stretcher." She tugged at the buckle on the back of my cummerbund. "You're not ever going to get married, are you Adam?"

"Not so tight, Mom. I can't breathe."

"Tell me you'll never get married, and I'll loosen it. Oh God. I'll be all right. I'll get it out of my system now, so I won't make a fool of myself during the ceremony." She went off to her dressing table to soak up a few more tears.

I have to admit, I was impressed with the image of the guy in my parents' full-length mirror. There he stood, long and lean, in a gray tux with a purple bow tie and a purple cummerbund, and a pleated shirt that didn't have buttons but fastened with fake diamond studs. I was transformed. I was Tom Selleck, Tom Cruise, all the great Toms of Hollywood.

"These blasted studs," muttered Dad. "Abby, help."

I pulled away from the mirror and took a few stiff steps in the black patent leather shoes. Not comfortable. Already my big toes were rubbing against the shoe leather. But how the total package looked was all that counted.

"Gorgeous," my mother said.

"I'm going to go pick up Miriam."

"Don't be late for the pictures. You know how Karen's family lives by the clock."

"That's because Karen's a dairy farmer," Dad said. "You've got to milk the cows at a certain time or they explode."

"I just never dreamed I'd raise a son to live with pigs and goats," Mom said, her voice going up a couple of octaves.

"Oh-oh, there she goes again. Adam, get out of here. I've got to shake some sense into your mother."

I glanced back as I left their room. My father held my mother in his arms, and they were both crying. I thought then that Eric and Karen would be lucky if they could be as close as my mom and dad, twenty-six years after their wedding.

* * *

250

I couldn't believe how beautiful Miriam looked. She still wasn't wearing any make-up, but her face glowed with color, and her eyes were as lively as they'd been that day she gave testimony at her church. She wore her hair pulled back and held at her neck with a big black bow. Little wispy curls fell in front of her ears. And the dress — it was a sort of ivory color with a high lace collar and long sleeves with lacey cuffs. Diana, of course, would never have been caught dead in anything like it, but it was perfect for Miriam, and it didn't make me sneeze.

"You look dashing, Adam. I'm used to you in jeans."

"Jeans are a lot more comfortable," I said, helping her into the car. She was very careful not to wrinkle her dress. She wore black patent leather shoes, sort of like mine, but hers had small heels and were probably a lot more comfortable.

She sat close to me in the car, using the middle seat belt instead of the one by her window. "It's been a long time since that day with Vincent van Gogh's ear," she said in a kind of faraway voice. Then reality struck. "Where are we going? Are you sure you can find this place? I remember your incredible sense of direction the day we went to the Indian Center."

"Of course I can find the synagogue. I had my bar mitzvah there, and the wedding rehearsal last night, and was over to see the rabbi for my essay." I watched the streets carefully, so I wouldn't make a wrong turn.

"I've never been in a synagogue, Adam. Do I have to do anything in particular, like kneel or anything?"

"No, that's the Catholics, not us."

"Do I have to bow or kiss the ground?"

"No, that's the Buddhists and the Muslims. Just act natural."

"And who will I sit with while you're up there being Eric's best man?"

I thought about that one a minute, and then it came to me. "With Eric's favorite teacher from Eisenhower, Mrs. Loomis."

"Oh, no, she's going to be there? Did I tell you I met a table that looked like her, out at the farmhouse?"

We posed for as many family pictures as possible without the bride and groom, while Miriam watched from the back of the sanctuary. During some of the shots of Karen's family, Miriam asked me, "Where are Eric and Karen?"

"It's supposed to be bad luck if they see each other before the ceremony. Isn't it the same in your church?"

"No, I don't think so. Your synagogue is lovely, Adam. It looks a lot like a church, but different. What's that lamp that hangs over the altar?"

"It's called the *ner tamid*, which means eternal light. It's kind of like the light in the refrigerator, only it doesn't go out when you close the door."

"This way, smile, smile, lady in the back, shift a little to the side. Bee-yoo-tee-ful!" bellowed the photographer.

"And what's behind those tapestry doors?" asked Miriam.

"That's where we keep the Torahs. Each one has the Five Books of Moses in it."

"Genesis, Exodus, Leviticus, Numbers, and Deuteronomy." Miriam rattled them off like a nursery rhyme.

"Right, I guess. But they're in Hebrew, and they're rolled up on two wooden poles, like scrolls, and they're all hand-painted and hand-sewn. Some little man in New York doesn't do anything else in his whole life but write Torahs. You could spend half your life doing just one."

"I'd like to see a Torah. Can I?"

I wasn't sure what Rabbi Fein would say about that, but at least I didn't have to answer, because my dad whistled for me. "The groom needs you, Adam. He's having an identity crisis."

"I've got to find Eric. Will you be okay?"

"Oh, sure. I'll just watch for the Great Wall of China."

We marched down the aisle to some slow music played by the *klezmer* musicians from Kansas City. Karen's sister Janet was the maid of honor, and we had to walk in together. She was at least four inches taller than me and took bigger steps. My feet were already killing me, but I had to look like I was having a good time and also count beats so I wouldn't screw up the whole wedding procession. When we passed Miriam's row, I rolled my eyes, and she smiled back.

It's hard to believe that it took a year to plan the wedding and fifteen minutes for it to be done with. At least it had something for everybody. To please my parents, they were allowed to walk Eric down the aisle. The bride and groom stood under the same *chupah*, or wedding canopy, that Karen's parents had stood under at their own wedding. To satisfy the great-grandmothers on both sides, Karen circled Eric seven times, according to the Jewish Orthodox tradition. And to please Eric and Karen, they wrote the whole ceremony themselves, so it wasn't as sappy as it might have been.

Rabbi Fein said, "This bride and this bridegroom who stand before us to proclaim their devotion to one another . . ."

I tried to focus in on the words, but I was concentrating really hard on details, like where I was supposed to stand, when I was supposed to come forward, and which pocket I'd hidden the ring in. Every so often I looked down at the congregation, especially at my mother, who maintained a bright little smile and never got hysterical, and at Miriam. I wished I could have been next to her, to explain what was going on.

A college friend of Karen's sang some song about fig trees and vines and fruit. It didn't make much sense to me, but it was supposed to be very romantic and sexy, from the Song of Songs. Then she sang an Israeli song, *"Erev Shel Shoshanim,"* which means night of roses. In other words, she sang about a lot of plants.

". . . According to the Mosaic Law and laws of the State of Kansas, in the presence of your families and friends, and with God as our witness, I now pronounce you . . ."

They kissed; you could hear it all over the sanctuary. Everyone laughed when they came out of the clinch. Then Eric stomped on a glass wrapped in a white napkin, signaling the end of the ceremony. Instead of the usual wedding march back down the aisle, the *klezmer* musicians played a bouncy Hasidic tune, and it was all over. My brother was a married man.

I broke out of the receiving line after about fifteen minutes, because I saw Miriam and Mrs. Loomis off in a corner, and they looked like they'd run out of things to talk about. I went to rescue Miriam. Rescue Miriam — it was getting to be a habit.

Waiters kept offering her champagne, but Brother James would have been proud to see how she stuck with the pink foaming punch. Mrs. Loomis drained a few champagne glasses, though. The band had set up their little combo in a corner of the social hall, and already, even before dinner, the old ladies were dancing with each other. The unrelenting beat of the music was hard to resist. Even Miriam's toe was tapping.

"Do you want to dance?" I asked, half-teasing.

"I'll pass," Miriam said, pulling her foot back. But before long, it was keeping time with the music again. "What happens next?"

"Well, we'll have dinner and some toasts and speeches and then the real dancing begins."

She tried to look stern and disapproving.

"It has been very interesting, Adam," Mrs. Loomis said. "I have never had occasion to attend a Jewish wedding before."

"I was wondering, Mrs. Loomis, I mean, since you have so many students, do you actually remember Eric from five years ago?"

"Oh, yes, yes. One does not forget a Bergen. I am frankly amazed that Eric has graduated from college and survived half a year of law school. I recall him being a student much like you."

"Lazy?"

"I wouldn't have said lazy. I would have said — casual. Charming, but definitely casual about academic matters. But looking at him standing so straight and purposeful under the wedding canopy gives me hope for you, Adam."

After dinner, I took Miriam around to meet people. "This is Aunt Ruth and Uncle Seymour, from New Haven." Miriam smiled while Aunt Ruth looked her over. I could see the question in Aunt Ruth's eyes: *This is a Jewish girl?*

Next came the two great-grandmothers. The first couple of years Eric and Karen went together, the great-grandmothers had a big rivalry going. But gradually they became the oldest people either of them knew, and so they were friends. Both hard of hearing, they were having a shouting match as we came up to them.

Karen's Great-grandma Sophie said, "So, Reba, be honest, did you ever think they'd stand under the *chupah* together?"

My Great-grandma Reba replied, "To tell the truth, Sophie, I never dreamed both of us would live long enough to see it happen. But, it was God's will."

"Grandma Reba, Grandma Sophie, this is Miriam." I knew that would throw them, because, while Miriam looked as WASP-y as girls come, she had a nice Torah name.

"Miriam?" The two grandmas exchanged looks, and we moved on.

"I want you to meet the rabbi."

Rabbi Fein put down his champagne glass to

shake Miriam's hand. "Hello. It's good to see you doing so well."

"I'm just fine now." Miriam did a little twirl to demonstrate her state of health. It seemed so light-hearted that it took me by surprise. I thought then that she was more relaxed around my rabbi than I was.

Rabbi Fein laughed. "Come back when there aren't so many people around. We'll talk some more." He waved and went off to charm the grandmas.

"I like him," Miriam said. "He seems so young for a rabbi."

"Well, he's probably about the same age as Brother James."

The musicians were really getting into the spirit of the occasion. My mother, past crying, was dancing and flopping around like a puppet. Now the men were lifting Eric on one chair and Karen on another. With only a handkerchief connecting them, they swayed and bobbed on the shoulders of the men, as the *klezmer* fiddle sped up.

And then it happened: the *hora*. It's the Jewish equivalent of "Twist and Shout." At any Jewish wedding, when the musicians play a *hora*, well I guess you could say all hell breaks loose. Talk about miracle cures: old ladies kick off their orthopedic shoes and grab the children, old men cast off their canes and grab young women, and they all make a circle. Everyone dances; it's irresistible. The music starts out harmlessly enough, just a nice Israeli melody, but after a couple of minutes you're going round and round and round to a frantic jungle beat.

Hearts are pounding, skirts are whipping around, and if you wanted to stop, you wouldn't dare because of the humongous number of sweaty bodies that would pile up on top of you.

I kicked my shoes under our table. "Come on, Miriam, let's do the *hora*!"

"I couldn't," she said, following me to the circle.

"Sure you can. Just do what I do. No one knows the steps anyway." The musicians were into the third or fourth round of the song, and the pace was picking up. We broke into the ever-widening circle, watching everyone's feet at first until our own feet went on automatic pilot.

By the fifth revolution of the melody, Miriam was right in step, with her hair flying around her head, twisting right and left, dipping and kicking with the rest of us.

You want the music to go on forever, but you know that if it doesn't stop pretty soon, you're going to have a heart attack. When the music finally stops, all you can feel is your heart beating about a thousand times per second and your face as hot as a pizza.

"Oh, Adam, that was incredible," Miriam cried. "I've never been so tired in all my life. Will they play it again?"

"Nope, just once. The old folks' pacemakers couldn't take it more than once." I led her over to the table, and we collapsed in our chairs, still holding hands and quivering all over, like you do after jogging a couple of miles. She tossed off her shoes and stuck her legs out in front of her. For a second, I thought about the curl of her toes that day in the hospital.

Still gasping for breath, she said, "I didn't dream I'd be able to do something so physical ever again. Remember when it hurt every time I breathed?"

"I remember."

"Oh, Adam. I'm so happy tonight."

Me, too.

We pulled up outside Miriam's house. I was pretty sure she wouldn't ask me to come in, because of the uncles. So, I slid my arm around her, and she backed up close to me. I'd waited so long for her to be healthy, for us to be alone, for some great stuff to happen. Here we were in the car, both of us feeling romantic. I don't think I ever loved anyone as much as I loved Miriam that moment. The clean smell of her hair and the crispness of her dress and the softness of her coat made me feel really cozy, really secure. I shifted her around in my arms, pulled her close against me. Just like I didn't want the music to stop, now I didn't want the evening to end. I thought she felt the same.

"I had a wonderful time," she said. Her words warmed my neck. "I'll always remember this evening, Adam. I'll remember how beautiful your synagogue is, how happy Eric and Karen are, how nice your parents are. I'll remember the rabbi and the dancing. Tonight when I'm falling asleep, I'll go over and over all the details to etch them forever in my memory."

"I'll call you when I wake up tomorrow," I promised.

I felt a change before I heard it; something shifted in her soft body. "No," she said.

"No, what? No, you're sleeping late? No, you have to go somewhere?"

"Just — no."

"No, *what?*"

"We can't see each other anymore."

It was like a slap, stinging my face, ringing in my ears. She pulled away from me and leaned against the car door.

"Remember our friend Emily Dickinson?" Miriam's voice was heavy with sadness. "She's got another poem. 'I cannot live with you, it would be life, and life is over there, behind the shelf.' "

"What? I don't get it." Oh, I was getting it, all right. I was getting tossed overboard, or shoved on a back shelf. "This is what you *want?*"

"Brother James said it, Adam. I'm fish, and you're fowl. We can't live in the same medium."

"Oh, yeah? It sure seemed like we were both fish tonight. We seemed to be swimming together just fine."

"While you were in there with Eric when he changed for the honeymoon, I talked to Rabbi Fein. I asked to see a Torah. He took me down to the small chapel, and he took out a Torah scroll and unrolled it for me. Every letter was a perfect creation of love. I couldn't believe how exquisitely beautiful it was, Adam. My eyes filled up, and I was afraid my tears would stain the parchment. And I thought about the little man in New York, the one you told me about, spending half his life creating this one sacred piece of art."

I knew this was spiraling downward. I felt chilled to my bones.

"The scroll was opened to Leviticus nineteen, the rabbi said. He called it the Holiness Code. I know, only because I know Leviticus, that somewhere in that passage it said, 'Thou shalt love thy neighbor as thyself.' But Adam, as beautiful as the scroll was and as well as I knew the passage, I could not read a single word, not even a single letter. That's why we can't see each other anymore."

"Why? Because you can't read Hebrew? Believe me, most Jews can't even read Hebrew, Miriam. Didn't the rabbi tell you that?"

"But don't you see, Adam? The scribe in New York, he made that Torah scroll for you, for all of you, whether or not you can read it. But he did not make it for me."

"You're making a big deal out of an anonymous guy 1,500 miles away. He's probably been dead for fifty years anyway."

"Adam, I promised Brother James that I would try to convert you." Her teeth were chattering; I wasn't sure I heard her clearly.

"To save you. To bring you to Jesus. Because I care so much about you. Don't say anything, don't say anything."

I tried to keep quiet, though the anger was rising. The cumberbund was tight, the bow tie was tight, my shoes were tight, my chest was tight.

"But Adam, now that I've met the grandmas and the rabbi, and now that I've seen you stand up there under the wedding canopy with that purple skullcap on your head — well, now I know I can't do what

261

I need to do. That's why we can't see each other anymore."

She unlocked the car door and pushed it open a crack. I felt a stab of cold air at my feet. Miriam reached back for my hand. "I've loved these weeks with you, Adam. You've been my best friend ever. Good-bye." She blew me a frosty kiss and was gone.

I couldn't find the keys. I couldn't remember how to start the car, which foot to use for the gas, how to shift gears. I didn't want to look up, but I saw her slip into her house and close the door against the night, against me.

I drove home automatically. I couldn't tell you what streets I took, because my mind was whirling off in the ozone. *Luminarias* glowed all over my neighborhood, points of fire, freezing cold.

I don't remember undressing, but out of habit I must have hung up the tux carefully. I only remember turning on my electric blanket and getting in between the icy sheets and waiting for them to warm me up.

Somewhere in the middle of the night I realized that Miriam was right, of course. We weren't six of one, half a dozen of the other. We were fish and fowl, apples and oranges. It had to end. Maybe it began ending when Miriam was healed. "Some say the world will end in fire, some say in ice."

Wasted potential? Not with Miriam, I wasn't. I'd pretty much given her my best. Mrs. Loomis would approve, even if Brother James didn't.

Around 4:00 a.m., with my head thick and achey, I told myself, "Adam, you'll survive. You're good at bouncing back. Debate trains you to take blows and come back fighting. You'll let the old sense of humor kick in. You'll squash down all the hurt feelings. They'll never show. Like my good old dependable hair, ninety-four percent of all those stubbed feelings will fall right back into place. And I can live with the other six percent." Once, not so long ago, I could shrug my shoulders and say, "Who cares?" I could do that again — as soon as I stopped feeling like a bag of bricks had been dropped on my chest. I was living proof that hearts hurt, even if you're not having a heart attack.

Diana was gone, Miriam was gone. Who would I wake up to, who would I fall asleep to every night? My insides caved in like an empty sack, growling, hungry, as if I'd never be filled up again. I fell asleep and woke up a hundred times; the monster of the night slowly crawled by.

With the sun just starting to ease its way up from behind Brent's house, I felt myself giving in to solid sleep. In that twilight zone between waking and sleeping, the last conscious thought I had was, I'm miserable, but . . .

At least Miriam's well.

About the Author

Lois Ruby makes her Scholastic Hardcover debut with *Miriam's Well*. A former young adult librarian, she is the author of several novels and short story collections, including *Arriving at a Place You've Never Left*, which was an ALA Best Book for Young Adults.

Ms. Ruby says, "Miriam's dilemma makes me wonder how we decide just what it is that we believe in. Can we believe something and its opposite at the same time? Can we love what we fear? And why is the forbidden always so appealing? The questions are far more interesting than the answers and are the only point in writing stories like *Miriam's Well*."

Lois Ruby was born in San Francisco, California, and now lives in Wichita, Kansas, with her husband, who is a psychologist. Their three sons are scattered at universities across the country.